DUKE OF PRYDE

SEVEN DUKES OF SIN
BOOK THREE

MARIAH STONE

Stone
Publishing

GET THE EARL OF CHANS FOR FREE

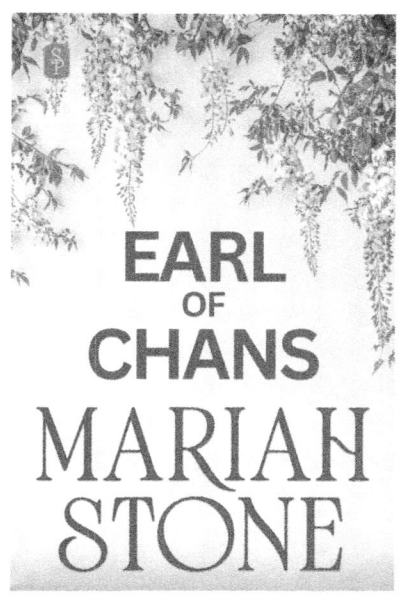

A torn dress. A sheltering gazebo. And four years of unspoken words between them. The Earl of Chans is about to risk everything for the mathematics genius who never left his heart.

Get the Earl of Chans now to believe in love again.

https://mariahstone.com/get-earl-of-chans/

EPIGRAPH

"Señor Don Quixote, your worship has, no doubt, perceived the beauty of my lady duchess..."

Miguel de Cervantes, *Don Quixote*

"I cannot fix on the hour, or the spot, or the look or the words, which laid the foundation. It is too long ago. I was in the middle before I knew that I had begun."

Jane Austen, *Pride and Prejudice*

CREDO

The Seven Dukes of Sin Credo
Three:

Secrets shared. Secrets sealed.

1

"Where the hell is he?" Constantine Buccleigh, the Duke of Pryde, paced down the aisle of All Saints Church. This could be the day his secret finally ruined his life.

The scents of dust and incense hung in the air around him. And weak sunlight filtered through the Gothic windows, casting his shadow across the stone floor. The locals of Shepherdsbrook, a village on the outskirts of London, had filed out after the Sunday sermon not a quarter of an hour ago.

Constantine's blasphemy bounced off the walls of the empty church like a bullet. His riding boots clicked against the flagstones, and he crossed his arms over his chest as he paced too fast for a duke who prided himself on his composure.

A crash behind Constantine had him spinning around, hand instinctively darting to the letter in the inner pocket of his coat.

But it was only Octavius.

At the back of the vacant pews, the Duke of Eccess flashed him a guilty look as he caught a bookshelf from which prayer books rained down.

Constantine raised a single eyebrow, forcing his shoulders back to their usual position. "Octavius, if you could save your talent of demolition for another day..."

Eccess straightened the shelf, his biceps bulging even through the layers of his tailored coat. While Constantine bent to pick up the books and return them to the shelf, Octavius gave the cross above the altar an exaggerated bow. "Pardon me, Lord. Just a tiny excess of wine. I'm sure you understand, with the whole water-to-wine business."

He retrieved a silver flask with the symbol of a boar engraved on it from his pocket. He raised it first to Constantine, then to the cross, and drank, his honey-blond hair falling over his forehead.

When all of the books were back in their places, Constantine eyed the flask. "Truth be told, I wouldn't mind a drop of that myself."

"Certainly. You look like a bowstring about to snap." Octavius extended the flask towards him. "As always, my best. Cognac Fine Champagne."

Constantine's hand twitched towards it. But then he let it fall back to his side. "Not today. I need every bit of control I possess."

Octavius's eyes narrowed for a moment. "Suit yourself. You could use a bit of loosening up, if you ask me."

"I do not."

Finally, footsteps sounded upon the floor like a cannonade. Constantine ran one of his sweat-dampened hands across his hair and corrected his cravat.

He ushered Eccess towards the sound until he could finally

see a movement in the darkness below the chancel arch. The footsteps stopped.

A baby cooed.

Constantine stopped breathing and went completely still.

A baby?

Two female figures in simple brown and gray muslin dresses and spencers walked out of the shadows, soft heels clicking against the worn flagstones. The one holding the baby was a fair bit taller than the other.

He and Octavius exchanged puzzled looks. Perhaps these were just two parishioners who had stayed after the sermon. These two couldn't have anything to do with the letter.

As it had done so many times, his mind returned to the letter he had received three days ago.

London, 20 September, 1814,

To His Grace, the Duke of Pryde,

Your Grace,

I trust my letter finds you in good health.

An important matter concerning your circumstances has been revealed to me. It would be most prudent for you to attend the sermon at All Saints Church of Shepherdsbrook this Sunday.

Your Grace's most humble and obedient servant,

A friend

Admittedly, a *friend* could be male or female. He supposed he just didn't think blackmail would be within a woman's purview.

When both ladies came to stand in front of him, he realized the one with the baby was even taller than he'd first thought, almost the same height as himself.

What reason might a mother with an infant have to engage him? He was not the Duke of Luhst. He did not whore around.

Eccess cleared his throat. "May we help you?"

The tall female focused her attention on Eccess. "Your Grace, Duke of Pryde?"

Now that she stood in the light, Constantine could see that she was lovely, with soft locks of copper-colored hair falling around her face from under a simple black bonnet. Her large green eyes looked gentle yet earnest. Her mouth was wide and sensual. And her nose was slightly pointy, making her appear young and adventurous. The shorter lady was in her midtwenties and had a conventionally attractive face under wavy black hair.

"No, I'm afraid not," said Octavius. "Duke of Eccess. At your service."

"I am Pryde," said Constantine, keeping his voice measured despite his heart drumming against his ribs. "How can I help, Miss...?"

"Miss Modesty Fairchild," she said. "This is Miss Grace Lockhart, who came as my chaperone."

Constantine gave a customary bow of his head while Eccess did the same.

Surely, they were not *blackmailers*, these ladies who seemed modest and respectable, albeit poor. He admitted he had imagined scoundrels from the rookeries of Whitechapel, wielding knives and pistols.

"Mr. Fairchild, the vicar who just did the sermon, is my father," she added.

He raised the letter. "Did you write this?"

Miss Fairchild's gaze darted to the paper as she bounced the baby. A slight blush crept up her cheeks. "Indeed I did, Your Grace. I was uncertain what to write in such a situation. When your own natural child is concerned—"

His own natural child?

What did she know about his mother's long-lost letter— the one that confirmed he was not his father's true son? She should have started the letter with that.

Wait—

Surely, she wasn't implying—

Goddamn it, not another attempted blackmail because of a secret child!

Not a few weeks ago, at his house party at Pryde Manor, his friend the Duke of Luhst had received a letter claiming he had a natural child. But Lucien had denied the allegations and refused to pay. The blackmailer had then sent Lucien's three-year-old daughter to Pryde Manor. The resulting scandal had roared through London, been covered in every society paper and gossip column. The ton's matrons still clucked their tongues over the Duke of Luhst's fall from grace.

Did the same blackmailer now attempt to incriminate him? Or was this woman implying it was *her* baby *from him*?

He was certain he'd never seen her before; he never would have forgotten those pretty lips.

For a moment, Constantine's carefully maintained façade threatened to crack. He forced a polite smile he had given countless times. "Pray tell, what am I accused of exactly?" he asked.

She exchanged a cautious glance with her friend, who raised her eyebrows at her. Then Miss Fairchild's eyes met his. "Augustus is your child, of course."

Constantine felt a fiery pressure building within his skull, threatening to shatter it. The complete nonsense of this situation was so obscene it was comical. He ought to be relieved. She had not mentioned his mother's letter nor his father's will, nor made any threat to expose his true parentage.

The only woman he'd ever slept with was a sex worker at Elysium, an elite gentlemen's club in Whitechapel. The club's owner, Mr. Thorne Blackmore, had assured Pryde his lover was barren.

He struggled and failed to keep his voice even. "*My* child?"

Eccess—the traitor—let out a laugh and craned his neck to look at the bundle in the tall woman's arms. "May we see the babe?"

"No," said Constantine while Miss Fairchild brought the bundle closer. "There's no need."

To his great dissatisfaction, he'd seen the adorable little face of a newborn—large dark bluish eyes landing on him, mouth smacking as the babe made sweet little grunts, adorable button nose and full cheeks—within the swaddle and a little hand with delicate fingers and translucent fingernails peek out by a round chin.

For the blink of an eye, warmth flooded his cold chest, and he wished the baby *was* his own flesh and blood. A tiny human to love and hold close. Should the baby be his son, he would bring him into his care. Provide for him. Support him.

In fact, a new kind of thrill ran through his limbs. Something strangely resembling affection.

But he was being manipulated. Lied to.

Someone was trying to prey on his feelings. Take him for a fool.

"Augustus's mother told me everything," said Miss Fairchild defensively. "You're the father. She gave me custody of Augustus before she died..."

Constantine could now understand the rage his friend Dorian, the Duke of Rath, must have felt his entire life.

Unlike Rath, the Duke of Pryde couldn't afford to unleash his rage.

"Miss Fairchild," he said. "I cannot emphasize enough how impossible this is."

"I assure you, it's true," said Miss Fairchild quickly. "I held her hand as she gave her last breath and she wanted—"

His chest grew tight and hot. She dared to put him through this? Three days of clawing at walls, three sleepless nights, terrified someone had the proof that would destroy him.

For what? To be extorted with nonsense?

The deceased woman's identity and cause of death were irrelevant to him. He suspected this self-proclaimed mother had fabricated the story—perhaps to blackmail someone after secretly giving birth.

She had selected the wrong man as her target.

"You read about the Duke of Luhst's misfortune in the papers, didn't you?" he asked, struggling to keep his voice calm. "And you thought you could fool another man. Except, I am beyond reproach. Fathering a bastard is one thing I have always meticulously avoided."

Miss Fairchild's pretty mouth sagged open for a moment before she spoke. "I am not attempting to—"

"This is not *my* child. I feel sorry for it, but I will not be drawn into a despicable scheme that has no grounds. If you contact me again, you will face court fees for libel so grave you will never be able to get out of debtor's prison."

Relief loosened the tight band around his chest. He turned on his heel and walked away. Octavius said a hasty goodbye and rushed after him. The doors of the church couldn't approach fast enough.

Miss Fairchild was unaware of his true secret and had no solid basis to make any demands. He and his title were safe.

As they strode away, Constantine kept his steps measured and unhurried, his posture impeccable.

He needed to breathe. Unclench his fists.

Now he could return to his normal life. There was no threat and no blackmailer.

But under the rigid mask of control, his mind was in chaos.

He may have deflected one false claim, but his secret still made him vulnerable.

If not Miss Fairchild today, someone else might use it against him tomorrow.

Walking by his side, Octavius opened his flask. "A redhead... Looked so timid but must be fire in bed."

An image flashed through Constantine's mind of Miss Fairchild's red hair spread across his pillow, those pretty lips swollen and open in bliss, her sweat-misted body arching beneath him.

Not beneath Octavius.

Him.

"Hold your tongue," Constantine said, more briskly than he'd like. "Never speak of her in that way again."

Octavius gulped from the flask and closed it. "Come now, I speak from experience."

Constantine shook his head. "Do stop."

Octavius sent him a puzzled look. "Fine. You and your pride..."

There was no point in getting angry over a strange woman's honor, knowing he'd never see her again in his life.

2

What sort of callous man would reject his own baby?

Anger burned in Miss Modesty Fairchild's chest as she descended from the hackney, cradling little Augustus tightly. The infant slept peacefully, unaware of his father's pitiless dismissal.

She hurried across the busy dirt path towards the women's almshouse, Grace following close behind. A chilly September wind cut through her spencer, but Modesty ignored it, indignation keeping her warm. Street children in ragged clothes darted between the buildings. A woman in a threadbare shawl rushed past, and a man shuffled by, eyes staring blankly from a worn-out face.

The duke was everything her father had warned her about —aristocratic perfection masking a heart of ice.

Yet her breath had caught when she saw him. His athletic, broad-shouldered frame tapered to a lean waist, narrow hips, and long, muscular legs. Beneath windswept dark brown hair, his face was more devastating still—all sharp planes and angular cheekbones softened only by the slight cleft in his strong jaw. Deep, penetrating, chestnut-brown eyes tilted upwards slightly at the corners, and were surrounded by long, dark lashes. But his mouth—with a full lower lip and a perfect Cupid's bow—seemed at odds with such commanding features, as if nature couldn't quite decide between severity and sensuality.

His companion, the Duke of Eccess, had at least shown some warmth despite the scent of wine on his breath. He'd tried to look at Augustus, but Pryde had remained unmoved. No doubt acknowledging his child would tarnish his spotless reputation.

Grace opened the door for Modesty. "What will you do now?"

A former tannery, Grace's women's almshouse was housed in a large brick building with grimy windows set high on the walls to let in light. It was in the depths of Whitechapel, on a broad street lined with crumbling buildings that leaned towards each other like drunken workers.

Modesty's arms tightening around her precious bundle, she passed through the doorway. "I'll do what the duke cannot. I will care for an innocent child who needs love more than status. First, I must find a wet nurse for Augustus."

The smell of damp stone filled her nose as she and Grace moved through the main room, her small heels echoing against the cold floor.

"After that, Papa and I will raise him as Ophelia would have wanted."

Her own mama had died in childbirth, just as Augustus's had. That was one reason she cared so much for the sweet boy who wasn't her own. She loved his button nose, and the full round cheeks, and the soft dusting of blond hair on his head, and the birthmark behind his ear in the shape of a wolf.

The other reason was unthinkable...

At the far end of the large space, women bent over old workbenches, now used for sewing, with bits of cloth and thread scattered about them. Three cooking grates had been set within a large fireplace on the other wall. A cauldron stood on one of them, bubbling with the comforting smell of stew.

She cuddled Augustus closer to her as a cold wind sliced by her cheek. The place was becoming increasingly drafty, the chill seeping through cracks in the windows and doors.

"You know," said Grace as they walked. "It is better for Augustus. You will give him so much love. A vain and prideful man like the duke could never care for him as you would."

Modesty remembered how Pryde's perfect features had hardened at the sight of Augustus, how that brief flicker of softness in his eyes had turned to stone.

"You're right," she said. "The duke would never love him."

They walked past women who sat at tables, busy with needlework, rocking babes or bouncing toddlers, or talking in low voices.

Modesty had met Ophelia two months ago, right at this table, as the other woman had struggled to patch a skirt—the primary way women here earned petty coin. She was pretty, with blond hair and sad, wet blue eyes. Her husband had died when she was three months pregnant. After his death, all of his possessions were sold to settle his debts, and she became homeless.

Modesty and her father had taken Ophelia in as they often did with homeless pregnant women—and even some from the almshouse. It was better to give birth in a clean, warm house than in the cold, drafty space that, despite all efforts, was not the best place for newborn babies.

How had a respectable married woman of her friend's modest status crossed paths with the Duke of Pryde? Perhaps, struggling with a husband who had always been drunk, and perpetually living on the verge of poverty, it had been easy for Ophelia to find comfort in the arms of a handsome, rich, and powerful man.

But when Ophelia had gone to the duke for help two months ago, he had cruelly rejected her, and she'd ended up in the almshouse.

Grace and Modesty proceeded towards the right side of the hall where curtains hung in a row, creating private small spaces, each of which housed a thin mattress or a wooden box serving as a cot. It wasn't much, but this was still better than the streets.

"You had to try." Grace nodded to a group of women who were gathered at a round table writing, while another woman read aloud. "The duke is Augustus's only family. You promised a dying mother you would keep her babe safe, and you're going to change your entire life for him. You're the kindest person I've ever known, but will you still be able to pursue your research while caring for a baby?"

Sorrow pierced her heart at the thought of giving up her antiquarian aspirations. She would never now trek through Egypt's ancient tombs or uncover the secrets of Rome's buried cities, never make the kinds of discoveries that could change how people understood the past. The Roman villa she'd found on the farm of one of the church's parishioners could have been her first step towards proving that women belonged in the field as much as men did. But dreams of academic recognition and breakthroughs in understanding humanity's past would have to remain just that—mere fantasies.

She could still see the cylindrical bronze jewelry box that had emerged under her shovel. And below that, tesserae forming a mosaic floor. Precipitation had helped to remove the topsoil, washing centuries of dirt from the box as she lifted it. She recalled grasping the cold, age-roughened metal with her freezing, wet fingers, blinking away the rain that gusted into her face. She opened the lid and swallowed a gasp at the treasures inside: a silver mirror, blue and green glass beads, a broken fibula...and, most intriguingly, a small carved stone. The stone was not Roman at all—she was certain it was an artifact from the Picts, a Scottish tribe!

She'd been so stunned by her find that time itself seemed to stop.

But time hadn't stopped for the pregnant woman waiting for her an hour's walk away to make the trip home together. Ophelia had stood in the elements until she was frigid and soaked before finally giving up and walking back to the vicarage on her own.

What Grace didn't know—what no one knew—was that Ophelia had died because of Modesty's distraction that day. So her silly dreams were a negligible price to pay for giving her friend's child a decent life...and it was her well-deserved penance.

"I won't pursue my research any longer," she answered, coming back to the present. "Your brother will be kind enough to continue the excavation."

"And assume all the credit?" Grace clicked her tongue. "I love George and want nothing but the best for him, but...that site...it's yours."

Modesty's wisest choice was to let George take the recognition, and she would do what a woman was supposed to do: support her papa and raise a child.

They stopped, and Grace pulled back a section of the curtain. Behind it, leaning against a cushion on a straw mattress along the wall, sat a woman who dabbed at her eyes with a handkerchief. She wore an old brown dress with patches, her tousled hair sticking out in wild strands around her tired face.

"How are you feeling, Mrs. Walcott?" Grace asked.

"Still proper sore, Miss Lockhart," she replied with a sad smile, "but gettin' better. Dr. Sterling said that's wot to expect."

Before Modesty could react, there were footsteps behind them.

"Ah, Miss Fairchild," a male voice said, and Modesty turned to see George, his face bright and his dark eyes crinkling kindly at the corners as he looked at her. "How did the meeting go?"

George was a tall, slim man with dark curly hair—the same shade as his sister Grace's—falling in unruly waves around a pleasant, open face. He wore a brown wool coat that had been carefully mended at the elbows, a simple linen shirt, and old breeches. He held a wooden board bearing a plate and a tin mug.

Modesty returned his smile. He had been the one who'd first sparked her interest in history. When they were children, he'd spent countless afternoons telling her tales of ancient civilizations and buried treasures. Now he brought those same stories to life by digging for antiquarian treasures.

"Not very well, I'm afraid, Mr. Lockhart," Modesty said. "Hence, little Augustus needs a wet nurse."

George frowned. "How disappointing."

"Would you consider nursing Augustus, Mrs. Walcott?" asked Grace.

The woman looked at the bundle. "I—er..."

Grace walked over and took Mrs. Walcott's hand in hers. "I am sorry, it must be so hard after losing your own babe."

"It is, but...me chest's full of milk, ain't it? Proper hurts, it does. If another little'un needs a mother...least where it comes to the feedin'...I'll do it. Right then."

Modesty cradled the sleeping baby closer. "Thank you. My father is a vicar in Shepherdsbrook, half an hour's carriage ride

from here. I'm charged with taking care of Augustus. A woman
from my father's parish fed him until now, but that was always
temporary. She already has six children of her own and can't
take another baby in. We have little, but we'll give you food
and a safe home."

The woman nodded, still teary. "What happened to his
mother, then?"

"She..." Modesty swallowed a painful memory of the afternoon five days ago that had changed everything. "She ran a
fever before the labor pains began. Shortly after the birth, her
illness worsened and...well... Before she died, she asked me to
look after him."

Quite distraught after Ophelia's death, Modesty had come
to the almshouse, asking for advice. Grace and George were her
closest friends, and she knew she could trust them like she
could trust herself.

Modesty smiled at Mrs. Walcott. "All of us will be this
child's family."

"I'm right grateful for the bed an' board," said Mrs.
Walcott. "Ain't got nowhere to go. Me husband's dead, too.
Ain't got no one, I haven't."

Modesty nodded and blinked away her tears. "Well. Now
you have me, my papa, and this little boy. You will never be
alone."

Mrs. Walcott stretched her arms out to take the baby, and
Modesty passed Augustus to her.

As she watched Mrs. Walcott rock the sweet child, her
heart filled with relief.

Her mind went back to the deep chestnut eyes, the straight
back, and the chiseled face—a beautiful mask that hid the
ugliest, most selfish person she ever met in her life.

Grace was right.

Perhaps that cold duke rejecting Augustus was the best

thing that had ever happened to him. She would dedicate her life to this baby. He'd be raised by a loving family with good morals.

The stab of regret and sadness that lanced through her heart at the thought of her forsaken dreams was nothing.

3

The scents of wet mud, rotting fish, and sour decay mingled with the crisp evening air by the entrance of Elysium as Constantine brushed his hand down the Andalusian's neck. Icarus's silky white coat was almost glowing against the darkness of the Whitechapel night—the light of torch posts giving the horse a warm yellow glow. The stallion's large, expressive eyes blinked as it sniffed at him softly.

"A stunning specimen." The Duke of Enveigh's light brown hair fell into his gray eyes as he looked over Icarus. The silver serpent buttons of his green coat glinted in the light. "No wonder His Royal Highness hates you for outbidding him. I'd hate you a little, too. Though, is it wise to bring such a valuable horse to Whitechapel?"

Constantine gazed up at the imposing building of three floors before him. "Mr. Blackmore's stables are guarded like a castle. I'm not concerned."

Petticoat Street stretched in either direction, its market—always bustling in the daytime—now empty. The windows glowed warmly with candlelight behind the panes. Above the entrance, six sharp triangles arranged in a semicircle formed the symbol of sunrays. In Greek mythology, Elysium promised eternal paradise for heroes and the virtuous. This Elysium offered its members a different kind of utopia—one where they could indulge their every desire without judgment or consequence. There was nothing virtuous about it.

Tomorrow, Constantine would retreat to his country estate. The blackmail scare three days ago had reminded him that he was long overdue for marriage. He needed a wife of impeccable breeding by the end of next Season. It had nothing to do with love. Love was so far from Constantine's ambitions, it was but the tiniest speck in the sky. The right alliance and his wife's excellent pedigree would give him even higher standing.

But all in due course.

Presently, he needed his lover Aphrodite's help to cast Miss Fairchild and little baby Augustus out of his head.

"That is not only why His Royal Highness harbors a grudge." Eccess took a long pull from his silver flask. His massive frame dwarfed the building's entrance, his rust-colored coat barely containing shoulders as broad as a doorway. Despite his perpetually disheveled appearance, his eyes remained as sharp as blades.

Enveigh narrowed his eyes. "You would know. You're the Prince Regent's dearest friend."

"I would not claim the Regent's friendship, in truth." Eccess cocked his head, stretching his neck muscles. "Let us just say we have similar tastes in all things pleasurable. Food and drink being among them. As for his feelings towards you, Constantine, I would argue that they have little to do with the Andalusian and much to do with your damned pride."

"Ah." Enveigh chuckled. "The famous House of Lords incident."

Constantine's jaw clenched. The Regent was famous for indulging in extravagances that had plunged him deep into personal debt. His Royal Highness had sought Parliament's approval for an extension of his Civil List to cover the shortfall. While Constantine, as a duke, had no vote in the Commons where the decision would be made, his sharp opposition in the Lords' chamber sent ripples through Parliament. Through trusted allies in the Commons and carefully placed public statements, he'd made his disapproval impossible to ignore. Now, the Regent—one of England's most influential figures— nursed a grudge. One word from him could destroy everything Constantine had worked so hard to keep.

His ducal friends understood him as no one else could. Among them, he didn't have to maintain his immaculate image. The need to appear flawless had been drilled into him since childhood. He had felt lonely and inadequate for most of his young years; his parents had restricted his contact only to his tutor and themselves, to keep his education pure.

Rath, Luhst, Eccess, Enveigh, Irevrence, Fortyne.

And himself. Pryde.

Seven Dukes of Sin. Friends he'd never had growing up. They knew his worst flaws and accepted his secrets, shielded them like their own. And he guarded theirs.

He'd die for every one of them if it came to it.

The doors of Elysium opened, and the owner of the club, Thorne Blackmore, appeared to welcome them. Two guards standing on either side of the entrance nodded to him with respect.

Blackmore was a tall man with inky hair and dark eyes. Handsome, with striking sharp features, he dressed like a duke and possessed the manners of a perfect gentleman. His calm demeanor was misleading—everyone in London knew how quick and deadly he could be.

The dukes nodded to him in greeting. "Mr. Blackmore."

"Welcome, Your Graces," said Blackmore. "As always, the club is ready for you." His gaze fell on the Andalusian. "Is that the steed His Royal Highness can't stop talking about?"

Constantine stroked Icarus's finely muscled withers. "It is."

"Let's get those horses stabled." Blackmore gestured to his head groom and two more who appeared from behind the corner of the building. As the three grooms led their horses away, Blackmore gestured towards the open doors from which soft golden light, the scents of vanilla and wine, and the sounds of a Haydn chamber piece emerged. "Please. A night of pleasures awaits."

The men walked into the large room with wood-paneled walls painted an elegant dark teal. Music flowed from the orchestra on the balcony. A marula tree stood behind glass, its silk leaves catching light from crystal chandeliers while a python wound around its trunk. Fifteen women of all shapes and forms dressed in gauzy silks waited near round tables. A panther paced in its cage by the wall. Along the walls were several alcoves hidden behind dark velvet curtains. The scent of roasted meat, delicacies, and wine drifted from copper serving trays held by footmen.

Constantine's gaze fell on Aphrodite, who stood wearing an indigo gown—his color. She was a beautiful woman with dark silky hair and deep eyes.

And yet for the first time in his life, he wished for another woman. Preferably a red-haired woman with green eyes.

"Stay in Pryde Manor for the hunting season, both of you," he suggested to Eccess and Enveigh as each of them accepted a glass of wine from a footman's tray. "And by hunting, I do not mean just foxes."

"What are you talking about?" asked Eccess.

Constantine took a measured sip. "It is time for me to choose a wife. I'd like to call upon the nearby families in the coming months to make acquaintances. I expect that will make it easier to decide on the lady and start courting in the upcoming London Season."

"We already lost Rath and Luhst," declared Enveigh. "Not you, too."

"I'll start making a list of marriage candidates this week. Will you help me, Archibald?"

Enveigh shuddered. "Forgive me, but Octavius is much more a connoisseur of current debutantes."

Eccess gave a low rumble of a laugh. "Indeed I am. Looking is an underestimated pleasure."

Constantine chuckled. "Marvelous. Then we will discuss my options, and you will accompany me on my visits. This will be my last time in Elysium, I hope. Now, if you'll excuse me, I'm expected elsewhere."

But before he could make his way towards Aphrodite, a footman appeared before him with a letter on a tray.

"Your Grace, this was just delivered for you."

Constantine blinked. Who would know he was here besides his staff and the dukes? He took the letter and, with a strange sense of trepidation, unfolded it.

London, 27 September, 1814,

To His Grace, the Duke of Pryde
  Your Grace,

. . .

I have in my possession your late mother's letter—the one that proves you are not the deceased Duke of Pryde's son but rather the product of her affair with a common parson.

Constantine stopped reading, struggling to catch a breath. They had his mother's letter. Ophelia's mother had stolen it as insurance when she realized Ophelia was carrying the duke's child. His father had hunted it for years.

Tensing his hands to stop the tremor, he resumed reading.

More importantly, I know that a true heir to the dukedom was born not a week ago. His name is Augustus, and he's the son of Mrs. Ophelia Lester, who was the natural daughter of the deceased Duke of Pryde.

As per your father's will, should this information become public, you would lose everything—title, lands, and your spotless reputation. However, for £1,000 in bank notes, delivered to the tavern Portside and set under the third table on the left in five days, the letter will remain our secret.

Fail to comply, and I shall forward it to His Royal Highness and the offices of all society papers.

Your Grace's most humble and obedient servant,
   Anonymous

Constantine's world shook and swayed on its axis. He kept staring at the precise, practiced handwriting, and couldn't quite understand.

His worst nightmare had arrived.

This was different from Miss Fairchild's letter. It was specific. All business.

Octavius was looking over Constantine's shoulder. "What is this?"

"My end," mumbled Constantine as he felt the paper being taken from his hand.

"What is going on?" asked Enveigh.

"Another blackmail letter," murmured Eccess as his eyes scanned the writing quickly.

"Another?" Enveigh's tone became serious.

First Lucien had been blackmailed over a daughter he hadn't known existed. Then Miss Fairchild had appeared with Augustus. Now this.

Constantine's mind reeled. He felt sick. "Goddamn it... It must be Miss Fairchild."

"Nah, not the redhead," said Octavius. "She believed Augustus was your baby. She thought Ophelia was your lover." He raised the letter. "This *Anonymous* knows Ophelia is your father's illegitimate daughter, and that she gave birth to Augustus."

Blood chilled in his veins as the memory of Miss Fairchild's words struck him. *She gave me custody of Augustus before she died.*

"Oh, God," he murmured as icy cold realization struck him. "Ophelia is dead...because of me."

Both of his friends looked at him sharply.

"Not because of you," said Enveigh. "What do you have to do with her death?"

He remembered the tired pregnant woman with his father's blue eyes and blond hair, high cheekbones, the straight Roman nose that had been passed on through the Buccleigh line for generations.

All features that he lacked.

Ophelia had been well-dressed, but her clothes were grimy, her hair in disarray. Clearly no maid had touched her for some time.

"She came to me not long ago. I wanted to help her. I should have. I would have given her a house, staff, a monthly allowance. But I required assurances first. In exchange for my aid, I demanded the letter her mama had stolen."

The letter that *Anonymous* was now using to blackmail him.

What was wrong with him? Was his pride really more important than a person's life? He was not a monster. He was supposed to be a gentleman.

Enveigh cleared his throat. "Well, not to rub salt in your wound, but having her near would have been wise. You could have kept her and the baby under your control."

Constantine hung his head. "And she wouldn't have died."

Octavius exhaled, sadness filling his eyes. "You don't know that. Unfortunately, many women die in childbirth, whether they're rich or poor."

"But now Miss Fairchild has the babe," said Enveigh, "and you've lost all influence over the situation."

"Precisely. All ducal titles are, strictly speaking, gifts of the Crown. I'm certain His Royal Highness would love nothing more than to agree with my father's will, strip me of every-thing, and install Augustus as the next duke. All just to spite me."

"With himself as guardian until the boy comes of age," Eccess added darkly. "Complete control of the Pryde fortune and influence."

"Indeed. I need to bring Augustus under my protection to prevent him from becoming a weapon that could be used against me."

His skin felt itchy and sweaty as he imagined the shame, the weight of the gossip, and the Regent's satisfied smirk.

"Miss Fairchild..." Constantine said. "She must be involved in some way."

"She did seem a decent person," said Eccess reluctantly. "A vicar's daughter."

Constantine's thoughts raced so quickly he couldn't catch them. "She knew Ophelia. She has the child... The child that threatens everything I am."

He pushed his hands through his hair. "Blackmore," he yelled. "My horse! Right away! I'm leaving at once."

Blackmore frowned as he slowly approached. "Of course, as you wish. Is everything all right?"

"Horse," Constantine said through gritted teeth. "Now!"

A dangerous glint flashed through the man's eyes. Blackmore surely didn't appreciate being barked at. But he was a better man than Constantine, as he let the insult slide and nodded his head. "Right away, Your Grace."

"What are you doing?" asked Octavius as Blackmore strode swiftly to one of the footmen. "Just stop and think for a moment. You can't accuse her again."

He's right, came a distant thought. But Constantine could barely hear it. All he knew was that the baby was a threat.

He needed to find out if Miss Fairchild was the blackmailer —and take the baby into his custody *now*.

"It cannot be a coincidence I'm receiving this letter after denying Miss Fairchild's claim. She didn't get what she wanted from me, so now she or her accomplices say they have my mother's letter. That must be her scheme!"

Eccess narrowed his eyes. "Is this even the same handwriting?"

"I do not care." He strode towards the door. "Miss Fairchild must be dealt with, and quickly."

4

HALF AN HOUR LATER, Constantine reined Icarus to a stop before the vicarage of Shepherdsbrook. The modest brick house sat in the shadow of All Saints Church, a single candle flickering in one of its windows. Eccess, who had insisted on accompanying him, stopped his steed before him.

"Think this through, Constantine. Be reasonable."

But Constantine shrugged him off. He was reasonable. He was right, as always. And he was not going to allow anyone to take his position from him. Fear and fury battled inside him like two wolves, and the cage he struggled to keep them in was weakening. He knew he had to neutralize the threat, and not even one of his closest friends could be allowed to stand in his way.

"Remain outside if you wish," he said, pushing all emotions down to keep his composure even.

Constantine dismounted and marched towards the poor door, which hung loosely on its hinges. By the sound of heavy footsteps, he knew Octavius followed him. He knocked, the sound resounding in the dark evening air, while Eccess stopped by his right shoulder.

Without looking at his friend, Constantine said, "If you choose to stay, I do not wish to hear another word about reason. I am perfectly reasonable."

"Of course you are," said Octavius quietly. "Banging on the door of a young woman at night in order to yell at her is the epitome of reason."

Feet shuffled behind the door. Then it swung open, and in the semidarkness of a narrow hallway stood Miss Fairchild. Her dark jade eyes were wide open under her long, curved eyelashes.

He shouldn't be noting the particulars of her eyelashes.

She blinked in surprise. "Your Grace? And Your Grace..." she said as her gaze drifted to Eccess.

"Miss Fairchild." Constantine gave her a short bow. Octavius did the same.

She hesitated, then gave a small curtsy.

She was dressed in a simple dark green woolen dress and a white apron. Her hair was tied in a tight chignon behind her head, with a few natural curls around her face. He should not be looking at her hair or her face or her dress.

She seemed so innocent, so pure... Could the daughter of a vicar really be a blackmailer? A strange pang in his chest didn't help his confidence.

The same pang pulled at his heart and grew into worry for her. Words escaped his mouth before he could listen to the voice of reason. "Why are you opening the door at this hour by yourself?"

His voice sounded harsher than he'd intended—cold. She frowned. "Forgive me, but we do not have a butler like the wealthy lords of Mayfair do."

He cleared his throat. The jab was fair, and he looked at

Eccess, who made a face at him. *She's right and you know it* was written clearly in his friend's expression.

He should not care for the well-being of a woman who might be his blackmailer. "Is your father not at home?"

"No. He's with a parishioner for her last rites."

"Right. Even better. Allow me to get straight to the issue. I will not be blackmailed, Miss Fairchild."

She seemed speechless for several moments, looking between him and Eccess. "You cannot be in earnest."

Eccess leaned a little closer. "Forgive the interruption, but would it not be better to talk of such sensitive matters inside? If that's not inconvenient."

A baby's cry sounded from deep within the house, and Miss Fairchild glanced over her shoulder into the dark hallway.

"You have some nerve." She threw a glare at him. "Coming to my house, accusing me yet again of blackmail...and now demanding to be invited inside?"

"Just to clarify"—Octavius pressed his large hand against his barrel chest—"*I* am not accusing you of anything."

The babe was wailing louder. "Miss Fairchild!" cried a female voice. "Fetch us some cloth for the little'un's nappies, would ya?"

Miss Fairchild's mouth twisted with the anger she was clearly trying to contain. "Very well. Come in."

She turned and walked a few steps, opened a drawer, and picked out a fresh muslin cloth.

"Do try to think with a cool head, Pryde," murmured Eccess. "You don't have proof she's the blackmailer."

Constantine's lip twitched. "I don't have proof she's not."

He followed her slender figure down the hallway.

"I know what I'm doing," he said in a low voice as they passed between white plastered walls decorated with small devotional paintings. "Even if she didn't send the letter today, she knew Ophelia. And, most importantly, she has Augustus."

Miss Fairchild led them into a modest sitting room that doubled as a dining room—a space no larger than Constantine's dressing chamber at Pryde Manor. A carved crucifix hung above the mantel, and religious engravings dotted the walls between shelves lined with books. A well-worn sofa and two armchairs flanked a wooden cradle, where Augustus lay, waving his tiny arms and legs as he wailed. A woman dressed even more modestly than Miss Fairchild was leaning over his cot, cooing at him.

Miss Fairchild handed the woman the cloth and she swiftly changed the baby, then swaddled him tightly. Miss Fairchild picked him up, rocking and shushing. In the candlelight, her gaze was a muted dark green, flickering with fury at him. An attractive blush spread over her cheeks.

"This is Mrs. Walcott," Miss Fairchild said. "Augustus's wet nurse. Anything you have to say, sir, you may say in front of her. I have nothing to hide."

The nurse curtsied.

His gaze dropped to the small bundle wrapped in muslin, to the bald head under a lace cap, the tiny ears. His stomach knotted.

He was Pryde's father's true heir.

Helpless rage clawed at him. Ever since he'd learned the truth at age ten, he'd spent his life trying to replace his tainted blood with perfect behavior—as if being the most honorable duke in England could somehow make up for being no duke at all.

But this baby didn't need to do any of that. He had the right to everything Pryde possessed simply because he existed.

Augustus was still a member of his family, though. And he needed to be raised as such. So as much as Constantine had denied him twice—once when Ophelia had come to him for help, and again three days ago—he had to accept the baby now. That way, whether Miss Fairchild was the blackmailer or not, no one else could use the boy against him by becoming his guardian.

"Is there a parish register with the record of the babe's birth?" he asked.

"Certainly," said Miss Fairchild. "Augustus was born in this house, and my father did everything right."

"How is he registered?"

"Papa and I were forced to christen him under the name of Lester before we ascertained your whereabouts. Mrs. Ophelia Lester is his mother. He was named Augustus Lester, the son of Mr. John Lester, Ophelia's deceased husband. But before she died, she said he's yours."

He couldn't imagine what twist of the dying woman's words could have made Miss Fairchild believe Augustus was his. But whatever the misunderstanding was, she had wanted him to take the child in. And he—as it turned out—wanted the same.

His head must have cleared. The fear had somehow subsided...perhaps from seeing Miss Fairchild again. So he realized his mistake.

Had she been the blackmailer, she'd have wanted to keep Augustus with her. Because whoever controlled the baby controlled the title and the estate.

His jaw tightened. He may have been wrong about her intentions. Her letter had been written more ominously than it should have been, but perhaps his own fear had made him jump to conclusions. And she had signed it as *A friend*, while today's letter was signed *Anonymous*.

The thought of her not being so evil as to use a baby to blackmail him was an almost physical relief.

But how could Constantine make sure she knew nothing of his true parentage without revealing too much?

"How were you acquainted with Ophelia?" he asked.

"She stayed with us for two months. We became trusted friends."

How trusted?

"Did she tell you anything...about her father?"

"Not much. Why do you ask?"

"And about an important letter her mother possessed?" he continued, ignoring her question.

Miss Fairchild shook her head, frowning. "Not that I recall. What letter?"

He couldn't say much more. Either she was a master of deceit or she truly knew nothing. Continued interrogation risked revealing more than he intended. Her eyes, though still blazing with fury, bore no secrets and held neither guilt nor malice.

He was almost certain she was not involved in the black-mail scheme. But, whether she was or not, his main concern now was assuming custody of Augustus.

He cleared his throat. "Very well, Miss Fairchild. You wished for me to take the infant in. I will do so. You may simply give him to me."

Miss Fairchild's expression shifted from furious to aston-ished in a heartbeat. "Excuse me?"

"I will take Augustus. Isn't that what you demanded of me not three days ago?"

"I— Well... Yes, but—"

"But what?"

She clutched the baby closer. "Forgive me, but I do not know you, sir."

"That shouldn't matter."

"That is the only thing that matters. I know Ophelia came

to you, poor, homeless, and alone, asking for assistance, and you refused her, sending her onto the street. And now she has gone to her rest and poor Augustus is left without a mother. I had hoped that you would be a man of honor, that you would atone for your sins. And yet you completely rejected a helpless newborn, called me a liar, and accused me of blackmail. You may be a powerful man, but it is I who have responsibility for Augustus as given to me by his mother. And I do not trust that you will give him proper care."

What a detailed list of his imperfections. Guilt and fear swirled in his gut as Miss Fairchild looked at him with distaste, condemning him. And she was right. Ophelia's death was on his hands. He had to at least do right by her baby.

"I should have never refused your request," he said. "I have come to realize I want to take him in and raise him."

She shook her head. "Forgive me if I do not believe such a sudden change of heart. Why don't you admit it's because of the potential scandal? Isn't that what you're afraid of?"

The muscles in his shoulders contracted. Right, the scandal. A scandal would attract attention. People would ask dangerous questions. "I need to protect my reputation like everyone else. Do you not, Miss Fairchild?"

"I do. But I would never put my own reputation above the well-being of a baby."

As he had...as he was still doing.

She must truly hate him, think him despicable. And yet, he'd always worked so hard to appear honorable, always tried to do the right thing.

Miss Fairchild's chest moved quickly up and down. "Augustus's health and happiness is my priority. I won't let anyone take him away from me, especially someone I don't trust."

A stone dropped into the pit of his stomach. It was his own

fault, really. Had he not dismissed her so easily at the church, had he not put his pride first, he could have learned what had happened, whose son Augustus was. He'd have had the baby under his protection already.

And now...now he could lose everything. And any scoundrel—especially the blackmailer—could get a hold of his father's heir and then...

There was one last thing he could do to save his position and keep his title.

If Miss Fairchild wouldn't relinquish Augustus...then they must be taken together, as one.

"Miss Fairchild, if you do not concede to give me the baby, I have no choice but to ask you to be my wife."

She frowned and blinked several times, her face slackening.

Eccess moved to stand in front of him, blocking the sight of Miss Fairchild. "Are you out of your mind, Constantine?" He lowered his voice. "Friend, I'm the drunk, and yet you're the one being reckless."

Pryde brushed past him and found himself almost eye to eye with Miss Fairchild. The features of her face were soft in the flickering light of candles. Her height allowed her to meet his gaze directly rather than peering up at him like most women did. The sight stirred a strange sort of burning in his blood. The thought of her being his wife transformed it into an inferno.

A sensation he had best ignore. He couldn't let himself get distracted. His goal was too important.

Fear drove him to choose all the wrong words, the part of him that knew how to charm and be a gentleman crumbling to ashes.

Instead, he became some kind of a brute, shielding himself from an invisible attack.

"I realize I'll be lowering myself by marrying a vicar's

daughter, but if that is the only way to bring Augustus into my family, then it is what I must do."

The irony, of course, was that he was the child of a clergyman himself. That thought made him bristle even more.

"Constantine!" Eccess cried out. "Think what you're saying!"

It was too late now. He had made his offer, and he'd offended Miss Fairchild immensely. He saw hurt and humiliation burning in her eyes, which made him regret his words immediately. But there was only one path forward now.

"I would like to offer Augustus my home and my protection," he said. "Therefore, I would like you to be my wife."

"No matter how low of a match I am for a duke?" she demanded, her voice quivering with rage.

The choice was simple: marry below his station or risk losing everything. With Miss Fairchild as his wife, he could father an heir, strengthening his position. Even if the truth about his parentage emerged, the Regent would be less likely to uproot an established family line.

Besides, an heir would be a way to buy time and slow down any legal proceedings, as the courts would have to consider the child's future as well.

Miss Fairchild narrowed her eyes at him. "And yet another change so quickly, Duke? What sort of man protects his reputation so fiercely he's willing to marry his presumed blackmailer?"

Eccess stepped closer to him, looking surprisingly sober. "Constantine, there must be another way. Marriage is for the rest of your life. You do not know this woman. What about the list of candidates, the visiting of the families, the courting of suitable debutantes? Your hasty marriage to a woman with a baby will be a massive scandal."

Constantine inhaled sharply, thinking fast. Until the blackmail issue was resolved, any hint of a scandal would be especially dangerous. "You're right, Octavius. I will claim Augustus is the child of a deceased cousin or family friend. Augustus will be raised as my ward. Miss Fairchild is the baby's temporary guardian, appointed by the deceased parents. Our hasty marriage will be explained by..."

What explanation could possibly keep his reputation intact? No one could be allowed to believe he was marrying Miss Fairchild because he got her pregnant. It all needed to be very respectable. And, though she was far below his status, she was clearly from a good family. Her father was a blameless vicar, preaching very strongly against sin.

He sighed. "It will have to be love. I will confess my sudden and true love for you, Miss Fairchild. It'll require us to act as though we're hopelessly smitten with each other. Sacrifices will need to be made, I'm afraid."

Miss Fairchild's gaze widened so much he worried she might insist he depart immediately and never return. "I do not know how you could be called a gentleman, Your Grace. Could you have given a more offensive proposal?" Her cheeks were blazing, her eyes dark and furious.

Constantine stared at her, waiting. He was such an ass. He didn't recognize himself. He, who was praised by the ton as a man of unblemished honor, the heir of one of the oldest and most respected English families.

Augustus squealed, and Miss Fairchild looked down at him with tenderness. Her eyes filled with tears as she bounced him gently in her arms, and the baby grew quiet.

"You cannot imagine how ardently I wish to deny you," she hissed.

Someone in her position declining a duke's proposal? The riches, the safety, the status and admiration? Her children would be nobles. She'd be a duchess. Who would refuse that?

Still, her rejection stung, hitting him deeper than he would have imagined. She was right, though. He had not behaved like a duke, like a man anyone would want to marry.

She took a deep breath then let it out. "But I promised Ophelia I'd make it my life's mission to care for this baby, and I'll do so. I know being raised by his rich and powerful father would be better for him than remaining here. He would have the finest tutors, an Oxford education, connections in society, and opportunities I could never provide. But I cannot just give him to someone who doesn't have his best interest at heart. So no matter how much I'm repulsed by you and your proposal...I will not be able to live with myself if I don't do what's best for Augustus."

She sobbed and exhaled.

"So...yes. I will marry you. But understand this—I do it only for Augustus. I will play the part of your loving wife in public, but in private, you'll never have my heart or my respect."

5

Modesty hated how her breath caught as she watched Pryde arrive. His white stallion thundered past the weathered church wall, scattering fallen leaves beneath its hooves, then followed the winding gravel path towards the vicarage. His back was straight, his hands steady on the reins as the powerful muscles of his long legs flexed beneath his breeches, holding the beast under perfect control. The wind ruffled his brown hair, softening the stark planes of his face. His cheekbones were flushed from the morning chill, his dark gaze glistening—and focused directly on her. Against the pewter sky and autumn colors, he cut a striking figure in his indigo riding coat.

Her fingers itched to muss that perfect hair, to pull on his pristine cravat, to wrinkle that immaculate coat—anything to crack that polished façade.

She clasped her hands as the duke dismounted and tied the reins to a nearby tree. Could one feel both the utmost vexation and flutters in one's stomach at the same moment? Even Papa grumbled something watching the duke walk towards them.

Tall, elegant, and graceful, he bowed to them, touching his top hat. He was as cold as stone. Beneath the polished exterior, he was arrogant and heartless, concerned with his image and nothing more.

As the duke stood before them, the scents of moist earth and decomposing vegetation mingled with his bergamot cologne, causing her skin to prickle with awareness.

"Your Grace," said her father grumpily. "Your proposal was very unexpected."

Papa had been shocked by the news and highly displeased. But he agreed the baby's future had to come first. That was how he had raised his daughter, to do what was right no matter the personal sacrifice.

"I am so very sorry about that, Mr. Fairchild," the duke replied with a polite nod. "I hope you can appreciate the circumstances."

Papa gave a reluctant nod. "Nothing is more important than the wee babe who lost his mother. At least he still has his father. And Modesty, of course."

Pryde's gaze settled on her, heating her skin. "Indeed."

"I only pray that you will return to your senses and will not let your pride and vanity come before doing what's right from now on."

"Forgive me, sir, I—"

"Do not pretend that you don't understand my meaning. Pride, sir, is the worst of the—"

"Deadly sins. I know, Mr. Fairchild. I heard your sermon this past Sunday. Lucifer, the fallen angel, etcetera."

Papa's scowl deepened. "Treat my daughter and your little son with the respect and kindness they deserve, that is all I ask. Come to church, too. I fear for your soul, Duke."

Pryde's eyes narrowed. "You do not know me, sir. How can you fear for my soul?"

"All of London knows of the Seven Dukes of Sin. You may think you're infallible, sir, but no one needs humility more than you."

Pryde's gaze grew dark. "I appreciate your advice, sir, we will be family, after all. But I am the best judge of my own needs. And right now, I'd like a walk with my future bride. You will chaperone us, of course. The weather looks agreeable, do you not think so, Miss Fairchild? You have a"—he looked back at a simple country road leading through the fields and into a grove of trees—"pleasant woodlands in your surroundings."

Last night after she'd agreed to his proposal, he'd said he would come to talk to her today so that he had something to tell the gossips of the ton—something to make their sudden love more believable.

"Would you not like to see your son first?" asked Modesty coldly. "He just woke up. He's with his nurse now."

Pryde didn't even flinch, his eyes chilly on her. "No, I wouldn't want to disturb the babe." He gestured towards a path that led behind the vicarage. "Shall we?"

Papa's bushy, unruly eyebrows knotted as he gave her a nod.

Suppressing a jolt of anger, she nodded as well and walked next to the duke. They passed the kitchen garden with its late cabbages and herbs, then the wooden henhouse where sleepy clucking drifted through the slats. Beyond that was the washhouse, where linens hung limply in the cool air. Farther ahead along the gravel path that wound towards the grove was a fenced meadow with an animal shed. Their goat, Bessie, stood in the meadow, chewing on a patch of grass.

Pryde's presence at her side was like an invisible force pressing against her, stealing her breath, quickening her pulse... How could she marry him, spend her life with the man, if she despised him so much already?

His purpose in this conversation was not to get to know her but to learn enough so that he could pretend to be in love with her. A wave of disgust shuddered through her.

Still. She needed to make an effort. For Augustus. And, perhaps, there were good qualities in this man, too. He couldn't be entirely horrible. No one was.

"The wedding is in three days," he said as they walked. "I already acquired the special license. We will be married in St. George's of Hanover Square by the Bishop of London himself."

She swallowed. "A big wedding?"

"Indeed."

She licked her lips. Apart from the Dukes of Pryde and Eccess, she had never been acquainted with anyone of noble birth. How was she going to be a duchess when she knew nothing of running salons, attending balls, and discussing politics with diplomats over dinner?

"How old are you, Miss Fairchild?" he asked.

Quite a direct question. She blushed. "Nineteen, sir." She looked him over. She estimated him being in his late twenties or early thirties. He should know better at that age than to engage in casual dalliances and look down his nose at the common people, should he not? "What about you?"

"I am thirty," he replied. "Pray tell, what is your favorite flower?"

"My favorite flower?"

"Indeed. I'd like to make sure the church is decorated with them."

"Uh..." She had no preference for flowers. She was busy with much more practical things. "Wildflowers, I suppose. That's what I see most often."

"Right. Very rustic. What accomplishments do you have?"

She felt intense heat creep into her face again. She couldn't entertain, sing, or play a musical instrument—yet another reason she would be inadequate in the role of duchess.

"I'm afraid there was little time left for any accomplishments after helping my father with the parish. I can, however, cook an excellent stew, bake bread, recite the bible, and tell you all about the Roman empire in Britain."

He frowned. "The Roman empire in Britain?"

"Yes. I'm fond of history books. My friend Mr. George Lockhart took me on archeological digs, and I haven't been able to satisfy my curiosity about ancient civilizations since. There is a ruin that I discovered only three miles away from here. I just lost track of time... And when it was already too late, I—"

When Modesty had finally arrived home that day—worried over Ophelia's absence at their meeting place and chastising herself for her distraction—she'd found her in the throes of a terrible fever.

"A Roman ruin?" he asked, genuine enthusiasm in his voice.

She glanced up at his profile, and even though his face remained cold, his brown eyes flickered with interest.

"Yes, indeed. We discovered a hypocaust system under the tesserae, and I found several fascinating artifacts—including what appears to be a small Pictish stone."

"A Pictish stone fragment this far south? I didn't know there was any evidence of Picts having reached this area. My father collected Roman artifacts, and I inherited his passion. I have several pieces myself—including a collection of Roman coins from Hadrian's time and a rather remarkable bronze mirror."

Interest sparked within her chest. "And you have these in your own home?"

"Among many other things."

She exhaled as a wave of excitement rushed through her. No, she couldn't give in to hope like that. If he was interested in antiquities and history, it only meant he was an educated man, as he should be given his status.

"Is that the time period that interests you the most?" he asked, his voice growing soft.

"Yes, I'm fascinated with ancient history," she said. "Especially the Dark Ages. Roman chronicles described the Picts. And I've seen drawings of their standing stones in Mr. Gordon's *Itinerarium Septentrionale*. What most intrigues me is their unusual social structure—their kings were crowned through the female line, something unheard of in other societies of that time. Personally, I have a theory that the mirror and comb symbols carved on their stones suggest women held positions of great importance."

He frowned, and she wondered if he was about to object to her suggestion that women could ever hold positions of importance. She wouldn't be surprised.

But instead, he asked, "Have you ever been to Scotland?"

"Never."

But oh, how she wished she could go. She had seen enchanting drawings and paintings of Scottish landscapes, castle ruins, and standing stones. Her mama's family was from Scotland, and she yearned to understand how her ancestors had lived and worked. Her father disapproved of her interest, but she had always dreamed that one day she could join an archeological expedition and be one of the first to discover the secrets of the past.

She longed to know whether her theory was correct, that Pictish women had held positions of power that went beyond just determining succession.

"What stopped you from going?" he asked.

"Duty, of course," she chuckled. "To my father and his parish. I help in Miss Lockhart's women's almshouse as well."

He nodded and looked into the distance, as though memorizing her words. "Naturally you do. Look, Miss Fairchild, I hope you understand that you may keep reading history books —God knows, I have an entire library of them—and organize charitable events in Mayfair. But digging around in the dirt and especially returning to Whitechapel, even to the women's almshouse, as a duchess will not be acceptable."

"Oh, indeed?" The words came out sweet as honey, but her knuckles hurt as her hands clenched.

"I'm afraid so."

As they followed the path past the paddock, Modesty spotted some late dandelions growing along the gravel's edge. She bent to pluck a few leaves.

"Would you excuse me a moment, Your Grace?" Without waiting for his answer, she approached the fence where Bessie stood watching them with her usual keen interest. She offered the leaves through the wooden slats. Bessie's lips tickled her palm as the goat delicately accepted the treat.

The duke came to stand by her side. "As I was saying, Miss Fairchild, a duchess must maintain certain standards of—" He broke off with an undignified yelp. Bessie, apparently finding the dandelions insufficient, had stuck her nose through the slats and latched on to his fine coat.

"Bessie!" Modesty called out, trying and failing to keep the laughter from her voice. "Do forgive her, Your Grace. She has excellent taste in fabric."

The duke attempted to shake off the goat while maintaining his dignity—an impossible task if ever there was one. The goat, now enjoying the game, clamped down harder and tugged. For a moment, Modesty allowed herself the pleasure of watching him struggle.

"Is this"—he grunted, dancing sideways—"a regular occurrence on your walks?"

"Oh, yes," Modesty said cheerfully as she leaned over the fence and distracted the goat by scratching around the base of her horns. Looking blissful, and immensely pleased with herself, Bessie finally released him. "Though usually it's just turnip tops she's after, not wool from London's finest tailors."

They continued walking, though the duke looked more than a little rumpled now, and she wondered if he was regretting his hasty offer of marriage. "Let's see," he said. "How much would I need to prepare you? Can you play any instruments? Sing? Paint in watercolors?"

It seemed as if he planned to move on and pretend the goat incident had not occurred, though she noticed him brushing at his coat surreptitiously. She forced her lips into a sweet smile that didn't reach her eyes. "I can whistle a jaunty tune and produce watercolors that would please any toddler. Will that suffice?"

His jaw muscles twitched. "How many balls have you attended? Even small country balls?"

She felt her cheeks burn. She should just reply sincerely. She didn't normally indulge in sarcasm, had always tried to be agreeable and unassuming, but there was something about this man that made her set barbs in every word she spoke. "Oh, countless ones, Duke. The turnip harvest festivals are particularly grand affairs."

He sighed. "So none? You cannot dance at all?"

"I was a little busy caring for people. Dancing is usually not very useful to the poor."

His eyebrows lowered. "Do you ride at all? I have some of the finest thoroughbreds in England."

"I'm more familiar with cows. Do they handle similarly?"

His profile was so still it could be minted on a coin. It

certainly was striking enough. She didn't care. She couldn't have felt more judged, lowlier than she did in this moment.

"Miss Fairchild, I am simply trying to get to know you better."

"So that you can pretend to be in love with me?" She scoffed and shook her head. "What is it that you appreciate, besides horses, balls, and saving your reputation?"

"History, Miss Fairchild. I also take great pride in breeding horses—I've recently turned my attention to pure-blooded Andalusians. And...I have my close friends."

"Yes, the Seven Dukes, I heard."

"I take my seat in the House of Lords and endeavor to serve the country to the best of my ability. I read extensively. I ride, hunt, fence, and engage in various sporting pursuits. My soirées and balls are considered among the finest in London, if I may say so."

"Your Grace," she replied. "I think you've realized by now what a mistake we're both making. It seems there could be no two people more different from you and me. You live for yourself. I live for others. You live in a mansion. I live in a drafty vicarage with crumbling walls. How do you think our marriage would work out? I think it will be a complete disaster."

He didn't say anything, but he didn't have to. The silence between them stretched as wide as the gap between their worlds—his of fine wool coats and leisure, hers of muddy boots and honest work. And somewhere in between lay Augustus's future, binding them together whether they liked it or not.

6

I T W A S the day of her wedding, and Modesty's hands were shaking as she looked at herself in the mirror. In her small bedchamber, with white walls, plain wooden furniture, and a couple of small watercolors, she looked like she belonged. Her place was not in the luxury and opulence of Mayfair.

Grace studied her with wide eyes. "How are you feeling?"

Modesty looked over the best gown she owned, a simple muslin one the color of lilacs. Was it the color that made the bags under her eyes so dark and prominent? Or was it just that she hadn't slept for three nights—not since the duke had rushed into her life with his insulting proposal? She should have demanded he never speak to her again.

Not marry him, for pity's sake.

Augustus slept soundly in his crib. *Let every night of your life be so peaceful, little one.*

If not for this tiny babe, she would have continued her modest and unremarkable life—stealing time to explore the ruins and brush her fingers along the stones and fossils George brought home from his excavations. Longing to discover something significant, to throw light into the dark corners of the past and understand better what made humanity the way it was.

She met her friend's eyes and forced a smile. "I'm perfectly fine."

Grace's gaze warmed as she squeezed Modesty's hand. "Not many would uproot their life for a baby that isn't their own."

Modesty let out a long exhale, attempting to relieve the tension squeezing her windpipe. She owed it to Ophelia to care for her child when she couldn't.

"Some would say I'm very lucky. From a vicar's daughter to a duchess."

She released Grace's hand and crossed to the dressing table, her fingers trailing over the ornate box Constantine had sent yesterday. Her hands trembled even more as she lifted the lid, revealing what lay within. Grace gasped softly. Nestled on midnight blue velvet lay the most exquisite necklace she'd ever seen. Diamonds and sapphires alternated in an intricate floral pattern. The gold setting was so pale it appeared almost silver, the metalwork so delicate it seemed to float between the gems.

She chuckled. "This must be worth more than the vicarage."

"It is beautiful," Grace said. "Did the duke send this?"

"He did."

"Why are you not wearing it?"

Modesty inhaled sharply. "I can't make myself."

"Don't you think it means he appreciates you? Wants to please you?"

"He wants to please himself. Wants to protect his reputation. We're to be madly in love. This must be what will show everyone the extent of his feelings."

Understanding softened Grace's features. "Right. So, will you put it on?"

Modesty chuckled. "Look at my dress, at my hair. I'm going to carry a bouquet of wildflowers, and I made my gown myself. How ridiculous would this necklace look on me?"

The day before, several boxes had arrived at her doorstep accompanied by an army of maids ready to transform her into a proper duchess. Inside were silk gowns in fashionable colors, delicate slippers, and bonnets adorned with feathers, flowers, pearls, and crystals.

"His grace insists," said the stern-faced woman who must have been the senior maid.

Modesty's fingers traced the fine fabrics. "Please thank his grace, but I will wear my own gown."

The head maid's mouth tightened. "Miss, a duchess cannot—"

"I am not a duchess yet," Modesty said quietly but firmly. "And this is the last choice I will make as myself."

And so here she was now. In her own dress.

Feeling like she may have made a mistake.

Modesty closed the lid of the box and placed it back on the dressing table. "The very idea of pretending is sickening. All I want is to protect little Augustus. I want nothing to do with the duke."

His vanity and pride repulsed her.

And yet, he stole her breath away every time she saw him. Why couldn't she stop looking into his eyes, drowning in them?

Grace picked up Modesty's bonnet, decorated with purple meadow saffron, and held it out to her. "Don't you think you could eventually be happy with him?"

Modesty inhaled and exhaled but the tension in her chest wouldn't ease.

She took the bonnet, placed it on her head, then began tying the lilac-colored ribbons. "One must always keep up hope, must one not?"

One hour later, Modesty's footsteps echoed against the marble floors as she entered St. George's, the sound swallowed by the vaulted ceiling high above. Morning light streaming through towering stained-glass windows in jewel-bright colors put her small church's simple panes to shame.

Her throat tightened as what felt like hundreds of eyes turned towards her. Silk rustled as the ton's finest shifted in their seats to stare—duchesses and countesses in morning dresses worth more than her father's yearly income, their necks and ears decorated with gems. In All Saints, she knew every weathered face, every patched Sunday best. Here, she recognized no one save the duke.

The aisle stretched before her, impossibly long. Each step brought her closer to the duke, who stood as rigid as the marble columns that flanked the pews on each side. His indigo coat was immaculate, his cravat a masterpiece of intricate folds. His dark eyes were intense on her, melting her bones. Was that supposed to be the look of love? Something in her chest fluttered. Was it his presence, how effortlessly he commanded the space around him? This was her future husband—this stranger who belonged so completely to this glittering world that felt as foreign to her as the moon.

The Bishop of London droned through his sermon. And it was time for their vows.

"I, Constantine Buccleigh," his voice carried through the church, "the Duke of Pryde, take thee, Miss Modesty Fairchild, to be my wedded wife..."

His fingers brushed against hers as he slipped the ring on, the touch sending a shiver down her spine. His hands were large, warm, and strong, but with elegant fingers, and she wondered why it felt so enjoyable to have them on her skin.

When it was her turn, she had to swallow twice before she could speak. "I, Modesty Fairchild," she said, her voice wavering slightly, "take thee, Constantine Buccleigh..."

She spoke the vow, barely able to remember what she said. She was acutely aware of his presence—the subtle scent of bergamot, vetiver, and leather that clung to him, the steady rise and fall of his chest, the way he seemed to tower over her despite him being only slightly taller.

Their eyes met over their joined hands. Something flickered in his gaze—pride? Satisfaction? For a moment, she thought she glimpsed vulnerability beneath his marble façade, the flash of a lonely little boy who seemed shy but hopeful. But it was gone before she could be sure, replaced by that familiar mask of aristocratic indifference.

"What God has joined together, let no man put asunder," the bishop intoned.

The duke's fingers tightened almost imperceptibly around hers. Was it meant to be reassuring or a reminder of their agreement? She couldn't tell, and that uncertainty made her heart flit about like a trapped bird in her chest.

What had she just done?

Half an hour later, the wedding breakfast took place in Pryde House in Mayfair.

She and the duke stood side by side in the grand room. The heat radiating from his body seemed to draw her closer, even as propriety demanded she maintain her distance. Mirrors with golden frames hung on walls of masculine indigo tones. White marble statues stood between paintings that bore scenes of maritime storms and naval victories. A large table was laden with cold game pies, glazed ham, bride cake, sweetmeats and preserved fruit, fresh bread and butter, cold meats and terrines.

While guests arrived, the duke never left her side. He introduced her to so many lords and ladies, dukes and duchesses that she couldn't remember their names and merely smiled with a wooden face.

She felt the duke's attention on her like the brush of hot air from a fire.

When all of the guests had gathered around them, the duke cleared his throat.

"I know many of you were surprised at the quick wedding announcement," he declared. "But I simply couldn't wait to marry this delightful young woman and make her rightfully mine."

Her stomach clenched at the words. Was he really saying them? Someone like him? She looked up at him, and he was staring straight at her, his expression bathing her in warmth.

"Beautiful," he said, his chestnut eyes darkening as they swept over her face. "Incredibly kind. Someone who loves history and antiquities so much. Someone with modesty and manners. I am so lucky to call you my wife."

She swallowed, her throat dry. The deep timbre of his voice vibrated through her, and she found herself swaying slightly towards him. His jaw tensed as he spoke, a muscle flickering beneath his skin, and her gaze was inexplicably drawn to the fullness of his lower lip. Surely, he was just pretending, but why did each word seem to strike directly at her heart?

"Someone selfless," he continued, his voice dropping to an intimate murmur that seemed meant for her alone. He shifted closer, the broad expanse of his shoulders nearly shielding her from the crowd, creating a private moment in the midst of the gathering. His breath whispered against her temple as he spoke. "Who helps in a women's almshouse, loves wildflowers, and cares for others so deeply there are no limits to what she would do to help them."

The intensity of his gaze held her captive as he raised his glass, his signet ring catching the light. A lock of dark hair had fallen across his forehead, softening his usually stern countenance, making him look younger. His free hand moved to the small of her back, warm and steady through the thin muslin of her gown. "To Modesty Buccleigh, the new Duchess of Pryde."

The touch of his hand, the heat of his body, the hypnotic depth of his eyes...she was light-headed, and she wasn't sure if it was the wine or something far more dangerous.

The rest of the room followed his exclamation, all toasting her, while she felt dizzy from the attention. She sipped her wine. This was the first time she had tasted champagne, and it was prickly on her tongue. The elation hitting her blood a moment later made her feel weak.

She didn't like it.

He drank, too, his eyes never leaving hers.

"Are you hungry?" he asked quietly. "Would you like something to eat?"

She turned to the table and was surprised to find wildflowers in vases standing among plates with cut meat, pies, and bread. Many of the bouquets had purple meadow saffron, and so they fit strangely well with her outfit.

"No, I do not think I could eat even if I wanted to," she said. "But thank you."

She shivered slightly. Her nerves were as taut as bowstrings. This was her new home, and these were the people she supposed she'd find herself entertaining, talking to perhaps every day. It was opulent and had every comfort. And yet, she yearned to return to her modest room with whitewashed walls, and windows with cracked glass, and her books on the Roman Empire, which smelled like old paper and dust.

"Are you cold?" he asked. "May I fetch you a shawl?"

She didn't know which she preferred, his coldness or his attention. At least when he was cool to her, she felt strong, alive with indignation. When he was warm, she felt weak and uncertain of herself.

"I'm quite all right," she said. "Thank you."

"Was the necklace I sent you not to your liking?"

She swallowed. "I—er—I couldn't put it on."

He frowned. "Was the clasp broken?"

"No. The necklace is lovely. But—I've never worn anything so valuable in my life. And I worried my current attire would mock the beauty of the necklace...and make it seem unworthy while it is so precious."

His gaze briefly dropped down her body, bringing an onrush of heat. "You were sent appropriate clothes, were you not?"

She swallowed. It was hard to imagine she would ever feel entitled to wear a fortune on her neck while others scraped and struggled for every coin and bit of food. "Yes. But I didn't think I could— They must cost a fortune— I couldn't imagine—"

He nodded. "I hope you will feel like you can wear beautiful gowns and jewelry in the future. You're a duchess now."

A duchess...the word felt foreign and strange.

Her gaze dropped to his neck and the pin that he wore in his cravat. "Who is this woman? She looks lovely."

He looked down on his chest. "My mama," he said. "This pin was her gift to my papa. I wanted her to be with me when I married."

Something tightened in her chest as she studied the lovely face of a woman in a high powdered wig. Despite herself, her heart reached out to him.

"She passed away many years ago," he added. "I fit her portrait into the pin after my papa passed away."

Sharp, needlelike pain pierced her heart. "I am sorry she's no longer with us. It must have been wonderful to have known her at all."

He gave a curt nod. "It was. I presume your mama passed away?"

She nodded, trying to breathe deeply through her tight throat. "She died giving birth to me. I wish I had known my mama, wish I had seen her face even once. It is very lovely you've brought yours to the wedding."

Something passed across his face, as though a curtain lifted, his carefully maintained mask cracking for just a breath. Their eyes locked, and in that moment, she saw past the duke, past the nobleman, into the depths of the man himself. She saw a boy standing at his mother's grave, just as lost as she had been as a child, that same ache of absence carved into his heart. There was a rawness there, an uncertainty that he kept hidden behind his stern countenance and sharp words. His eyes, usually so guarded, held an echo of old pain, and something else—a desperate, almost childlike longing for connection, for someone who understood this particular wound that had never quite healed.

Earlier, he'd looked at her with such warmth, spoken of her with such seeming admiration. It had felt so real. Even more so now. For a heartbeat, she let herself see it: Augustus taking his first steps in the garden while Constantine steadied him, his large hands gentle around the baby's middle. The three of them in the library, Constantine showing Augustus the Roman coins while she sketched the artifacts in her notebook. Summer afternoons beneath the oak trees, a blanket spread with treats, Constantine's deep laugh mixing with Augustus's happy squeals as she wove them both flower crowns...

But then he blinked, and the walls came rushing back up, leaving her wondering if she'd imagined that glimpse of his true self, that profound understanding between them.

He had just opened his mouth to ask something when there was a whisper of silk as someone came to stand by their side, and the spell was broken.

"Here's the new duchess," said a stunning golden-haired woman in an exquisite crimson satin dress. Her smile lit up the room. "I cannot wait to get to know you better, Your Grace."

She stood next to a very tall, dark-haired man in a crimson waistcoat. He looked fierce but there was warmth in his sky-blue eyes. By their side was another lady who had his coloring. She wore a yellow gown and was accompanied by a man with soft blond curls and a mischievous violet gaze. They had been introduced earlier, but to her shame she couldn't remember their names.

"I thank you..." she managed.

"Patience, Duchess of Rath." The golden-haired woman smiled broader. "I know you can't remember our names. Trust me, I've been in your position. There's no shame in it. This is my husband, the Duke of Rath. My sister-in-law and my brother-in-law, the Duke and Duchess of Luhst. These three men"—she indicated Pryde, Rath, and Luhst—"are as thick as thieves. Just be warned."

Something about the Duchess of Rath was so warm and welcoming, the tension in Modesty's throat and her chest melted a little.

She remembered what her father had said about the Seven Dukes of Sin, and she wondered if she should be afraid. But instead she felt more at home than she had a few moments ago.

She smiled back, a little relieved. "I shall consider myself warned." She glanced at Rath and Luhst, who regarded her with kind curiosity. The Duke of Luhst, she realized, was the man Pryde had mentioned being blackmailed because of an illegitimate child. Would it be impolite to ask about that? She wasn't sure, and she didn't want to embarrass anyone.

"Is this right? You interest yourself in history and ancient studies?" asked the Duchess of Rath.

Modesty nodded. "Indeed I do. Whenever I have time, of course."

The Duchess of Luhst lit up with enthusiasm. "Perhaps you might wish to join me and Patience in our club."

Modesty blinked. "Your club?"

"Indeed," said the Duchess of Luhst. "Patience is a botanist. I do medical research. If you wish to deepen and enhance your knowledge, or discuss your findings and challenges, you're very welcome. We call ourselves Misses with Microscopes and want more women to join. It would be our pleasure if you do."

Modesty felt a jolt of excitement she had rarely experienced in her life. Discussing antiquities? History? Theories, proof, evidence, hypotheses... She couldn't do much of that in Shepherdsbrook, only sometimes when she spoke with Mr. Lockhart. Could she speak of such things regularly, without looking over her shoulder, afraid of her papa's disapproval? He had always felt she should be helping him and others, not reading about the past.

"I—" She looked at her new husband, who stared at her with raised brows.

What about Augustus? The entire reason for her marriage was the well-being of the baby. He was now with Mrs. Walcott, settling in somewhere upstairs. She should spend any spare time with him. Besides, she needed to learn so much about being a duchess—manners, correct addresses, dances, and so on.

The Duke of Luhst grinned, his eyes crinkling with mirth. "Beware of these two. They're quite serious about their science."

"I thank you," she said with a polite nod. "I do not think my knowledge is as vast as yours. It's merely an amusement for me." Or a dream that would never come true. "I would not want to waste your valuable time."

Both of the ladies' smiles fell a little. "Well," said the Duchess of Luhst, who threw a careful glance at Pryde. "If you ever change your mind, Duchess, just one word from you is all that's needed."

The Duchess of Rath beamed at her again. "Or if you need anything else. A friendly ear. Or just some company for tea. It can be quite daunting to learn everything one must to be a duchess."

Modesty smiled politely as the gentlemen and the ladies retreated to give room for other guests wishing to congratulate them.

But the Duke of Luhst lingered a moment and leaned towards her. "I know he can seem cold and insufferably proud. But give him a chance. In time you may find, as we all have, that he is the most loyal of friends."

Before she could reply or think more on what he said, he followed his wife and the Duke and Duchess of Rath to another corner of the room, looking carefree and practically glowing with happiness.

An older lady with a silvery mane of hair was introduced as the Dowager Duchess of Grandhampton. She was dressed in the fashions of the previous era, but still looked beautiful. With a twinkle in her kind blue eyes, she asked how she and the duke had met and how their love had blossomed so quickly.

"We met at the church where Mr. Fairchild preaches," said Pryde, completely calm and collected. "All Saints of Shepherdsbrook. And Miss Fairchild completely charmed me. From that day forward, the thought of a future without her was unbearable."

The dowager chuckled. "Clearly. I have not known you to visit churches...especially those on the outskirts of London."

"Quite right. Call it destiny. Providence. It was as though someone beckoned me to come to the church."

The duchess's eyes sparkled with humor and she smiled kindly. "Providence. Of course. Marriage for love is a rare thing, I should know—all my grandchildren were so fortunate, though not without their challenges... In any event, I hope you both realize that and cherish each other always. I wish you every happiness."

Happiness...

Modesty looked up at Pryde, and he stared into her eyes. She has seen glimpses of something softer beneath his hard exterior. Would she be so naïve as to believe they might truly love each other someday...or at least enjoy moments of happiness?

Everyone sat at the grand table for breakfast. She forced herself to take a few bites of the game pie, more because she didn't want the food to go to waste than because she was hungry. And then the guests began departing. While she was saying goodbye to Papa, Grace, and George, the duke left her side to say goodbye to his six ducal friends. As she waved to her papa, who was the last guest to leave, she allowed herself a moment of weakness while no footmen were in sight. She leaned against the large bay window in the sitting room adjacent to the entrance hall. The hours at the center of so many distinguished guests' attention had left her shaken and exhausted. She let herself sink down onto the window seat, enjoying the partial privacy that a heavy indigo and golden curtain gave her from the rest of the drawing room.

She'd go to see Augustus in a moment. Her heart quickened at the thought of him alone in this strange house. Would Mrs. Walcott know to keep his blanket close, the one that still carried his mother's scent? Would she remember he needed to be held upright for a few minutes after feeding or he'd get that terrible colic that kept him crying all night?

She should have asked where they had put him. Pryde House was a maze of corridors and closed doors; she'd have to find a servant to guide her... Yet another reminder of how out of place she was in this grand house.

She watched as one of Pryde's carriages drew up. He had insisted on providing transportation to return Papa, Grace, and George to Shepherdsbrook, despite her father's initial protests about accepting such a favor.

After watching the carriage pull away, she made to descend from the window seat. But the sound of male voices coming through the open sitting room door stopped her.

She'd recognize Pryde's voice anywhere. Low, rich, velvety. It always caused an unmistakable tickling sensation in her lower belly.

"She seems lovely, Constantine," said a deep voice, and she thought this must be the Duke of Rath. "Are you sure you made the right choice by marrying someone the Regent will disapprove of, though—especially so quickly? As amiable as Miss Fairchild is, and as much as Patience and Chastity long to have another friend who shares their passion for scientific pursuits..."

"Beware," said a man she thought must be the Duke of Luhst. "Dorian and I are testaments to how love can change a man."

"Love," her husband chuckled. "Believe me, there's no chance of that."

Modesty held her breath, the words hitting her harder than she had ever thought they could.

"She's nothing but a means to an end," he continued. "A way to take control of the baby and avoid a scandal. A vicar's daughter will be the perfect wife—quiet, obedient, and invisible. She won't protest as I go on with my life unbothered. She has secured a rich and noble husband. What else can a woman of her birth wish for in life?"

She couldn't breathe. Hurt slapped her hard as she tried to blink through the tears. She tasted copper—she'd bitten her lip to keep from making a sound. That was what he thought of her?

The bay window's cushion felt like stone beneath her. She wrapped her arms around herself but couldn't stop shaking. What a fool she'd been to let herself hope, even for a moment.

There could be no hope for this marriage.

She could never love someone like her husband—insensitive, pompous, and self-centered.

And he could never love someone he believed was so far beneath him.

7

Constantine knocked on the door that connected his room to that of Miss Fairchild and listened.

He needed to stop calling her Miss.

She was his wife now, for better or worse.

But she didn't seem like the Duchess of Pryde...not yet. She'd been so shy and so timid at the wedding breakfast. The poor lilac gown hung on her slim frame, too short for her height and completely unflattering for her fair complexion. She needed to wear gowns that would bring out her remarkable forest-green eyes and that mesmerizing color of her hair —like burnished copper. Bright and fiery.

How could a woman so striking stand with her hands clasped before her and her shoulders tense and slouched, looking as though she wanted to make herself smaller, to hide?

He knocked again.

"Duchess?" he said. "May I come in?"

The silence beyond the door clawed at his nerves. He was supposed to bed her tonight—for the sake of this bloody marriage and to ensure she was pregnant as soon as possible. But he'd had only one lover before.

An experienced one.

What was he meant to do with a virgin? He'd have to hurt her, and that was last thing he wished.

"Yes," came a quiet reply from behind the door.

He licked his lips, then clasped the door handle and entered. She was standing in the middle of the room, still in her wedding dress. Her stance was almost as stiff as the muslin fabric. He wished he had Lucien's charm and the ability put others at ease with just one glance.

Would she, perhaps, loosen up if he brushed gently against her tight shoulders or kneaded her muscles?

He cleared his throat and walked towards her slowly, licking his lips again. The windows were dark, the light of candles in candelabras reflecting against the glass. A black coal grate emitted warmth and soft light from the large fireplace on the opposite wall. A grand four-poster bed dominated one wall, its elegant canopy draped in pale blue silk, and the blue counterpane adorned with golden patterns.

His new wife looked so domestic, so fragile, with her eyes round and her lips parted as she stared at him.

He cleared his throat. "I came to..."

Goodness, he was overcome with shyness. What ailed him? He had every right to bed her. He wanted to. Why was he feeling like an adolescent before having his first woman?

"I need an heir," he said simply, and she blinked.

"You need an heir?"

"Yes. There are currently no other heirs to my title. No cousins, no uncles, or anyone else. Just myself...and Augustus, of course."

She swallowed visibly and sucked in a breath. Her gaze darted towards the bed. "Oh."

She blushed crimson.

He stepped closer to her. She retreated, maintaining the distance between them.

A whiff of her scent brushed against his senses. He'd caught it earlier, as well, in the carriage on the way from St. George's to Pryde House, and during the breakfast when she'd stood by his side. Wildflowers. Clean skin. Her own aroma, which was fruity and feminine and elicited a memory he couldn't quite grasp—an echo of joy, ease, and pleasure.

She had such lovely full lips and high cheekbones, and her expressive eyes were slanted slightly at the edges. Standing so close, he could see that tiny freckles dusted her cheeks, adding a youthful innocence that tugged at something deep inside him.

Would she taste as sweet as she smelled?

He wanted to kiss her. To run his tongue along her plush lower lip and feel her shudder in his arms, to hear her moan in surrender as her breath mixed with his own.

With his heart slamming hard against his ribs, he raised his hand towards her, slowly, as one would with a young fawn. He expected her to flinch and step away from him, and he wouldn't blame her if she wanted to do so. But she didn't. She stood unmoving, her lips still slightly parted, pale pink like delicate petals. He picked up a strand of her gorgeous hair and tucked it behind her ear, and an intoxicating current rushed through his every nerve ending.

Like touching stars...

Then he brushed her face with his knuckles. Good God, such soft skin. Now it felt as if he'd plunged his entire hand into a pool of stars. His skin tingled, suddenly alive in every spot where he'd touched her.

Their gazes were locked, and he saw her pupils dilate, making the green of her eyes darken to the color of forest moss.

The blush that swept over on her cheeks made him wonder if her chest would look just as rosy when she squirmed with pleasure as he brought her to her release.

Oh, this duty of making an heir with her wouldn't be a chore at all.

"Such silky, delicate skin," he said as he stepped even closer, his fingers trailing along her jaw. "You're beautiful, Miss Fairchild. Beautiful bride. Beautiful wife."

She blinked at the words, as though not quite sure she'd heard him right. Before she could retreat again, he closed the distance between them. His lips brushed hers, gentle as a whisper, testing. The softness of her mouth, the small gasp that escaped her—it was heaven itself. She tasted of the wedding wine and honey and wildflowers.

For one glorious moment, she melted against him. Her hands came up to rest on his chest, and he felt her fingers curl into his waistcoat. He deepened the kiss, drawing her closer, one hand cradling the back of her head while the other settled at her waist. She made a small sound, half sigh, half moan, that sent fire racing through his blood.

Then, as though waking from a spell, she stiffened. Her hands pushed against his chest. She wrenched away from him, stumbling backwards until the bed stood between them like a fortress wall.

"No," she said, her voice shaking. Her lips were a deeper pink from his kiss, and knowing he'd done that to her made him want to cross the room and claim them again. She wrapped her arms around herself. "I would like you to leave."

He swayed a little, struggling to find his balance. He had a strange sense that he'd just come so, so close to tasting heaven...and now had been violently pulled away from it.

"Forgive me," he said, though he wasn't sure what he was

apologizing for—the kiss, his presumption, or everything that had led them to this moment.

As the draw of her body began subsiding, his head cleared. Her rejection stung. He had never been rejected by a woman. His lover in Elysium was always willing, and he didn't pursue women outside of that arrangement. Young widows and unhappily married ladies tried to catch his attention at balls, but he never entertained them, unwilling to father natural children. He had avoided debutantes and their mamas like the plague, wanting to wait until he was ready to choose a bride himself.

And now that he had one, she didn't want him.

It hurt like the slash of a red-hot saber across his gut.

"May I inquire as to why?" he asked, struggling a little to return his breathing to normal.

"You may not," she said, her head high, her shoulders rigid.

He nodded. Naturally, a woman wouldn't want to be bedded by a man she despised. "Is your objection to me?"

Her eyes blazed. "It is hard to accept a man who pretends at love while, in truth, believing I'm far beneath his status. Who imagines he is doing me a favor by wedding me. Who is more concerned with his reputation than the well-being of his child. A man who turned away a pregnant woman asking for help."

Her words lashed him like a whip. "Quite a list," he said.

He supposed he had behaved like a brute.

But how could she understand the pressure he was under? Every perfectly executed bow, every flawlessly delivered pleasantry, every impeccable item of clothing was another brick in the wall protecting his secret. One whisper of his true parentage, and everything would crumble. Maintaining his reputation wasn't about vanity—it was about survival.

He couldn't show her how much her words affected him.

She was unaware that he was but a counterfeit duke. But she seemed able to see past the façade he'd created, the stone-cold armor he wore every day. She saw the flaws he hid from the world.

Good heavens, what would she do if she ever discovered the truth?

"Very well," he said, his voice poised as always. "I will not press my attentions where they're not wanted. But do know you will lie with me. It is your duty as my wife whether you wish it or not. Still, I will not take you against your will, as that is not in my nature. I will leave you now. Tomorrow you will start learning how to be a true duchess."

8

THE CARRIAGE WHEELS rattled over the cobblestones as Constantine approached the modest town house in a quiet corner of London, one of many properties tied to his estate. He stepped out, his polished boots gleaming in the weak autumn sunlight. The air was crisp, carrying the scent of fallen leaves and smoke.

"Please give the babe to me," he said to Mrs. Walcott, who was about to descend from the carriage as well. Augustus was swaddled tightly in white lace and clutched to her chest. "It will be easier for you to climb down."

Mrs. Walcott's mouth pressed into a tight line. She had been in complete disagreement with his decision, he knew, from the moment he and Mrs. Higgs entered the nursery early that morning. As two maids had begun packing Augustus's and Mrs. Walcott's things, the nurse had continually asked if Modesty was aware they were leaving and if she would come to say goodbye.

He needed to hide Augustus away for the sake of his title. Avoiding a scandal around the marriage and the arrival of a baby in the house was paramount. Any scandal meant attention. Meant questions. And questions meant the Regent might start digging for answers.

For the truth.

"I am not going to eat him," Constantine said, staring the nurse down.

The most annoying thing was, part of him agreed with her. He should have told Modesty. He should not separate her and the babe at all. Modesty would be furious. Hurt. Worried.

But this was the best thing. He'd return the child as soon as the threat to his title was eliminated.

Mrs. Walcott nodded. "Right then, Your Grace."

She handed him the bundle. It was the first time he had held Augustus, and he was surprised by how little he weighed. The babe frowned, studying him as though through frosted glass. Constantine's heart thumped against his chest. Good Lord, what was he doing? Being so afraid of a tiny newborn, innocent and pure. Was this really him—the honorable Duke of Pryde?

Mrs. Walcott descended and stretched her arms out. "If you could, Your Grace?"

"I'll carry him," he said, strangely reluctant to release the baby so quickly. "Your arms must be tired."

She frowned but nodded. "If you wish."

"I do. And I cannot stress enough that the duchess is not to know Augustus's location. I appreciate that you owe her your loyalty, but you're now under my employment. If my desire for secrecy was to be violated, I'm afraid Augustus will need to have a new wet nurse who is more loyal to the man who pays her wages."

Anger flashed through her eyes. "As you wish, Your Grace."

He nodded, and they all turned towards the house. Two

footmen and a maid were unloading things from the back of the carriage.

Constantine climbed the stairs first. The entrance doors were already open. He nodded to the footman who stood ready to greet him. "Good afternoon, Thomas. How is Mr. Hawthorne today?"

Thomas's weathered face creased with concern. "Not one of his better days, Your Grace. He's been talking about sending out advertisements searching for tutoring positions all morning."

Constantine's heart sank, but he kept his face impassive. "I see. Perhaps he'd like to see this little boy."

A warm smile lit Thomas's expression as he craned his neck to look at Augustus. "I'm sure he will. Surely, that would do him good."

Thomas and the rest of the staff had been notified of the plan with Augustus last night when Constantine had made the decision. And the arrangements were made that morning, before Modesty was awake. The staff had been asked to set up a nursery and hastily purchase any furniture and other supplies required for a newborn and his nurse.

The interior of the house was spotless and warm, a stark contrast to the chill outside. Soft carpets muffled Constantine's footsteps as he made his way to the sitting room. It was a modest but well-maintained house, one of the buildings his family had owned in London for generations. The walls were lined with bookshelves, filled with volumes on history, litera- ture, and the classics. Constantine always made sure there were plenty of books for Mr. Hawthorne, whose lifelong passion for learning kept his spirits up.

Mr. Hawthorne sat in an armchair by the window, a woolen blanket draped over his knees. His once-sharp blue eyes were clouded with confusion as he looked up at Constantine's entrance.

"Ah, young man," Mr. Hawthorne said, his voice quavering. "Are you here to hire me as a tutor for your child?"

Constantine swallowed the lump in his throat. Mr. Hawthorne was the only friend he'd had as a boy. With his papa resenting him and controlling his every step and his mama anxious for him to be something he could never be—his papa's natural son—the loneliness he'd felt as a child had been bone-deep. Except when he'd had lessons with his tutor, Mr. Hawthorne.

"No," he said as he took a seat across from the elderly man. "This is little Augustus, my ward. I've come to visit you. How are you feeling?"

Mr. Hawthorne's gray brows furrowed. "Visit me? I don't... I'm sorry, I don't seem to recall who you are, Mr...."

He never did, not for the past two years. "It's all right," Constantine said gently. "We're old friends. I come to see you every week."

Mr. Hawthorne nodded, though uncertainty still clouded his features. His face was wrinkled and pale, the light reflecting off his bald head.

As Mr. Hawthorne's gaze drifted to Augustus, his face brightened. "Is this not the most exceptional young fellow? Just look at the inquisitive light in his eyes! My brother was the same way as a babe."

"Would you mind if Augustus stayed with you for a while?" he asked. "He'll have a wet nurse and a maid to keep an eye on him."

"Do I mind? Not at all." He stretched out his arms, and Constantine gave him the bundle. "I'll read to you, Augustus, and tell you stories of Robin Hood, and Red Riding Hood, and

Cinderella. You need your curiosity fulfilled. I already see that. We will have the best of times together!"

As Constantine watched the old man coo to the baby, his chest tightened even more. As the babe fussed, turning his head this way and that, his cap shifted to reveal a birthmark behind his ear, visible through his wispy golden hair—a mark in the shape of a wolf's head. Constantine's breath caught. A wolf's head had been on the coat of arms of the dukes of Pryde for generations. How fitting. Here, written upon Augustus's very flesh, was an undeniable sign of his birthright. Providence itself had marked him as heir to the dukedom.

Constantine tore his gaze away from Augustus. "How have you been, Mr. Hawthorne?"

"Very well, indeed." Mr. Hawthorne's eyes wrinkled as he smiled. "I expect to receive a good position any day now. It will be wonderful to teach young minds about the mysteries of the world."

Constantine's throat clenched as he pressed out a smile. It was heartbreaking to see a man he dearly loved in this state. "Of course you will."

They spoke a little more, Constantine asking what he had done today, what he had read. And they discussed poetry that had been published forty years ago. As the conversation drifted, Constantine's mind returned to his wife and Augustus. His gut wrenched in worry. Only yesterday he'd married Modesty and accepted the babe into his home.

Later today, he would pay the exorbitant sum of £1,000 to the drinking establishment Portside. It was situated near the docks in Whitechapel and also served as a boxing club with illegal fights. After he paid, the blackmailer should leave him alone.

If he lost his title, his wealth, who would care for Mr. Hawthorne? Who would provide for his new wife, his household staff, the families who depended on his estate? This man, who had been more of a father to him than the duke ever was, would end up in a workhouse. And Modesty—who deserved so much better—would be ruined by association.

"I will leave you, Mr. Hawthorne," Constantine said, rising to his feet. "I will return to see you and Augustus soon."

Mr. Hawthorne looked up at him, a flicker of recognition in his eyes. "Of course, Constantine. Do come again. It's always a pleasure to speak with bright young men."

As Constantine left the town house, the weight of his decisions pressed heavily upon him. Was he truly protecting others or just disguising his self-preservation as nobility? Perhaps both were true. He climbed into his carriage, his resolve wavering. He would protect those he cared about, yes, but he couldn't pretend his own survival wasn't at stake.

How would he look into his wife's eyes when she learned he'd hidden the child from the world...and from her?

⁂

Modesty stood before the ornate gold-framed mirror in her grand bedchamber, feeling like an imposter. The pale blue silk wallpaper still felt alien, as did standing idle while Graves, her lady's maid, arranged her hair. The chignon was admittedly beautiful, but the hours spent preening could have been better used helping at the women's almshouse or baking bread for the parish's sick. Her old muslin dress looked particularly shabby now, contrasted with her carefully styled hair. It was like plaiting silk ribbons into a work horse's mane.

The new duchess's wardrobe was folded in drawers in her dressing room—silks and satins, the value of which could support Grace's almshouse for months. But her world had shifted beneath her feet, and everything felt so strange. Her familiar muslin was like armor. She couldn't bear to touch those grand gowns, didn't want to betray the person she was behind her new title.

She could barely sleep last night after the duke had kissed her... The avalanche of sensations he'd caused... He had taken her by surprise, and she'd taken herself by surprise by allowing it, by not stopping him sooner. But it was so strange how right she'd felt in his arms at first. The warmth and pressure on her lips, the way his tongue stroked hers. Her breasts had ached to press against him, and a tingly heat had spread between her thighs.

She'd been so shocked by her own reaction that she had to stop it. If she'd let him go on, she didn't know what else would have happened between them...

Just remembering the kiss caused similar sensations to course through her now.

Her rational mind had saved her from her treacherous body.

How could she let a man she barely knew into her bed? All her life she'd been taught to be dutiful, to put others first, to accept what came her way with humility. But something about Pryde made her want to fight back, to demand more. Perhaps it was because of Augustus—having someone else to protect had given her the courage to stand up for herself. Or perhaps this fire had always been inside her, tamped down by years of her father's stern expectations.

"There, Your Grace," said Madeleine, stepping back to survey her work. "The chignon suits you beautifully."

Modesty met the young woman's eyes in the mirror. "Thank you, Madeleine. Though I confess, I'm not used to being still for so long."

Graves smiled kindly. "You'll grow accustomed to it, Your Grace. And if I may say, you look every inch a duchess."

Ready for the day, Modesty walked out of her grand bedchamber to go and see Augustus. The nursery was the first room she'd visited after the wedding guests left. These past two weeks, back at home, she'd fallen into a routine with Augustus. Every morning after breakfast, she'd take him to the garden, singing to him as they walked among the bushes and flower beds. She'd read to him from her books about Roman Britain while he cooed in his cradle, and rock him to sleep herself despite Mrs. Walcott's protests. Even her papa had remarked on how the baby seemed to know her voice, how he settled instantly in her arms.

When she approached Augustus's nursery, she froze and frowned... There were no sounds: no baby's cry, no cooing, no soft tones of Mrs. Walcott humming a lullaby.

Her heart began to race. Was Augustus still asleep? *Please let him be asleep.*

When she opened the door, the nursery was empty. Augustus's crib stood bare, the blankets folded neatly at its foot. His toys—the wooden horse from her childhood, the soft rabbit Ophelia had made—all gone.

At first, she thought Mrs. Walcott might have taken him out for a stroll. But his things would have been here, then. The nurse's bed was also stripped of linens, and there was no sign of her clothes, either.

What in the world? A sharp, icy shiver coursed through her veins as a horrible realization crept into her psyche.

"No," she whispered. "No, no, no."

She ran from the room, not caring about the impropriety of running through the house. After opening almost every door, she finally found Pryde in his study, writing.

"Where is he?" she demanded. "Where is Augustus?"

Pryde looked up, his face a mask of calm. "Good morning, Duchess. I trust you slept well?"

"Where is Augustus?" she repeated, her hands clenching into fists at her sides.

He set down his pen, unhurried. The audacity! "I've sent him away. It's for the best, really. Having a baby here, when we're newly wed, would create quite the scandal. People would assume he was born out of wedlock."

Modesty's chest felt constricted, as though bound too tightly. A hot flush surged up her neck, prickling her skin. "You...you sent him away? Without consulting me?"

"It's better for everyone this way," Pryde continued, his tone maddeningly cool. "He'll be raised there, with everything he could need—doting nurses, toys, fresh air. When he's older, we can reintroduce him as a young cousin or ward."

"Better for *everyone*?" Modesty's voice rose to a high pitch she didn't recognize. "Or better for you and your precious reputation? How dare you make such a decision without me! I am his guardian, I promised Ophelia—"

"You are my wife now," Pryde interrupted. "And I am the head of this household. It is my duty to make decisions for the good of our family and our standing in society."

Modesty felt tears of frustration pricking at her eyes. "*Our* standing in society? *Your* standing, more like! Is that all you care about? What about what's right? What about keeping an innocent baby with the person his mother charged with his safety and well-being?"

Something flickered—doubt? Regret?—across Pryde's face, but it was gone in an instant.

"He will be well cared for," Pryde said firmly. "And when the time is right, we will bring him back."

"When the time is right for you, you mean," Modesty spat. She turned on her heel, ready to storm out, then paused. "Where exactly did you send him? Which estate?"

Pryde's jaw tightened. "Why do you wish to know?"

"You cannot separate us. I promised his mother on her deathbed I'd make sure he's all right."

"Of course. And he is. Do you think I'd endanger a baby in any way?"

She shrugged. "I do know that for you, many things come before Augustus's well-being."

His brows twitched, and for a moment she saw hurt cross his face. She almost wished she hadn't said it... Almost.

"His nurse is with him," he said. "The house is fully staffed to care for his needs. You do not have to worry."

She shook her head. "How can I not worry when you keep me in the dark? Where did you send him?"

He held her gaze, watching her coolly from under thick eyebrows. "I think it's best if that information remains private for now. To avoid any...impulsive actions."

Modesty scoffed. "First, you sent Ophelia away when she needed you most, and now you've done the same to her child —to your own flesh and blood!"

She saw Pryde flinch at her words, but she was too angry to care. "Why won't you let me go with him?"

"You are my duchess, or at least the beginning of one. You will train with me to become a true duchess, and I will show you off like a prized diamond all around the city. We must convince the ton of our love match—anything less would create whispers, speculation. Such a scandal would harm not only us but Augustus as well. Society must see us as the perfect duke and duchess, above reproach in every way."

She turned and fled the room, her mind already forming plans. She would question every servant in the household, from the highest butler to the lowest stable boy. Someone must know something. And if that failed, she'd write to every estate agent in England, checking property records for Pryde holdings.

In the kitchen, she cornered the housekeeper. "Mrs. Higgs, do you know where they've taken Augustus? I need to know he's safe."

Mrs. Higgs's kindly face creased with sympathy, but she shook her head. "I'm sorry, Your Grace. I can't tell you even if I want to."

Modesty ran to the butler, Simons, and asked him, but received the same refusal. The maids. Her own lady's maid. The footmen...

Everyone told her the same thing.

Finally, she retreated to her room, not in defeat but to think. As tears rolled down her cheeks, she pulled out paper and a pen. She would start her letters to those estate agents now and make a list of every Pryde property she could discover, every connection she could utilize. Pryde might have power and wealth on his side, but she had truth and justice on hers.

As her tears subsided, determination took their place. Whatever it took, she would find Augustus and run away with him if she had to.

She would keep her promise to Ophelia, no matter the cost.

But she didn't have to face this alone. She needed her friends, the only people who'd understand. The only ones she could trust to help her find the baby. Wiping her tears, she left her room and called the butler to ask for the carriage.

9

MODESTY ENTERED through the large doors of the women's almshouse, twisting the fabric of her gown in her chilled hands. Familiar sounds echoed through the large brick building, a stark contrast to the comfortable silence of Pryde House. A breathtaking but lonely place.

Since the butler had refused to call the carriage for her trip to Whitechapel, she'd had to hire a hackney which she paid for with her pin money. Her husband was not going to be the end of her freedom.

She saw Grace sitting with a group at one of the large tables in the common area, reading aloud while the women took notes. She must be giving a lesson in calculus or writing. This was one of her ideas to help women acquire more sellable skills and find work as a maid or a housekeeper, even if it would be in a modest household.

George was slicing bread in the kitchen area while two women peeled potatoes at the large kitchen table. His face brightening, he excused himself and hurried to her. Grace beamed at her but couldn't come leave her lesson just yet.

"Miss Fairchild," George greeted her.

His dark hair needed a cut, his once-white shirt had seen better days, and his waistcoat was dusted with breadcrumbs and flour. He was a stark contrast to the perfectly dressed and coiffed duke. She wished she could tear her husband out of her mind, but he'd become imbedded in her thoughts like a mollusk attached to a rock.

"Please, forgive me," he said, frowning. "I meant to say Duchess. What brings you here?" His eyes widened as he took in Modesty's distress. "What's wrong?"

"I—I don't know why I came here. It's just...I have no one in that house. This is the only place where I feel like I have friends."

George led her towards a small area that served as a parlor with three old sofas and several threadbare chairs. He directed her towards one of the sofas and sat next to her, though not too close for propriety's sake.

"What did he do?" he asked gently.

Grace appeared and sat on the sofa on her other side. "Modesty, darling, what's the matter?" she asked, holding her hand.

Modesty appreciated the warmth of her friends, the concern. Her own husband had very little regard for her at all —for anyone but himself. It must be nice to live that way, within the safety, the protection, of selfishness. He must feel so proud of himself. While she was writhing from worry for Augustus.

The words tumbled out, a torrent of pain and anger. "He sent Augustus away. Without even telling me. He won't say where. I—I don't know what to do."

She'd always loved this sitting area, surrounded by book-shelves arranged like walls. There was a large window here, letting in plenty of light to read any of the volumes on botany, natural science, astronomy, and even mechanics, not to mention novels and poetry. The scents of old books lingered in the air. Modesty sank back into the sofa.

Ophelia had passed only two weeks ago. Two weeks since Modesty's life had been forever altered. And then it had changed again yesterday when she'd married the duke. She didn't even know who she was anymore—though she knew very well who she was supposed to be. Who her husband wanted her to be. A duchess. A woman eager to give her husband an heir. An elegant hostess for balls and grand dinners, and an excellent conversationalist.

She was probably supposed to be a little like him. Confident. Knowing her worth, her position, and her status. Being proud of herself and her heritage.

God knew, she wished she could be that way, could put her needs and wishes first for once in her life. Could feel she had the right to do so.

That was most definitely how the duke lived.

And now, poor Augustus had been torn away from her. She felt his absence like an amputation. She was so used to cradling his little body, to nights with interrupted sleep, to washing and changing his nappies, to worrying if he'd begun to feel lighter.

"Oh, Modesty," Grace murmured, squeezing her hand. "I'm so sorry. How horrible!"

George's expression darkened. "That's unconscionable. Miss Fairchild...Duchess...Modesty, if I may be so bold."

She nodded. She didn't care for titles, anyway. They'd known each other since childhood, and he had called her Modesty as they were growing up.

"You should have never married him!" he said, his eyes blazing. "I have always known it was a mistake."

Grace gave him a stern look. "That is none of your concern,

George. Modesty can make her own decisions. She did what was best for Augustus. Wouldn't you have done the same thing in her place?"

"It doesn't change anything," Modesty murmured. "I thought it would be best for Augustus to be raised by his father. That is why I married him. But his father wants nothing to do with him. So what am I to do now? Can you help me find Augustus?"

"Of course we will—" began Grace, but George shifted closer to Modesty on the sofa.

"I know what you can do," he exclaimed. "Word has reached me of an expedition departing for Egypt in a few weeks, to explore the ancient ruins near Thebes. I intend to apply for a position with the party, and if it pleases you, I shall put forward your name as well. I have no doubt they would greatly benefit from someone with your knowledge of antiquities."

For a moment, Modesty's heart soared, and she sat up straighter. Egypt! The land of pharaohs and pyramids, of hidden tombs and ancient mysteries. She could almost feel the desert sun on her face, taste the excitement of discovery. To be free of societal constraints, to pursue her passion without judgment...

To escape the cold duke...

She imagined a different life. George was kind, gentle, shared her interests. If he had proposed... But even as the thought formed, her traitorous mind recalled Constantine's commanding presence, the way his deep voice made her skin tingle, how his mere proximity in a room left her breathless. George's friendly smiles had never made her pulse race like Constantine's intense gazes. Had never made her wonder what it would feel like to be held, to be kissed like the duke had kissed her last night...

And that realization made her angry with herself. How could she still be drawn to a man who clearly held her in such contempt? Who could cast aside a baby without a second thought?

Augustus's face swam before her eyes. His tiny hands, his toothless mouth crying for her. No. She couldn't abandon him, not when he'd already lost so much.

"I...I can't," she said, her voice barely above a whisper. "I made a promise to Ophelia. I can't leave Augustus."

George nodded, understanding in his eyes. "Of course. I shouldn't have suggested it. Running away won't solve anything."

"What will you do?" Grace asked gently, breaking into her thoughts.

Modesty squared her shoulders, feeling a new resolve settle over her. "If the duke doesn't return Augustus soon, I'm going to find him. I cannot be separated from the little boy."

But she didn't trust that he would ever bring the baby back to her. There was something in Constantine's eyes whenever Augustus was mentioned. Not just cold indifference but real fear. What secrets was her husband hiding? What could make a powerful duke so terrified of a child?

"And then," she continued, stiffening her spine, "then I'll take the boy and get as far away from Pryde as possible."

"An admirable endeavor, Duchess."

His deep voice made her blood freeze.

She turned her head.

Constantine stood in the doorway, his tall frame filling the entrance, his expression unreadable, his dark gaze on her.

10

CONSTANTINE STARED at his wife across the hall of the almshouse. Their words about Egypt and escape had reached him clearly given the building's excellent acoustics. His jaw tightened as he watched Mr. Lockhart shift closer to Modesty and he directed a deep glare at him. Mr. Lockhart had offered her a way out—everything Constantine had denied her.

Oh, he recognized a rival when he saw one. Whatever Modesty thought of the man, he wanted to be more than just her friend.

"Duke..." she murmured, jumping to her feet.

He saw the calculation in her eyes—she was attempting to gauge how much he had heard, and what he was going to do.

Slowly, he strode closer to her.

"Duchess," he returned. "I must say, I was surprised when Simons informed me you wished for a carriage to bring you to Whitechapel. I specifically forbade you to come here."

"With all respect, Pryde," said Mr. Lockhart, who rose from the sofa and stepped between him and Modesty. "The duchess is a grown woman and should not require your permission to move about town."

Constantine stared down the fool. "With all respect, Mr. Lockhart, my marriage is none of your business. Stand aside, sir."

George glared at him with a helpless rage, not moving, and Constantine clenched his fist in his glove.

Another moment and he'd need to move the man himself, and then—God help him—he wouldn't be surprised if he'd be challenged to a duel for disrespecting a gentleman.

He supposed, he thought coldly, dying might not be the worst outcome of his situation.

But not today.

Before he was compelled to shift Mr. Lockhart from his path as he would a tall bookcase, his wife came to her senses and stepped out from behind her protector.

"For pity's sake," she murmured. "Mr. Lockhart is right, and I wouldn't have been forced to come and seek their council if you hadn't sent Augustus away."

She turned to Miss Lockhart and her brother. "Thank you for listening and for your friendship." She opened her purse and took out a generous amount of money she'd been given by Mrs. Higgs that morning, then pressed it into Miss Lockhart's hand. "Please use this for the almshouse. It's my duchess's allowance, but it's much better used here than on dresses and jewelry. Forgive me. As you see, the duke objects to my coming and helping at the almshouse. This is one way I can still do that."

Miss Lockhart squeezed the money and nodded. "I know, darling. We'll be here if you need us." She threw a sideways glance at Constantine. "Despite the circumstances."

Constantine's heart churned. He did feel like a proper

villain. Modesty was pure of heart, and of course, no amount of money would replace a kind word and a listening ear.

"My carriage is just outsi—" he began, but she brushed by, throwing him the most venomous glance, and hurried outside.

As she swept past him, the scent of wildflowers tickled his senses, making his pulse quicken.

He cleared his throat. No one behaved this way with him. Especially not a woman. Now a simple country girl was not only spurning his advances but ignoring him completely. His wife, the one woman he had every right to bed and who should want nothing more than to abide by his wishes.

He nodded politely to Miss Lockhart and her brother and calmly walked after his wife. His pride wouldn't allow him to chase her like a brute.

As he made his way to the front entrance, he noted what he hadn't before—the poor state of the almshouse, the women struggling to work, and how cold it was even for October. Although the money Modesty had given them would do a lot of good, it wouldn't be nearly enough. He'd make sure to send more.

He exited the building into the acrid Whitechapel air to see her crossing the muddy street a few steps ahead of him, though his carriage stood right here. Stubborn woman, he thought, grinding his teeth.

As he strode after his wife, a fight broke out in a nearby gin shop, and a rough-looking man bumped into her, sending her stumbling. Before she could regain her balance, the thundering approach of a brewer's dray made Constantine's heart stop. The massive horse reared, spooked by a sudden shout from the gin shop. The cart's wheels slid in the mud as the driver fought for control.

Constantine didn't think. He lunged forward, grabbed Modesty around the waist, and yanked her back against his chest. The dray's wheels splashed mud where she'd stood moments before. She shuddered in his arms, her breath coming in short gasps.

"You could have been killed," he growled into her ear, his heart hammering. The thought of losing her made him tighten his grip.

His clever, defiant, fascinating wife.

"I—I'm fine," she said, but didn't pull away.

The warmth of her body against his, the way she fit perfectly in his arms, was dangerously distracting. He needed to focus.

"My carriage. Now."

His footman had the carriage door open, and Constantine led Modesty towards it. When they were both seated, the horses lurched into motion. The confines suddenly felt too small for Constantine's warring emotions. Her intoxicating scent filled the space between them. Even mud-splattered and furious, she was breathtaking.

"You were absent from your morning instruction," he said.

"I was rather preoccupied with finding my son."

"Augustus is not your son. And for now, he must remain where he is."

"Why? Because he threatens your standing in the ton?"

He leaned forward, fighting the urge to pull her into his arms again. The memory of her pressed against his chest moments ago was dangerously distracting.

"Because I cannot risk—" He stopped himself. Good God, he'd almost revealed too much. She seemed to see straight through his carefully constructed walls. "Because right now, discretion is essential."

"You mean your reputation is essential."

"Yes." The admission tasted bitter. He watched her face, wondering if she could understand how everything—his position, his ability to protect those who depended on him—balanced on the knife's edge of society's approval.

"I demand to see him."

Her quiet determination twisted something in his chest. She looked so young, so fierce in her loyalty. Red locks framed her face beautifully, her green eyes blazing in the dim light. Her cheeks were flushed—no doubt from the thrill of the near accident. Or from her anger with him. She was nothing like the cold, calculating women of the ton he was used to.

He remembered how sweet her lips had tasted. God, he wanted to kiss her again. Inhale her, drink her down in mouthfuls. Toss aside all honor, good behavior, and years of schooling and be an animal with her.

"Three weeks," he found himself saying. "Give me three weeks to arrange matters properly. Lady Virtoux is hosting an antiquarian auction next week. Attend your lessons, learn to be a proper duchess, and I'll take you. I'll buy anything you like, for whatever price."

He knew she was tempted, saw it in how her breathing increased, how her gloved hands twitched. "Do you think trinkets can replace Augustus?"

"No. But I'm offering you both. We will go to the auction, and in three weeks Augustus returns—if you commit to becoming the duchess this title requires."

He would then have three weeks to resolve the issue with the Regent, find the letter, and come up with a believable story about Augustus's identity and why he was taking the child in.

She studied him, and for a moment he feared she'd refuse. What then? He couldn't bear to see that lost, betrayed look in her eyes again. Why did her good opinion matter so much?

"I cannot agree to this. You took away the only reason I married you. Augustus needs me."

Her words stung more than they should have. Constantine

fought to keep his voice level. "He has his nurse. And a maid. He's safe."

"I want daily reports about his health and well-being," she declared. "Two weeks at most. And if you break this promise" —she held his gaze—"I will find him myself, even if I have to search every estate in England."

He believed her. The thought of her traveling alone, vulnerable, made his blood run cold. "Very well. But you must apply yourself to your lessons. Society will be watching us closely."

She lifted her chin. "I'll learn to be your perfect duchess. But understand this. I'm doing it for Augustus, not for you."

Her concern for the child squeezed something in his chest. If only Augustus's very existence didn't threaten everything.

"And I want him christened," she said. "Papa and I had to christen him as soon as he was born, but now he has you. I know it is unusual, but there's no rule against presenting him again. He should be properly christened into your house. In All Saints. And my father should do it. I want you to be his godfather, and I'll be his godmother."

"I don't want to draw any attention," he said through gritted teeth.

"We will keep it small. Only our closest friends."

"Fine." He held out his hand. "Do we have an agreement?"

She placed her small hand in his. The touch sent heat racing up his arm. "Two weeks," she repeated. "Not a day more."

Would two weeks be sufficient? Before coming to the almshouse, he had stopped at Portside and left the money where the letter had indicated. So the blackmailer should be satisfied. But the letter that could ruin him was still out there. Fortyne's investigators were working hard to find it, but their efforts would need to be accelerated. He would hire his own people if necessary.

He should have released her hand. Instead, he found himself drawing her closer. Their eyes locked, and he couldn't look away. His skin tingled with pleasure when he looked into the depths of her eyes...into her very soul. He knew then he had made the right decision.

"We should seal our agreement properly," he murmured, watching her pupils dilate. The intoxicating blend of wild-flowers and her natural warmth tested the very limits of his control.

"I still despise you," she whispered, but her hand curled into his lapel.

"I know."

He wrapped his arms around her waist and pulled her to him. Then, still without breaking the eye contact, he leaned down to her lips.

He brushed his mouth against hers, gentle at first, testing. When she didn't pull away, he deepened the kiss, drinking in her soft gasp.

She kissed him back, their lips coming together in a small collision, and he thought he'd die right there from the intoxicating sensation. Her slight moan made his body tighten. As he stroked his tongue over her lips, she parted them, and he dipped into her depths. She arched her torso, bringing herself close to him, and he lifted her onto his knees. She wrapped her hands around his neck, and he ran his arms down her back, pulling her in even closer.

His lips left hers, trailing down her jaw to the delicate curve of her neck. Her breath hitched, a faint tremor running through her body. Oh, she was enjoying this. He wanted to give her more. Maybe Eccess was right, and this timid vicar's daughter was fire in bed...

His mouth moved lower, brushing the skin just above her flushed neckline, where her pulse fluttered wildly. They were both breathing hard, and he was ready to tear her clothes off when he became painfully aware they'd come to a halt, and the driver's footsteps were approaching the door.

He reluctantly tore himself away. Her eyes blazed as she gazed at him, her lips full and swollen from his kisses.

His kisses, not those of Mr. George Lockhart or any other gentleman. She was his and only his, and he wanted to show her how much pleasure he could provide—that he wasn't the monster she thought him.

"We've arrived, Your Grace," came a hesitant voice from outside.

Perhaps the driver saw through the window that they were occupied...smart man. Constantine should give him a raise.

"This is far from over," he said to his wife with a grin he couldn't stop. "This is just the beginning."

11

"You summoned us—here we are," said Eccess as the six dukes walked into Constantine's study three days later.

Sitting at his grand mahogany desk, Constantine looked up, the letter gripped too tightly in his hands. No matter how certain he was that he could solve any problem on his own, seeing his friends arrive on short notice lifted some weight off his shoulders.

He stood up from his armchair as Rath, Luhst, Eccess, Enveigh, Irevrence, and Fortyne spilled through the room. Autumn twilight poured through the large window framed with heavy curtains in Pryde indigo. The room smelled pleasantly of wood polish and books.

Dorian took a seat at the settee placed between two floor-to-ceiling mahogany bookcases full of leather-bound volumes. Above him, the large dark oil portrait of one of the previous Dukes of Pryde glared at Constantine, skillfully rendered eyes full of judgment.

Dorian's gaze was on the letter in Constantine's hands. "What happened?"

Constantine started pacing about, a thick rug with a blue floral pattern softening his steps. "I paid the required sum not three days ago," he said. "However..." He raised his hand with the letter higher. "This arrived this morning."

Enveigh took the letter from Constantine's hands. "Let me see." He began to read aloud:

London, 5 October, 1814

To His Grace, the Duke of Pryde,

I trust my letter finds you well, though I suspect it may disrupt your newfound marital bliss. You have taken the first step to secure your position, but I'm afraid your troubles are far from over.

The sum of £1,000 was merely a test of your willingness to protect your secret. Now I require £2,000 to be delivered in bank notes to the ragman's old sea chest filled with discarded rags at Whitechapel Market by noon tomorrow. This sum reflects naught but a fraction of what you stand to lose.

How much is your pride truly worth?

I remain, sir, your most humble and obedient servant,

Anonymous

Fortyne leaned next to the fireplace, staring pensively into the amber liquid he'd poured into a crystal glass. "Two thousand pounds... Only one tenth of your yearly income, but an exuberant sum for most."

Indeed, as a rural vicar of a small parish, Mr. Fairchild's income was only fifty pounds per year. It would take a lifetime for him to earn £2,000 with honest work. Constantine's jaw clenched. "And I'm not certain this Anonymous will stop if I pay."

Dorian rose to his feet and strode over to glare at the letter. "He intends to ruin you."

Eccess slammed his hand on the desk, making ink jars clunk against each other. "All of us. One by one. Lucien was first. Now you. Who will be next?"

"We all have secrets," said Fortyne quietly.

"Allow me to be the voice of reason once again," said Irevrence as he sank onto the settee Dorian had abandoned, sprawling out like a Roman emperor at a feast. "Though I notice no one ever thanks me for it. There's no evidence Anonymous knows all our secrets. We can't just assume that."

"So you suggest doing nothing?" demanded Constantine.

Enveigh snorted. "Of course he suggests doing nothing. Hiding himself from the world, from life, denying everything, lest he discover some emotion and get hurt in the process."

Anger flashed in Irevrence's soft blue eyes for a moment, then he turned away and lazily emptied the contents of his glass down his throat. "At least I don't think my lot in life is insufficient, while my peers have everything better. And I do not suggest inactivity. I suggest considering this carefully and not jumping to conclusions that might jeopardize everyone in the group."

Lucien cocked his head. "Whether they're a threat to all of us or not, it is very clear that we do need to find this person. I am proof that doing nothing is pure foolishness, though I am grateful to have my daughter in my life."

"Let's devise a plan." Fortyne walked over and sat behind Constantine's desk. He dipped the pen into ink and poised it above a piece of paper. "My investigators could learn nothing about Lucien's blackmailer. Whoever this is, they're very clever and practiced as they leave no clues behind. It's entirely possible you and Luhst aren't the blackmailer's first victims, that other members of the ton may also have paid thousands to keep their secrets hidden."

Dorian licked his lips. "We will speak to the clothes broker and watch his stall, though I doubt this will lead anywhere. It would be too obvious if the blackmailer turned out to be the merchant himself. But perhaps we may learn something."

Constantine exhaled slowly. "I wish to do it myself."

Enveigh frowned. "Did you not tell me you forbade your new wife from going to Whitechapel? And you yourself are going there?"

The mention of his wife sent hot awareness rushing through his body. He ached to hold her close again, to kiss her, to finally bed her. Despite Modesty going to see her friends in Whitechapel, he couldn't find a single flaw in her.

During the past three days, she had done his bidding—she'd gone to the modiste, spent time with Mrs. Higgs to learn how to run the household, and dined with him, learning the art of conversation. She took everything in with no word of complaint. But the light that he'd once seen in her eyes was dimmed, and he found himself trying—quite awkwardly—to cheer her up. He made sure she received daily reports of Augustus's health, which were written by Thomas, the footman who had looked after Mr. Hawthorne for years. He wouldn't betray Constantine by adding an address or a hint of how to find them.

Even worse, he found himself thinking of her, wondering what she was doing. Last night, he'd stared at the door separating their bedchambers so hard, his control had snapped once again, and he'd knocked. When no reply had come, he'd opened it to see his duchess asleep in a pool of moonlight. He'd longed to curl his body around her sleeping figure, but instead he'd returned to his bedchamber, feeling lonelier than he had in his entire life.

"A man is a very different thing from a woman," he said to the dukes. "I used to frequent Elysium in Whitechapel—just like you did and still do. But, given our hasty marriage and the blackmail, my duchess must not draw criticism or arouse suspicion of anything untoward."

"Very well. Interviewing the merchant," said Fortyne, who began scribbling. "What else?"

Eccess focused bleary eyes on Constantine. "How could the blackmailer have found your mama's incriminating letter in the first place? Could any servants know something?"

"Good thinking," Constantine said. "My father always ensured he knew the location of Ophelia's mother and later Ophelia, so I have their former addresses. If we track down the servants, we may find the blackmailer, or someone who knows something."

Fortyne continued writing. "Very good."

Constantine unfolded the map of England across his desk and put his finger at a location near Cambridge. "I'll go to Millbrook myself. It's a village ten miles north of Cambridge."

Fortyne wrote it down. "It's a little far-fetched, perhaps, but worth looking into. Wouldn't you rather send someone?"

"The fewer people who know about it the better."

"Allow me to come with you, then," said Eccess.

Irevrence chuckled, whirling his drink around. "What about your wards? Shouldn't you be trying to find yet another governess for them?"

Eccess threw him a deadly glare. "Believe me, they prefer I'm not there. All four of us do. And the governess...the advertisement is always running in the papers. The governess-hiring business has become my housekeeper's most important occupation."

"Very well, thanks for offering to come with me," said Constantine.

Fortyne looked up. "Anything else?"

The dukes all looked at each other.

Constantine folded the map back. "This is a good beginning. Tomorrow around noon, I'm going to wear a disguise and watch the blackmailer pick up the money at the merchant's stall. Perhaps one of you could do the same. A few footmen will accompany me to give chase if the culprit is spotted."

"I'll help," said Eccess.

Enveigh shook his head. "It's quite difficult to disguise you, Octavius. There aren't many men in England of your height and build."

"I could hunch," Eccess offered.

"Yes, because a hunched giant is so much less conspicuous than an upright one," Enveigh drawled. "I'll do it, Constantine."

Eccess rolled his eyes and drank. "Suit yourself."

As they talked through the details of organization, a cold certainty settled in Constantine's gut. This wouldn't be the end. The blackmailer had tasted blood, and they would keep coming, demanding more, until Constantine had nothing left to give.

Unless he caught them first.

The very idea of prowling Whitechapel's dangerous streets in disguise should have been an affront to his ducal dignity. Instead, he felt a grim satisfaction. For once, he would be the hunter rather than the hunted.

And God help whoever had dared threaten not just his position but his chance at real happiness with Modesty.

12

"No, Your Grace. A deeper curtsy for a marchioness." The Dowager Duchess of Grandhampton sat regally in her chair. She tapped her cane against the parquet floor, its sharp sound echoing through Pryde House's spacious drawing room.

Autumn sunlight streamed through the tall windows, catching on gilt-framed mirrors and making Modesty squint as she attempted the movement again. Then a tall clock in the corner struck the hour, reminding her how long they'd been practicing these countless curtsies.

Her neck ached from the endless repetitions; her feet protested the hours of standing. A silver tray of tea and untouched biscuits sat forgotten on a side table. The richly decorated room felt like a prison, despite the incredible kindness of the dowager and her friend, Lady Buchanan.

Two days ago, the six dukes had come to visit her husband in such haste and with such grim faces, she'd thought there must be another war starting. After they departed, he'd been in a poor mood. He'd been absent all day yesterday, and she had no notion where he'd gone. Of course. Why should he inform her of his actions? She was just his wife. Someone he could forbid from doing certain things and demand to do others. She had no say over his comings and goings.

"Just so," Lady Buchanan said. The Duke of Rath's aunt executed a smooth curtsey and lowered her head. "Deep enough to show respect for her rank but not so deep as to diminish your own position as a duchess."

Her silvery gray hair in an elegant chignon, Lady Buchanan was somewhat younger than the dowager, though equally regal and dressed just as old-fashioned. But both ladies certainly made the tailored waists and full skirts popular twenty years ago look spectacular.

"Again," the dowager commanded. "I am Lady Rutherford, a marchioness."

Modesty inclined her head, mentally measuring the angle.

"Not quite, dearest," Lady Buchanan interrupted. "You just treated a marchioness like a duchess. The ton will eat you alive if you make such mistakes."

"But I've done worse at my wedding!" exclaimed Modesty.

"The Duke of Pryde invited only close friends to your wedding breakfast. They would never judge you or gossip. Now, I am Lady Kenworth, a baroness..."

"Does it truly matter?" Modesty burst out. "Surely they don't carry measuring tools to social events."

The dowager duchess's eyebrows shot up. "My dear girl, we've been practicing these distinctions since we were in leading strings. Every lady in London will be watching you, waiting for the slightest misstep. The Duke of Pryde's sudden marriage is already the talk of the ton. You cannot afford errors."

"Try again," Lady Buchanan said. "Remember, the movement must flow from the upper chest, not the neck. Your spine must remain straight. Think of yourself as a swan—elegant, controlled."

"A swan who must measure precise angles with her neck," Modesty muttered.

The dowager's lips twitched in an echo of a smile. "You're doing it very well. Now, imagine I am the Marchioness of Exeter entering your drawing room. Extend your hand exactly halfway, and..." Modesty tried again. "Better. Though your eyes dropped. You must maintain eye contact throughout the movement. It shows confidence in your rank. Remember, you are a duchess now. No one but the royal family rank above you."

Modesty felt a little bit of encouragement, though she ached to take a carriage and return home to Shepherdsbrook. As she kept curtseying and greeting imagined ladies and gentlemen of different ranks, another ache pierced her heart.

She imagined herself by Constantine's side at Lady Virtoux's upcoming event... It had felt so wonderful in the carriage, when he had his arms wrapped around her. Her stomach squeezed in longing for her husband, heat rushing through her in a wave.

But he'd sent Augustus away, she reminded herself. She'd told him she despised him, and that was true, wasn't it?

"Now," the dowager duchess said, interrupting her thoughts. "Let us tackle the next complicated topic. Precedence."

She and Lady Buchanan stood and started arranging name cards on the table.

"You're hosting the French ambassador, Baron de Montigny, the Danish ambassador Count Leopoldus, and the Neapolitan ambassador, Duke di Serra Capriola. Among your British guests are the Marquess and Marchioness of Somerham, Earl and Countess of Suffton, and, of course, several members of Parliament."

Modesty's head spun. "The French ambassador would enter first?"

"I'm afraid not, dearest," Lady Buchanan said. "Foreign ambassadors, while honored guests, rank after British peers of equivalent rank. The Marquess of Somerham and his lady enter first, as the highest-ranking British peers present. Then..."

"Then the earl and countess," Modesty ventured.

Lady Buchanan smiled brightly. "Excellent. The ambassadors follow, in order of their seniority at the Court of St. James's. The French ambassador first, as he's been longest in London..."

"And where do I seat them?" Modesty stared at the dining table layout.

"You, as hostess, are seated at the foot of the table," said the dowager, pointing at the cards with her cane, "while the duke sits at the head. The marchioness must be on his right, as the highest-ranking lady present. The French Ambassador's wife to your husband's left..."

"And at my end?" Modesty asked.

"You place the Marquess of Somerham on your right," the dowager duchess instructed. "The French ambassador on your left. The Earl of Suffton next to the French ambassador's wife, and his countess beside the marquess."

"But wouldn't the earl be offended to be so far from the head of the table?" asked Modesty.

Her mind whirled. What in the world would she talk about with the ambassadors? She couldn't wait to discuss Icelandic sagas with someone from Scandinavia, but what were the chances he would share her passion for history and ancient cultures? As she'd learned yesterday from her lessons with both ladies, acceptable topics included the latest operas at King's Theatre, notable concerts, royal exhibitions, weather and its effect on hunting/riding seasons, court fashions, recent society weddings, upcoming balls, latest portraits by prominent artists, and new additions to noble collections. Bringing up fascinating archeological finds and getting too enthusiastic about historical topics would be seen as vulgar and unfeminine and most certainly not suitable for the Duchess of Pryde.

She felt a deep longing to hold Augustus in her arms again, to return to her boring but meaningful life with her papa. There she'd actually made a difference in other people's lives, even if she didn't go on expeditions.

She dreaded a dinner where she had to discuss topics she cared not a bit about.

"Less offended than the Danish ambassador would be to be seated below a British earl," Lady Buchanan said. "Foreign diplomacy requires delicate handling. One wrong placement and you could cause an international incident."

"That happened at a dinner I attended," the dowager reminisced. "The Swedish ambassador was seated below a viscount at Lady Jersey's dinner. The diplomatic fallout lasted months."

"And what of the Neapolitan ambassador?"

"Ah." The dowager's eyes gleamed. "Now there's the true challenge. Being the most recently arrived to Court, he's lowest in diplomatic precedence. However, being a duke in his own country..."

"Creates an interesting predicament," Lady Buchanan finished. "You must find a way to honor his rank while maintaining proper diplomatic order."

Modesty's mind reeled. She should approach this as an anthropological study, she decided. See this world like a scientist wishing to understand it and—even though it was not her natural environment, and it felt strange and unpleasant—try to blend in.

"Do you have an idea how to solve such a puzzle?" Modesty asked. "I have no notion."

The dowager nodded, a satisfied glint in her eyes. "Place him near enough to the head of the table to acknowledge his ducal status, but not so close as to offend the other ambassadors who outrank him in diplomatic precedence. Between the earl and the Danish ambassador's wife should suffice."

A knock sounded. Constantine stood in the doorway, and her breath caught at the imposing effect of his tall, broad-shouldered frame. Immaculately dressed as always, he stared intently at her, a meaning she couldn't decipher in his dark eyes.

How long had he been there? And when had he returned?

"How goes the schooling?" he asked.

"Her grace is progressing very well," Lady Buchanan said.

Modesty felt her cheeks burn. She knew what everyone thought—that she was hopeless, that she'd never master these ridiculous rules.

"Show me," Constantine said.

"I beg your pardon?"

"Pretend I've just entered with the Marchioness of Herfordon. How do you acknowledge us?"

Modesty's heart pounded. She curtsied and inclined her head to him first—that much she knew—then turned to give what she hoped was a perfectly calibrated curtsey to the imaginary marchioness.

"Better," the dowager said. "Though still a touch too deep."

"At least I didn't mistake her for a duchess this time," Modesty muttered.

To her surprise, Constantine's lips twitched. "Indeed. Though Lady Herfordon would probably forgive the error."

Was he teasing her? His eyes crinkled slightly at their edges, and warmth swirled deep in her gut.

"I should say the duchess has had enough schooling for today," said the dowager as her gaze darted between Modesty and the duke. "Lady Buchanan and I shall take our leave. Shall we return tomorrow?"

"Of course," Modesty said with a polite smile. She enjoyed the company of the two ladies. And despite disliking the subject, she couldn't have found better teachers. "Thank you both."

They said their goodbyes, correcting her curtseys and the order in which she addressed them, and left. Silence fell between Modesty and the duke, and her cheeks heated as his gaze slid over her from head to toe. She wore a newly fashioned gown in a burgundy that—the seamstress had assured her—would bring out the coloring of her hair and eyes. Intricate lace of the same color surrounded the neckline—which was much lower than she was accustomed to. The silk felt soft and weightless on her body, highlighting the details of her figure much more than her simple woolen and muslin dresses did. And she felt uncomfortably visible.

His slow perusal sent hot awareness throughout her body.

"When did you return?" she asked, feeling both the urge to defy him and the desire to hide. It was an impossible contradiction, and he was the only person who'd ever made her feel this way.

"Just now," he said. He was still in his riding clothes— gleaming hessian boots stretched to his knees, buff-colored riding breeches molded to his thighs, and a dark blue riding coat emphasized his shoulders. A few spots of mud marked his boots, and the crisp autumn air still clung to him, mixing with the leather-and-horse scent that followed him into the room. "I was in a hurry to see my wife."

The words, said in a velvety tone, made a thrill rush along her spine. He approached her, and she stood, breathless, her head devoid of any thoughts. He offered her his hand.

"Come with me. I'd like to continue your duchess schooling myself."

She swallowed hard, her throat dry. "How?"

"You'll see."

She sank in his deep brown eyes, unable to move. Finally, she managed to lay her hand in his, the heat of his skin scalding her. Never breaking the hold of his eyes over hers, he took her hand and wrapped it around his forearm. Then he led her through the door and down the hallway.

They arrived at a set of ornate doors she'd never before entered. "Now," he said, pushing them open to reveal a grand ballroom, "shall we begin with your dancing lessons?"

The ballroom took Modesty's breath away. It was empty, save for a trio of musicians sitting next to the fireplace: a violinist, a flutist, and a harpsichordist. The three men jumped to their feet and nodded as she and the duke walked in. Painted in a lovely pale blue, the room was grand and vast. White moldings decorated the high ceiling and the wall panels, and gilded mirrors hung between the panels. Though unlit, the crystal chandeliers were still beautiful in the daylight seeping through the tall windows.

"We'll begin with an English country dance," the duke said, his lips close to her ear. "It will be important for Lady Virtoux's antiquarian event."

He led her to the center of the room, positioning them facing each other. "We'll start with a simple set. Watch my movements and try to mirror them."

The trio began a lively tune. Constantine bowed, and Modesty, recalling the instructions of the two ladies, attempted a curtsy.

"Good," he murmured. "Now, we'll step forward, touch hands, and step back."

His hand was warm against hers as they touched palms, and even that brief contact sent a shiver down her spine.

Her husband had been the object of quite a few of her dreams lately. Dreams where he kissed her, held her in his arms, his body and his weight like a decadent pleasure of its own against her. The glide of his hands down her back, his lips and tongue against her bare neck, his firm chest under her palms... She often awoke overheated and perspiring, feeling a strange longing, an ache she couldn't soothe.

"Next, we'll do a turn," he instructed. "Take my hand, and we'll walk in a circle."

Modesty placed her hand in his, noting the contrast between his calloused palm and her softer skin. Yet another part of him that surprised her. She wondered why a duke's hand would be so rough. Riding? Fencing? As they circled each other, she caught the bergamot and musk scent that was distinctly masculine and uniquely him.

The dance required them to weave between other imaginary couples, and Constantine guided her gently with a hand at the small of her back. Even through her dress, she felt the heat of his touch, and her breath hitched.

"Now, we'll do a figure eight," he said, demonstrating the steps.

Modesty followed, concentrating on her feet but acutely aware of his movements. When their paths crossed, bringing them momentarily close, a brush of his coat against her arm made a shiver rush through her.

There it was again—the longing in her body, the ache deep down in her belly.

As they repeated the sequence, Modesty found herself relaxing into the rhythm. She caught glimpses of their reflection in the mirrors—her russet hair a vibrant contrast to his dark locks, her burgundy gown against his indigo coat. The elegant, graceful woman in the mirror looked at home in this stately room and in the arms of the handsome duke. But that woman wasn't truly Modesty, the girl who wanted nothing more than to dig in the dirt, to uncover relics from the distant past. She reminded herself that no matter what costume she put on, what mask she wore, she didn't belong in this world.

"Very good," Constantine said, his voice a low rumble that she felt more than heard. "You're picking this up quickly."

Despite her reservations, pride bloomed in her chest at his praise. She looked up, meeting his gaze, and her breath caught. His dark eyes were intense, focused solely on her. The room seemed to fade away, leaving only the two of them, moving together in perfect harmony. Her breasts tingled, her nipples hardening to sharp, painful knots. Sweat misted the back of her neck. Her face burned. All that just from the touch of his hands, from the presence his body emanated.

As they twirled and stepped in time with the music, Modesty felt light. Her earlier anger and frustration melted away, replaced by a heady mix of excitement and nervousness.

The music swelled, and they came together for the final figure, hands joined as they spun in a circle. As the last notes faded, they slowed to a stop, hands still clasped. For a moment, neither moved, and she found herself reluctant to step away.

"Very well done, Duchess," Constantine said softly, his thumb brushing lightly over her knuckles before he released her hand. "You're a breath of fresh air. I had an important appointment yesterday, which didn't go well. I'll need to go out of town for a few days, to Cambridge. But memories of dancing with you will help time pass more quickly... Will you dance with me again and give me more recollections to warm my cold, lonely bed?"

Breathless, Modesty nodded. As the musicians began a new melody, she knew there was more to the duke than she'd thought... Was there a beating heart in this man of stone?

13

MODESTY STARED at the household ledger before her. Five days of duchess schooling had passed alone, without Constantine, and she was doing her first task of reviewing the household expenses. Written in her husband's neat hand were regular expenses for a London town house she'd never heard of. It was in Bloomsbury, on John Street, and included a footman's wages, a housekeeper's salary, and weekly deliveries of food and wine.

Her stomach lurched. This was no business property or investment. This was a house maintained for someone's comfort—someone who required privacy.

She turned her head to look at Mrs. Higgs, who was standing behind her, instructing. "Mrs. Higgs," she tried to keep her voice steady, "are you familiar with this address?"

The light in the library was dim today with the heavy rain outside, but Modesty could still see discomfort flicker across the housekeeper's face. "I couldn't say, Your Grace. His grace isn't obliged to explain the purpose of his expenses to a housekeeper."

Of course, the irreproachable Duke of Pryde would ensure such arrangements were handled with utmost discretion. Her throat burned. He told her he'd be in Cambridge, but he could have lied. Was this where he'd been these past five days? In the arms of a woman who didn't challenge him, who didn't reject his advances or question his decisions?

She shouldn't care. She had told him she despised him, after all. He'd shown his true nature when he sent Augustus away, when he'd abandoned Ophelia in her time of need. She should have expected this.

But the ledger's damning evidence blurred before her eyes, and she realized with a start that she did care. Far more than she should.

While he spent his nights in another woman's bed, she was longing for him, dreaming of his hands, his mouth, his body, remembering how they'd danced, reliving their kisses.

During the days, she was distracted by her training with the dowager and Lady Buchanan. They were very good company, really, and she had begun to feel as if they were both her fairy godmothers. Especially when they finally acknowledged that she was almost ready for the next grand ton event. Though they'd assured her most of the ton was out of town, so she would have the opportunity to practice on a smaller scale.

But she felt lonely. Without Augustus, without her husband, and without any friends, she'd never felt lonelier.

And now this...

How could one live in such a grand house and yet be so completely miserable?

She slammed down her pen and stood up. "Mrs. Higgs, please have a carriage prepared for me. I should like to go and see my papa."

As the carriage carried her through the rain to Shepherdsbrook, she closed her eyes, praying to forget the word that made her heart wrench.

Mistress...

That word made her feel so insignificant, so betrayed. For the first time since her wedding day, she felt her wounded pride and wanted to roar.

Although Papa was glad to see her, he seemed to have become accustomed to life without her. Papa and she agreed on Augustus's christening date. She helped him with correspondence and helped cook some stew and bake bread for the parish poor.

But eventually everything was done, and she returned home like a good wife and a woman who knew her place, though her loneliness had not abated.

To cheer herself up, she sat at the library window and reread the reports on Augustus...until she her vision was blurry from tears. The pain in her heart took over, and she just couldn't stop crying. Outside, raindrops slowly slid down the glass of the window.

As she stared numbly into the grayness, she saw the duke stride out of the house. He must have returned while she was visiting papa. And now he was leaving again!

As she jumped to her feet, his carriage stopped before him. If she hesitated a second longer, she'd miss him.

The mistress. Either he had just spent time with his mistress, or he was going there now. What other reason could he have for such secrecy?

She hurried out of the library and towards the door.

As she rushed past the butler, Simons cried out, "Your Grace, is anything the matter?"

She ignored him as she opened the door, but she heard his footsteps behind her and more questions. Didn't she need her bonnet and her spencer? Was there anything wrong? Where was she going?

She didn't stop.

She had money in her reticule—thank heavens she'd grabbed it—so she ran across the street, rain quickly soaking her gown. She could see the duke's carriage turning the corner to the right. She waved down a passing hackney.

"Follow that carriage!" she commanded. "I'll double your fare!"

The driver nodded, and she climbed up, pulling the door closed behind her as they started moving.

She could no longer see the duke's carriage, and only hoped the man had seen which one she meant. She was shivering from the rush of the chase and the cold, wet October weather.

What would she encounter at the end of this journey? Was she truly ready to meet the other woman face-to-face? What would she say?

All of her instincts begged her to turn around, to return home, to hide and make herself small and agreeable once again.

But she couldn't sit there alone and in ignorance for another second. She wanted the truth. She wanted him to be faithful to her as his wife. She wanted a true family.

She wanted to roar her pain and her loneliness in his face.

Finally, the hackney stopped. Through the window, she saw the duke's carriage across the street. She watched him descend, his coat quickly getting wet in the rain, and rush up the stairs of a respectable town house. This was the address she'd seen, where the food had been delivered, and the wages of the footman and a housekeeper were paid.

Her heart beat hard as she looked up the three-story building in the row of similar town houses. There was candlelight flickering through the window; a shadow moved. Her heart was pierced with pain.

Was this where he found love? Warmth? An understanding woman who praised him for his pride and confidence?

Everything she did not. No wonder he looked for happiness elsewhere.

She shivered harder.

She could turn around. Ask the driver to take her back.

But no. Anger roiled in her stomach. Pryde had taken everything away from her. Her freedom. Her purpose. The child she loved.

She was making herself into everything she was not to meet his demands. The least he owed her was loyalty.

Opening the carriage door, Modesty carefully descended the fixed step. The rain immediately assaulted her, drops stinging her cheeks. She fumbled with her reticule, her fingers numb with cold as she withdrew the fare.

Then she crossed the street, her head spinning, her knees wobbling a little, and her stomach quivering with rage. The biting cold gnawed at her whole body through the thin layers of her silk gown and chemise as she climbed wet steps to the front door. Seizing the knocker, she pounded it against the door with all the force her chilled hands could muster.

Moments ticked by slowly. After what felt like an eternity, she heard heavy footsteps from behind the door. Then it swung open to reveal a footman in his fifties, his graying brows arched in mild confusion as he took in her drenched, wind-whipped appearance.

"Yes?" he asked.

"I'm the Duchess of Pryde," she said. Then she pushed by him into the hallway. "I'm here for my husband."

Constantine smiled and cooed over Augustus. He didn't know why his voice sounded so high or why he suddenly wanted to remove every piece of lace from around the baby's face, bbut he'd missed the little boy for the four days he spent in Cambridgeshire.

He'd missed Modesty even more.

The grate in the living room of Mr. Hawthorne's house radiated warmth, the glowing coals within crackling faintly. Mr. Hawthorne sat in his favorite chair with a book of fairy tales and read, his voice soothing and calm, taking Constantine back into his own childhood.

Mr. Hawthorne had an excellent voice for reading, just perfect for a tutor. Mrs. Walcott sat in the corner, snoring very softly, lulled by the story, a cup of tea at her side. Rain drummed quietly into the window.

The only one missing was his wife. Each time Augustus made a new sound or expression, Constantine found himself turning to share it with Modesty before remembering she wasn't there. That was his own fault, he knew, keeping the baby's location a secret from her. But he wanted to hear her delighted laugh, to see the way her eyes would surely light up at Augustus's achievements. Every house felt hollow to him now without her presence.

And what a pity she'd been in Shepherdsbrook when he'd arrived home. He'd decided then to make a quick visit to Mr. Hawthorne and Augustus hoping to return before she would be home.

But now he wished he had waited for her, had seen her just for one moment.

Six days ago, they had watched the spot in Whitechapel—Constantine, Enveigh, and four footmen. They'd been instructed to note anyone who lingered near the stall where the money had been left and especially anyone who'd try to grab something from the chest.

But the market had been its usual chaos of bodies and noise. Hundreds of people had passed through, none paying obvious attention to that location.

They couldn't spot the blackmailer, but the money was gone from the sea chest when Constantine checked it half an hour later.

Though their attempt to catch the blackmailer had failed, his investigation in Ophelia's hometown of Millbrook had yielded promising results. He'd tracked down a maid who still lived there, one who had served both Ophelia's mother and later Ophelia herself. At first, she'd refused to speak, but when he'd offered her an astonishing sum of two hundred pounds—twenty times the average yearly wage for a laborer—her resolve had crumbled.

She admitted to knowing about the letter in question, describing it as a prized possession that required careful guarding. It had always been kept in a precious rosewood box inlaid with delicate silver patterns and adorned with small pearls. The box itself was a treasure, given to Ophelia as a wedding gift when she'd married Mr. Lester.

The box, together with every single thing they owned, was repossessed by a firm in London since most of Mr. Lester's debts were from gaming halls in the city.

Constantine had asked Simons to inquire into the address of the company.

Once he had the address, Constantine would go to their offices and ask for the box. With any luck, they would have the address of whomever had bought it. Then he'd follow the buyer and hope they were the blackmailer.

Augustus made an adorable coo that sounded like

"Goooo," making Constantine's chest squeeze with some warm and wonderful feeling. He chuckled.

"I know," he said. "Goooo. What an exciting word."

He was so glad only Mr. Hawthorne and Augustus heard him speaking high-pitched like that. Mr. Hawthorne probably wouldn't remember. Neither would Augustus. No one would recall the cold, proud duke cooing like a mother hen.

Distantly, he registered a knock at the front door but paid it no heed. Footsteps sounded from the hallway. That must be Thomas accepting a delivery.

He devised a new game to amuse Augustus, one that involved pressing his lips together and blowing forcefully to create a loud, sputtering sound. The noise made the little boy's eyes widen and his lips purse with curious concentration. It was embarrassing, truly, how happy such a childish action made Constantine feel.

He barely registered the slight squeak of the door opening and realized all too late that Thomas must have come in, and he would most definitely remember the duke making silly sounds and faces.

"What on earth are you doing?" came a voice that was most certainly not Thomas's.

He startled, leaping to his feet so abruptly that Augustus let out a squeal of surprise. Constantine turned to face Modesty, his heart lurching.

Her eyes, hard and bright as emeralds, glared at him; her arched eyebrows knit together; her copper hair hung limply from a formerly intricate chignon, tendrils sticking to her face; her cheeks were flushed with anger, her sensual lips in a straight line. The high-waisted red silk gown she wore was wet, too, and clung to her body, drawing his attention to her upper chest, which moved quickly with her ragged breaths.

She was the only woman arresting enough to leave him lost for words.

His wife.

The very person he'd been longing for, more than he'd even allowed himself to admit, stood there. His heart seemed to shift, a knot within it unraveling, softening. The tension that had settled in his chest over the past few days eased, leaving a sense of relief and quiet joy in its place.

Augustus began fussing in his arms, perhaps unhappy about the sudden change. Mrs. Walcott woke up and jumped to her feet.

"Miss Fairchild!" she exclaimed with a huge smile. "Oh, forgive me, Your Grace! You're here, finally!"

Mr. Hawthorne stopped reading and was frowning at Modesty. "Are you here to hire me for your children?" he asked over his spectacles, the book lowered to the blanket on his knees.

Modesty looked at everyone around the room. "Where's your mistress?"

He was stupefied at the very word coming out of her mouth. Of all reasons for her to be here...it was this?

"My...mistress?" he asked.

"Yes! Mistress. Lover. The woman you've been keeping here..." Her face distorted in a grimace of hurt. "Oh, God, please don't tell me she has been watching over Augustus!"

He belatedly realized she wasn't wearing a bonnet or a spencer, and that she was shivering.

Still wondering what had possessed her to chase him down here and demand to know about a mistress, he approached her, Augustus snug in his arms.

Looking into her eyes, he held the baby out for her, and she hastily took him. The expression of fury mixed with hurt dissolved into one of pure love and wonder as she cooed at the baby. A stab of guilt in his gut made him wince inwardly. He'd been so cruel to have separated them.

But before he addressed that, and the mistress misunderstanding, he needed to get her warm.

He gently touched her elbow. "Come here, closer to the fireplace," he said, guiding her to the empty chair next to Mr. Hawthorne. "Would you like some hot tea?"

She settled into the chair, talking to Augustus with the same high-pitched voice he had used.

"Would you please fetch tea for Her Grace?" he asked Mrs. Walcott.

The woman sprang to her feet and poured tea from the teapot into a fresh cup. "Of course, Your Grace. It's still hot."

Modesty was still shivering. Deciding to send all propriety to hell, he removed his coat and wrapped it around her shoulders, covering both her and Augustus. Seeing her shining eyes on the baby made his heart melt.

He sank down to sit on the edge of the sofa next to her chair. "There's no mistress," he said gently.

She met his gaze, frowning. It pained him to see the softness with which she'd been looking at Augustus disappear, anger and betrayal filling her eyes.

"Do not lie to me, Duke. Not anymore. I've seen the bills you've been paying. You should have been more careful."

"This home is not for a mistress." He looked at his old tutor, who was still staring at Modesty over his spectacles, his gaze slightly cloudy. "It's for Mr. Hawthorne, my old tutor."

Surprise and realization filled her eyes. She looked at him like she was seeing him for the first time. While Mrs. Walcott brought over the tea and put it on the side table next to her, her gaze drifted to Mr. Hawthorne.

"Thank you, Mrs. Walcott," said Modesty with a distracted but sweet smile.

"You're not cross with me?" Mrs. Walcott asked. "For coming with Augustus?"

"On the contrary, I'm pleased you were allowed to come with him."

Mrs. Walcott looked relieved as she returned to her place by the window.

"Mr. Hawthorne," said Modesty. "How wonderful to meet you."

"And you, too," he replied. "Though I have trouble remembering your name, young lady."

"Modesty," she said.

"Modesty. You must be the mother of this little devil."

Her face changed, a flash of sadness passing through her—grief that resonated in him. "No, but I am as close as I can be to one."

Constantine leaned closer to her and said softly, "He was my only friend as a child. He's been living here for years."

"What are you talking about, sir?" Mr. Hawthorne chuckled. "Your old tutor! I'm only just beginning! I just sent out my advertisement for positions in good homes. I have plenty of excellent recommendations."

"Is he unwell?" she asked quietly, so only Constantine could hear her.

She wasn't angry with him anymore, thank heavens. A mistress? She'd come here, furious, through the rain without even stopping to put on a bonnet...

Had she been jealous?

The thought was strangely warming. He hated to cause her any vexation—God knew, he'd caused her enough of that already—but if she was jealous... Did that mean she wanted him for herself?

She didn't know he'd been hers since the moment he met

her. No woman had ever occupied his mind and soul so completely as his wife.

"This entire time, since you took Augustus away, have you been coming to visit him and Mr. Hawthorne?"

"I have. I had to make sure the babe was well while you couldn't."

She hugged the boy, inhaling his scent, just as Constantine had done a few times.

"There's no mistress," he murmured again, tenderly, and his heart split open in the most wonderful way when her eyes softened and she didn't look away. "There never was. There never will be."

Now she'd met Mr. Hawthorne. Caring for the old tutor was his weakness, a connection to his painful past. The tender underbelly he'd spent years hiding. He hadn't wanted her to see this part of him because it was dangerous for her to know him better.

Dangerous for his heart.

And yet, the gentle look in her eyes—now a moss green—made it all worth it.

Mistress...what a ridiculous notion. Why would he ever want a mistress when he was married to *her*?

14

CONSTANTINE PAUSED in the library doorway, his breath catching at the sight before him. Modesty lay curled on the sofa, a book resting forgotten upon her chest. Her copper hair had come partially loose from its pins, spilling across the cushions in gentle waves. She had drawn her legs up, wrapping herself in the soft folds of her shawl like a sleeping cat. The only light came from a five-branched candelabra on the side table, its flames casting a golden glow across her peaceful features.

His throat tightened with an emotion he couldn't quite name. There was something achingly intimate about finding her like this—her guard completely down, her face softened in sleep, trusting and vulnerable in a way she never allowed herself to be in waking hours. The domesticity of the scene struck him with unexpected force. This was his wife, in his home, surrounded by his books. The thought filled him with a possessive tenderness that both thrilled and terrified him.

Earlier today, he had visited the pawn shop that had acquired Mr. Lester's worldly goods. The box had been sold, but with financial encouragement, the shop owner had agreed to give him the name of the buyer: the Marchioness of Virtoux.

Nothing had prepared Constantine for this twist of fate. The marchioness was one of London's most notorious gossips. And she was the same woman hosting tomorrow's antiquarian soirée, where half the ton would gather to examine her latest acquisitions.

If Lady Virtoux had found the letter, she certainly had the power to ruin him. He had gone to call on her directly, but she was not at home. The possibility that she might be the black-mailer gnawed at his thoughts, disturbing his joyful reflections of happy times with his wife—like their dance lesson...like yesterday, with Augustus...

Quietly, Constantine moved through the library towards Modesty, not wanting to wake her. He stood by her side and allowed himself the secret pleasure of simply watching her sleep. He marveled at the way her long eyelashes cast shadows, the way her translucent eyelids trembled slightly as she dreamed.

She was...

His.

His to protect. His to cherish. His to crave. He may not deserve her, but she was his wife.

Though he had vowed not to insist she take him into her bed until she was ready, his body betrayed him. Heavens, even just thinking of her... He feared another rejection, yet his blood burned for her.

Driven by an impulse he distantly thought was a bad idea, he picked her up from the sofa, cradling her in his arms. She sighed, settling against his chest as naturally as if she belonged there. The slight weight of her tall, slim frame felt right in his arms.

As he carried her from the library, he was intoxicated by

the whisper of her sweet breath, the silk of her hair against his cheek, the subtle perfume that mingled with her own scent. In the weeks since their wedding, she had transformed herself with remarkable dedication. Her bearing had grown more assured, her manner more refined. Though she now dressed with all the elegance her position demanded, he found her most beautiful like this—unguarded, utterly herself.

Halfway up the stairs, she stirred in his arms. Her eyes fluttered open, confusion turning to awareness as she found herself cradled against his chest. He expected her to pull away, but instead she held his gaze, the candlelight from the wall sconces casting golden shadows across her face.

Her pink lips parted slightly, her breath warm against his chin. The firelight reflected in her green eyes drew him in until resistance became impossible. With exquisite slowness, he lowered his head and claimed her mouth with his own.

⚜

When Modesty opened her eyes, a tingling sensation ran through her entire body. She was in his strong arms—pressed to his warm, incredibly solid chest.

Candlelight showed the stark lines and shadowed angles of his face, his chestnut eyes so dark they seemed bottomless.

This man, usually as cold as ice, as sure as an arrow, always in control, now stared at her with naked desire. The heat in his eyes made her weak.

And so when he leaned down to her, she couldn't stop him—because she didn't want to.

Every day and night since the wedding she had dreamt of that first kiss in her chamber, and then the second one in the closeness of the carriage.

His lips were firm yet tender, and she surrendered to his

kiss as he claimed her, devoured her, teased her. She wrapped her arms around his neck to bring herself closer. How could she not?

Her body melted against his as he lifted his head and continued up the stairs. She could barely breathe, heat pooling low in her belly, dampness gathering between her thighs.

He resumed kissing her as he strolled down the hallway. Her bedchamber door stood ajar—the maids must have left it so when turning down her bed—and he shouldered it open without breaking their embrace. She was aware they'd reached her bed only when her back met the mattress.

And then he was on top of her.

Still kissing her.

And she was burning.

His hands roamed her body, and even through her corset and gown, each caress sent shivers along her skin. When he cupped her breast, a moan escaped her. His tongue deepened their kiss as he pressed against her, the hard length of him creating a delicious friction that had her arching instinctively, seeking more of that unfamiliar pleasure.

He moaned as her hips moved. "Modesty..." he murmured. "You're going to make me lose all control..."

What a bizarre notion. Normally, he was the one with all the power...and now she felt like the one in control. A rare feeling in her life.

She liked it.

"Tell me to stop and I will," he murmured hoarsely, barely tearing his mouth from hers.

"No," she managed through ragged breaths, and she'd never been more sincere about anything. "Don't stop."

He gave a sound of male distress and returned to her mouth. And all she could think was...more. She wanted more of his lips, and tongue, and hands, and legs, and that hard thing that was pressing into her.

He pulled back just enough to untie his cravat, shrug out of his coat, then his waistcoat. She reached up to help him tug his shirt over his head, eager to stroke the skin beneath. His chest was broad and well-muscled, dusted with dark hair. She ran her fingers over his silky, hot skin. Stroking him felt like touching a flame without being burned.

When his hand traced up her leg, she knew she should be scandalized. With no mother to guide her through these mysteries, she'd heard only whispers from the women at the almshouse about what happened between man and wife. But this felt natural, right. Timidness and desire fought within her. He brushed his hand up the inside of her leg, leaving a trace of intensely exquisite sensation. And she gasped when she realized he was going to reach her—

Oh!

He moved to the side and lay next to her, cupping her sex with his hand. She jerked as delicious warmth spread through her most intimate parts. And she had a strange urge to press against his hand, to move against it like she had just moved against the bulge in his breeches. His fingers spread her folds and he explored her, rubbing gently, dipping into her entrance.

She gasped as waves of bliss surged through her. Oh, his touch...

"Hmmm," he murmured hoarsely against her neck. "You're soaking wet."

She licked her lips, moving her hips, searching for his fingers. "Is that good?" she asked.

"Very," he rumbled softly. "It means you want me and are ready to take me in."

His finger found a secret spot that sent rapture coursing

through her veins. Her back arched on its own, and she clawed
desperately at the blanket beneath her.

"Take you in?" she rasped. "How?"

He chuckled as he changed the position of his hand, and
one of his fingers began probing inside her while others kept
rubbing at the wondrous place he had found. "Like so," he said,
gently exploring her tight entrance. His skilled fingers found
places that made her gasp, while his thumb stroked that sensitive spot that sent sparks through her body.

She was in heaven. No, in some sort of hell bathing in pleasure and yet wanting more, and it was all building and
building.

"But it wouldn't be my finger, my sweet girl," he
murmured.

"What would it be?"

He chuckled. "Something big..." He increased the pressure
and speed of his movements. "Something hard..." His finger
was diving deeper into her. "You'll see..." His fingers were
stretching her with an exquisite tension that balanced between
discomfort and bliss as he reached some spot inside her that
intensified everything.

"So innocent," he purred as he kissed her ear, and more
sensations danced through her. "So pure. Mine. Mine alone."

She shivered at that, and something happened deep within
her core. The ecstasy reached heights she never knew existed.
She couldn't do anything. Only feel it, ride it, as her muscles
tensed, and she cried out.

She burst with it, into millions of stars, as his hands drew
out every last tremor of her release, her entire body spasming.
And then she felt warm and heavy, and all she could do was
roll onto her side. Held close in his arms, she breathed in his
delicious scent...and slept.

15

MODESTY'S PALMS were sweating in her gloves when Constantine took her hand. She'd just reached the bottom of the stairs. They were about to leave for Lady Virtoux's antiquarian soirée.

What a shame that her first public event as a duchess coincided with a nasty gossip piece in today's society pages. It was about the late Duchess of Pryde's intimate friendship with a country parson. The tone had been innocent enough, but Constantine's face had gone rigid when he'd read it, and she couldn't shake the sense that something had shifted.

She pushed her worry down and focused on the thought that always lifted her spirits—in two days, Augustus would be home.

Last night, Constantine had slept in her bed for the first time, their limbs entangled after he'd brought her to the peak of pleasure...with nothing but his fingers...twice!

Tonight, she was clad in Pryde indigo. Her hair was expertly arranged and accented with jewels and silk flowers.

Earlier that evening, in the privacy of the drawing room, Constantine had presented her with a long leather box.

"This is for you," he said. "It belonged to my mother."

She frowned, staring at the box. "What is it?"

"Please, open it."

Her gloved hands shook. For her? Something his mother wore?

As she opened the lid, she inhaled a sharp breath. It was the most beautiful necklace of blue sapphires, each of them surrounded by diamonds. They glittered like stars in the candlelight.

"Constantine, this is...this is too much. I could never be so bold as to—"

He shook his head. "My mother would have loved for you to wear it. Especially to your first ton event. Please... Will you?"

She swallowed as she stared into his dark, liquid eyes. "I just can't fathom how valuable this must be."

"It is. But this is your life now. You're the new Duchess of Pryde, and I'd like you to have it."

She hesitated. How could she ever wear something so precious? "It must be the most beautiful thing I've ever seen."

"Certainly not I," he murmured. And when she looked up at him, his attention was fixed on her. "You are the most beautiful thing I have ever seen. The necklace will have found its perfect home."

A shiver ran over her skin, and she had a strange feeling of flying.

"Very well," she murmured.

"Please, allow me."

She turned around, lifting the locks of hair her lady's maid had arranged to fall over her shoulder. When his fingers brushed her heated skin, she closed her eyes. Tingles rushed through her body—and straight to her sex. She clasped her thighs together. Even from his lightest touch, she became damp, achy, and hot.

The necklace settled into place, and he gently took her by the shoulders and turned her to him.

"Look at you." His gaze swept over her before slowly, hungrily, returning to hers again.

Serious. Intense. Overwhelming. Like him.

As she looked in the mirror and caught the reflection of them both, she didn't recognize herself. They looked stunning together—a tall, handsome duke and his duchess.

But inside, she still felt like an imposter.

Twenty minutes later, they arrived in front of Lady Virtoux's house.

Though most of the ton had retired to their country estates, several prominent families remained in London for various political obligations. Lady Virtoux's autumn antiquarian auction was a rare social gathering for which many returned from the country for two weeks. Some even stayed until Christmas.

This made it even more crucial for the new Duchess of Pryde to make a good impression.

Constantine supported her as she descended the carriage steps, doing her best not to get entangled in her stunning gown and fall into a puddle. Her knees jittered as she stepped onto the ground, but Constantine's steady hand never wavered, and she felt his reassurance like a warm blanket.

She looked up at the grand walls. The home had five stories, tall windows, and Palladian architecture. The breeze was slight, the humid air scented with fallen leaves, dying grass, and wet stone. Torches lit every step leading up towards the entrance.

Constantine took her hand for a moment. "Do not be

afraid, Modesty. You're the Duchess of Pryde now. They will all want to be on your good side."

She licked her lips as her gloved fingers tightened around his briefly before he released her.

His gaze hardened. "And if someone isn't properly respectful, they'll have to answer to me."

She nodded, and he extended his arm. As her hand settled lightly on his forearm, a thrumming energy seemed to radiate from him, coursing through her palm and spreading warmth through her body.

They ascended the steps, and two footmen stepped forward to open the doors. Inside, the butler and two additional footmen efficiently relieved Modesty of her spencer and Constantine of his long coat.

"His Grace, the Duke of Pryde, and Her Grace, the Duchess of Pryde," the butler announced as they approached the ballroom where Lady Virtoux received her guests.

The change in Constantine was dramatic. He'd been soft with her alone, but now he stiffened and seemed to grow taller with his back so straight it could be a wall. His face became stone-cold, his eyes losing all warmth, just like the day she'd met him. He had been so close, so intimate when he'd brought her pleasure.

And now, it seemed, he'd put on his armor like a costume and stepped into the role he had to play.

The change made her heart shrivel. He felt distant, and even his arm under his fingers seemed as hard as a rock.

The marchioness and the marquess stood near the doorway, as was proper for the hosts. The marchioness's impressive height and proud bearing made her seem to tower over the other guests. Her modern, imperial cut gown set her apart from the more conservative ladies of her age. She assessed Modesty with sharp eyes.

"Your Grace." Lady Virtoux curtsied to Constantine then to Modesty, her smile never faltering. "And our new duchess. We've all been quite desperate to meet you. The one who claimed the heart of the most desirable bachelor in England."

Modesty inclined her head at the precise angle she'd practiced countless times with Lady Buchanan and the dowager— just deep enough to show courtesy to a marchioness, while maintaining the dignity of her ducal rank. "Lady Virtoux, thank you for including us in your gathering."

"But of course." The marchioness's smile didn't quite reach her eyes. "I do hope you'll find my little antiquarian event engaging. Though I daresay it's nothing compared to the duke's own collection at Pryde Manor."

"Lady Virtoux," murmured Constantine as he leaned closer to her, "once you have a moment, I'd very much like a word alone."

Modesty wasn't sure if she'd heard him right. Why would he want a word alone with the lady?

Before she could dwell on it, Lady Virtoux was already turning to greet the next arrivals, having given them exactly the appropriate amount of attention.

"Ah, there you are," said Eccess, who appeared from a group of guests, looming over most of them, and yet moving surprisingly quick with an animal grace about him. He quickly crossed the space towards them, a shadow of worry passing over his features.

"Octavius?" asked Constantine, collected and cool, a stark contrast with the storm in Modesty's chest.

Eccess stepped closer to his friend. "I must warn you, His Royal Highness is here."

Constantine paled slightly despite his stern expression. "Didn't you say he was otherwise engaged?"

"He was at one of his country estates. But he returned,

declaring the country was boring in October, and the antiquarian auction, though not enticing, was the only decent
gathering to attend."

Constantine's lips flattened, and his gaze hardened. "Very
well. Sooner or later, I'd have to introduce him to my duchess.
Let us go, Modesty."

He was going to introduce her to royalty. Her—a poor
vicar's daughter! Her mind raced as they made their way
through the ballroom, and her chest tightened even more with
anxiety. She recited everything she could remember her two
fairy godmothers having taught her about greeting a royal.

"Is there something amiss with the Regent?" she asked.
"Should I be aware of something?"

"Nothing," Constantine said as they followed Eccess
through the world of glittering jewels, shimmering silks,
straight backs, curious gazes, craned necks, and fluttering fans.

She maintained a polite smile, though she wished she
could return to Pryde House and curl up in the library. She had
just come upon a book filled with fascinating research into the
Picts and theories about their social structure. The author had
even drawn recently discovered ancient stones, which were
covered with simple yet beautiful carvings.

Instead, she tried to keep her head high and her back
straight as Constantine presented her to this lord and that
lady.

While they stood talking to one group of people, she
noticed whispers and stares from the other groups in the room.
A fragment of conversation reached her: "...his mother's indiscretion..."

She frowned, remembering that morning's paper. And
Constantine stiffened every time he caught a whispered word.

Finally, they stood in front of His Royal Highness, the
Regent of Great Britain. *Make the deepest curtsy while keeping*

your eyes modestly lowered until addressed, she remembered Lady Buchanan's instruction. The Regent must be allowed to speak first.

He was in his early fifties, though his excesses had aged him beyond his years. His round belly strained against an elaborately embroidered waistcoat—the evidence of countless elaborate meals and bottles of fine wine. Despite his size, he carried himself with the natural authority of one born to rule. His face, though full-cheeked and florid, retained traces of the legendary handsomeness of his youth, and his blue eyes were sharp with intelligence beneath their heavy lids.

"Your Royal Highness." Constantine bowed deeply.

The Regent's eyes swept over them coolly, lingering on Modesty in a way that made her skin crawl. "Pryde," he acknowledged, then turned his attention to her. "And this must be your new duchess."

"Indeed, Your Royal Highness. May I present Her Grace, the Duchess of Pryde."

"Your Royal Highness," Modesty murmured, executing the deepest curtsy of her life.

"You certainly have good taste, whether it's in horses...or in women."

Modesty smiled politely at the jab.

Constantine inclined his head. "I suppose I do."

"I'm disappointed I wasn't consulted."

Constantine remained perfectly collected, but his eyes sharpened into shards.

The Regent looked at Modesty's stomach. "A special license was acquired in a rush, I heard?"

Constantine shifted very slightly towards her. "The rush was because we are in love and could stay apart no longer."

"Ah. Of course. Love." He assessed her carefully. "When

love is so strong, no other considerations are allowed. Family. Wealth. Lineage. Where is your family from, Duchess?"

She shivered and wished she could disappear.

"My wife's family is unreproachable," said the duke.

"Forgive me, could you please bring me a glass of punch, Pryde?" asked the Regent, staring at him coldly. "I'm suddenly very parched."

Constantine stared straight back. "I am sure there are much more competent punch bearers here than I."

"I insist."

They glared at each other like two wolves, bristled and growling.

Finally, Constantine gave an obedient nod and left after very covertly squeezing her gloved hand.

As he hurried through the crowd towards the tables that held punch, Modesty's heart beat hard in her chest.

"Would you like a tour around the room?" asked the Regent.

"Certainly, Your Royal Highness."

"Very well," said the Regent and indicated the direction with his arm—opposite of where Constantine had gone. What was going on between the two of them?

"Where did you come from, oh innocent rose?" asked the Regent.

Oh innocent rose? She resisted the urge to snort. If he knew she'd spent her days studying ancient burial practices and Roman battlefield tactics, he might reconsider his assessment. "I come from Shepherdsbrook. My father is a clergyman, since you asked about my family. So, indeed, the duke married much below his station. But, well, as he said"—she swallowed—"our love couldn't wait."

"I cannot blame the duke. Had I met a beautiful rose like you, I couldn't have resisted snatching you away."

She chewed on the inside of her bottom lip. Was this how the ton was? The Regent had a reputation for being reckless and for overindulging. But openly flirting with a married woman in public, while her husband was in the same room? What in the world could she say so that she didn't offend the Regent, but also removed herself from his attentions?

"You honor me."

"I would like to do much more than honor you. Much, much more. In fact, you have an open invitation to visit me in private. Whenever you please."

Modesty couldn't believe her ears. Surely, he wasn't propositioning her with something so intimate, so base within minutes of having met her. If this was the life of the ton, she wanted no part of it.

She longingly thought of Augustus's warm, slight weight in her arms, of the books and the artifacts in Pryde's library. And most of all, she thought of her husband, longing for him to return and take her away from this odious man.

"I am sure that is much too generous a way for you to spend your time."

As they continued to walk through small groups of ladies and gentlemen, she caught more conversation fragments that made her heart pound: "...the late duchess's letters..." and "...that country parson..." and "...the affair..."

The whispers seemed to follow them like shadows through the room. But why would anyone question Constantine's mother's reputation?

"Your refreshment, Your Royal Highness," said Constantine, appearing with a glass of punch in each hand.

His voice rang with steel, his face impenetrable, and yet Modesty saw fury blaze in his chestnut eyes. Constantine passed him both glasses of punch.

"If you'll excuse me, my wife has promised me a dance."

He extended his hand to her, and she placed hers in it with such relief she could fly.

His eyes were warm on her, the fury extinguished. And she melted at the protective way he wrapped his fingers around hers and led her towards the dance floor. The couples formed two lines, one of ladies and the other of gentlemen. She felt all eyes on her—heavy, sharp, penetrating. Everyone seemed grander, more elegant, and more deserving to be here in this glittering world of beauty and riches than she.

Yet, when she looked into her husband's eyes, staring at her like he saw no one else, the world around them dissolved.

And she felt like the most deserving one of all.

Then the music began.

She remembered the steps he'd taught her and followed them. Coming together, hands touching, gazes locking, scents mingling. She found herself smiling at him, grateful for how he'd trained her. The hours they'd spent together in the private ballroom were now put to the test. But all she felt was joy at the rhythm of their bodies moving with the music, their steps, touches, turns. It was flirtation itself.

When his fingers found hers, she remembered them touching the most intimate part of her body. She remembered the bliss he could elicit from her.

That pleasure, that connection, that tenderness was now in his every touch and every turn of his body—in the way he held his neck, the way his torso turned to her, the way his lips were settled in a small, private smile.

As they came together, palm to palm, and made a circle around each other, he murmured, "You're the most beautiful woman in the room, Modesty."

Her breath hitched, color flooding to her cheeks. They stepped back and made a figure eight around the people standing to their sides. No. A duke could never truly appreciate her, admire her—she who was born to a simple clergyman, who was never anything spectacular, who existed only to help her father.

"You flatter me," she responded when they came together again.

"No. I am proud to call you my wife."

Heavens, how wonderfully those words tickled down her spine.

There it was again, the heat, the longing. Her body always betrayed her when he touched her. She wanted more of him. More of his body. More of his soul. More of the way his chestnut eyes had warmed and glimmered last night when he'd brought her such pleasure.

He didn't know it yet, but she'd be selfish tonight and wouldn't let him sleep in his own bed. The next time their hands met, she looked straight into his eyes, sank in them. Her heart, she knew, was beating in unison with his. Heaven help her.

Who was this woman he was awakening?

16

Later that evening, when Lady Virtoux unveiled a bronze mirror, Constantine heard Modesty's soft gasp.

Lady Virtoux stood on a small dais at the front of the drawing room, slightly elevated above the seated guests. To her left, a long sideboard displayed items yet to be auctioned, carefully arranged under glass domes or on plush velvet cushions, guarded by two attentive footmen.

The bronze disc the size of a lady's palm caught the candlelight in its dull golden-brown surface. The mirror's handle was in the shape of intertwined serpents, and it looked to be cast iron. Around the mirror's edge, a binding with intricate spirals and geometric patterns flowed.

Modesty's fingers twitched at her sides as though longing to touch it, to examine the spiraling patterns that matched the drawings in her books. She bit her lip, and he knew she was trying to maintain composure. He'd get it for her. Then he'd go and speak to Lady Virtoux about the rosewood box.

The article published in that morning's paper was a knife in his back. He had no idea why the blackmailer would attack his reputation when he'd paid everything that had been asked. Perhaps it was to make sure Constantine knew they were serious, and a new demand for more money was surely about to come.

With the attention brought on by the gossip about his mother's indiscretion, it wouldn't be safe to bring Augustus home as he'd promised Modesty.

He'd need to break his word to her...which was going to kill him.

Although if Lady Virtoux was the blackmailer, his struggles would be over. He wouldn't leave without his mama's letter.

Whatever it took.

Then he could bring Augustus home early—today, even— and have the pleasure of watching his wife's face glow with joy.

Lady Virtoux lifted the mirror in her gloved hands, turning in a circle so everyone could see it clearly. "A rare artifact which was found near Inverness, this bronze mirror shows the distinctive patterns of Pictish craftsmanship. Bidding begins at five pounds."

The starting bid alone was worth half a footman's yearly wages. Constantine raised his hand. "Five pounds!"

The Regent's voice cut through the crowd. "Ten pounds."

Constantine's jaw tightened. The Regent knew very well Constantine had led the opposition to increasing his annuity just last month. This wasn't about the mirror at all.

"Twenty," Constantine said, his voice carrying across the suddenly hushed drawing room.

The Regent's lips curved. "Forty."

Constantine's fingers dug into his palm. He knew he should yield. The practical choice would be to let the Regent have his victory. But then he caught sight of Modesty from the corner of his eye, watching her struggle to hide her disappointment behind a duchess's mask, and something in his chest twisted painfully. He'd denied her so much already. He couldn't bear to see that light die in her eyes—not when he had the power to keep it burning.

"Eighty," he said.

"Ninety," the Regent countered.

A ripple went through the crowd. Everyone knew of His Royal Highness's mounting debts, his struggles with Parliament—and Constantine's actions against increasing the annuity.

"One hundred pounds," Constantine said. Modesty turned to him, her eyes wide.

The Regent's face flushed deeper. "Two hundred."

Damn his pride, but Constantine couldn't back down. Not with Modesty watching, not with the Regent's smug certainty that Constantine would yield. Just as he was expected to yield about Augustus, about his marriage, about everything.

Constantine's jaw tightened. "Four hundred."

Just as he said it, part of him wondered if he was being reckless. The blackmailer would surely demand more money soon, and here he was, spending a fortune on pride.

A collective gasp echoed across the room. The Regent's fingers whitened on his glass of wine. Constantine could practically hear his own future crumbling. But Modesty's face, the naked hope she couldn't quite hide, had his heart squeezing with determination.

"Constantine, that is too much!" she whispered. "It's not worth it. You can put this money to much better use...give it to the almshouse...or anything else."

She was right. Four hundred pounds could even fund a small excavation somewhere in Britain. Was it really worth it to spend that much on one mirror?

Around them, ladies fanned themselves, whispering

behind their hands at each escalating bid. The rustle of silk, the clink of wineglasses, the sparkles of jewels shifting as they turned their heads to watch the battle between duke and Regent.

"Six hundred!" the Regent proclaimed.

Constantine met his gaze, keeping his composure perfect. They both knew the Regent couldn't go higher without causing a scandal because of his debt. Both knew Constantine had forced this moment. It was exactly what had happened at the bidding for Icarus. The Regent must be finding it unbearable.

"Constantine, don't," Modesty whispered. "Truly, I'm thankful, but let him have it."

He heard her. But he couldn't let it go. He had to have the mirror. He couldn't let the Regent win, not like that. It was a matter of pride.

"One thousand pounds."

Silence fell. Constantine could feel the weight of every eye in the room. It was more than most families saw in a year, more than he'd planned to spend on updating the tenant farms this season. Distantly, he wondered what other sacrifices his pride would demand of him. The bidding had started at five pounds, and here he was, offering a small fortune.

The Regent's face purpled, but after a long moment, he inclined his head with deadly grace. "Yours, Your Grace. Though I wonder if you'll find it worth the price."

The threat wasn't subtle. But then Modesty's hand found his arm, trembling with suppressed excitement, and Constantine couldn't bring himself to regret a single pound.

"One thousand pounds," said Lady Virtoux, "going once... twice...sold to the Duke of Pryde."

Modesty dug her fingers into his arm, obviously fighting to maintain composure. But her eyes... God, her eyes were luminous, like emeralds on fire.

As Lady Virtoux's footman brought the mirror for their inspection, Modesty's careful duchess mask cracked. She leaned forward, her breath catching as she traced the air just above the bronze surface.

"I know it was much too much, but... Oh, Constantine, look at the spiral patterns here... They are usually carved on objects of importance. And the serpents on the handle... Serpents often represent wisdom or transformation in Celtic art. A regular mirror wouldn't have such elaborate metalwork. I think it wasn't just practical—it was symbolic. A woman who carried it could have been seen as powerful in her own right."

"Fascinating," Constantine said. He'd pay another thousand just to see that light in her eyes again.

But to his disappointment, she looked around and schooled her features back to demure appreciation.

"No, go on." He squeezed her hand secretly, unable to stop his smile. "I believe you were about to revolutionize our understanding of ancient Scottish society."

She looked up at him then, really looked at him, and the naked gratitude and joy in her expression made his chest ache. For a moment, he forgot about the Regent's threatening glare, forgot about Lady Virtoux possessing the rosewood box, forgot about everything but the way Modesty's whole being seemed to glow with enthusiasm.

"Thank you," she whispered. "For taking me seriously. For letting me be myself, if only for a moment."

He'd been a fool to try suppressing this side of her, to try molding her into some perfect, passive duchess. This was who she truly was—brilliant, passionate, alive. Let tomorrow bring what consequences it would. Tonight, he'd given his wife a piece of history to unravel, and her smile was worth any price.

But he couldn't rest yet. The box awaited and with it, perhaps, answers about the blackmailer. He'd need to tread carefully with Lady Virtoux, approach the subject with more finesse than he'd shown when accusing Modesty. One wrong word could send his carefully constructed world tumbling down.

After the auction finished, Lady Virtoux came to him. "Shall we discuss payment in my study?"

Perfect. He'd ask her about the box right after he settled the payment. "Of course."

Leaving Modesty under Eccess's care, he followed Lady Virtoux into her study. It felt too warm, despite the chill October night beyond the windows. At her desk, she produced a ledger bound in leather, the gilded edges catching the light. Constantine dipped the pen she provided into the inkwell, then signed his name with a practiced flourish on the page where she indicated—the official record of the sale.

"I thank you, sir," she said as she put the ledger away. "Now, what was it that you wanted to talk to me about?"

His fingers clenched behind his back. "I understand you recently acquired an interesting piece," Constantine said carefully. "A rosewood box with silver inlay and pearl work."

Lady Virtoux's perfectly shaped eyebrows rose. "How curious that you'd know of such a specific item."

"I have an interest in fine craftsmanship."

"Do you?" Her smile was razor-sharp. "How intriguing. Your mother shared that passion, didn't she? Though her interests tended more towards...spiritual matters."

His fingers dug into his palms behind his back. "My mother had many interests."

"Oh, yes. She was particularly captivated by theological discussions, as I recall. Spent quite a lot of time with that country parson... What was his name?"

Constantine's throat tightened. "I'm afraid I don't follow."

"No? Strange. One would think a son would remember

such things. Though perhaps not all sons have reason to remember their mothers' spiritual advisors."

The threat in her words was clear as crystal. Constantine fought to keep his voice steady.

"Tell me," she said, "how is married life treating you? Your new duchess is quite…unconventional. A clergyman's daughter, isn't she? How fitting."

The deliberate emphasis on "clergyman" made his blood run cold. "My marriage is not the topic at hand."

She leaned forward. "But it's all so riveting. The hasty wedding, the mysterious woman no one has ever heard of… Is she a suitable match for a duke? And now this stunning display over a Pictish mirror. One might almost think you were trying to make amends for something."

"If you have something to say, Lady Virtoux, say it plainly."

"Oh, but where would the fun be in that? Though I must say, your new duchess's scholarly enthusiasm is quite charming. So passionate about uncovering secrets of humanity. Would she be as overjoyed to uncover hidden truths in family histories?"

The room seemed to close in around him. Was this elegant torture preparation for a blackmail demand? Or was she simply amusing herself with his discomfort?

He was in quite a pickle. He couldn't plainly accuse her of blackmail, because if she wasn't the blackmailer, the ton would know everything tonight.

"The box was my mother's family heirloom," he lied. "I simply tracked it through the seller and wish to buy it from you. I do not have many happy memories of my childhood. That box is connected to one of them."

He was falling deeper into his own trap. How could he find out if she was the blackmailer?

He could ask her to write something and compare her writing with that of the letter.

"Oh," she said, smiling. "I see. I wouldn't want to keep a cherished childhood memory from you. What was it about, if I may inquire?"

He cleared his throat. "A wonderful day out with my mama. She used to keep her necklaces in the box. My wife wears one of them tonight."

"Right. I noticed. Your mama's taste was exquisite."

"It was."

She nodded then rummaged in the drawer of her desk and withdrew an ornate rosewood box. His heart beat hard against his chest at the sight.

"A rather unique piece," she said, setting it before him. "Though perhaps not as valuable as your new Pictish mirror."

His throat tightened at the sight of the silver inlay, the delicate pearl work—exactly as the maid had described. "May I?"

She gestured permission with a practiced flourish. As he lifted the lid, his heart pounded. There were pens inside. Discreetly, he lifted the false bottom the maid had mentioned and suppressed a curse. The secret compartment was empty, no trace of the letter that could destroy everything.

If Lady Virtoux had found the letter, she would, of course, keep it in a different location. So he still needed to find out if she was the blackmailer.

He nodded and placed the box on the desk. "How much would you like for it?"

"Take it for free, Duke. As my gift and appreciation for your mama."

"Thank you," he said tightly. "Might I impose on you for one more favor? Would you write a short note gifting it to my duchess? She's quite meticulous about documenting her growing collection of antiquities. I'd love to surprise her with both the mirror and this beloved family piece, properly authenticated by such a renowned collector as yourself."

She chuckled. "Of course. Anything for your new duchess. As long as she doesn't have her own spiritual friend."

She began writing while Constantine clenched his jaw hard enough to crush his teeth in an attempt to not say something he'd regret.

Handing him the note with a sly smile, she said, "Do give my regards to your lovely duchess. Such a refreshing addition to our circle."

Constantine's hand tightened around the box until his knuckles whitened. "Very kind of you."

He strode out, his mind racing. The box was empty. He stopped at the candle sconce on the wall and studied her writing. He cursed. Completely different. Her handwriting was round and curly. The blackmailer's was sharp and long.

He supposed she could have changed it, but what were the chances of that?

The investigation had hit a dead end, despite his friends' help. And now the ton's most notorious gossip was circling like a vulture, ready to tear him apart.

The smartest thing he could do was to avoid gossip and questions. Which meant keeping Augustus hidden. The look of hurt and disappointment on Modesty's face would kill him.

Unless...

There was only one person left who might be able to help —a man who dealt in secrets darker than his own. Thorne Blackmore. The thought of going to him made Constantine's skin crawl, but he was out of options.

17

BACK AT HOME, in his wife's bedchamber, Constantine poured port into two glasses and stilled, gathering the strength to face Modesty. He didn't want to think about the blackmailer and the gossip piece. Didn't want to think about how to convince Thorne Blackmore to help him.

He wanted to push the whole world to the side for just one night.

Modesty called to him like a siren.

Resisting her would be the hardest thing he'd ever done, but he owed her the truth before anything more happened between them. Honor demanded it, even if his body screamed at him to take what she so freely offered.

He'd always wanted to be honorable, but he was a bastard. His very existence was a lie. So his actions didn't always match his intentions. But something about Modesty made him long to be a better man.

God knew, he was already walking a very thin line. At the soirée earlier tonight, he'd been torn between his duty to the Pryde title and his wish to finally be free of the lie that had burdened him his entire life. Free to allow himself to be happy with his wife. He'd been torn between needing to break his word to Modesty and aching to see joy shine in her eyes as she held Augustus...

So he'd settled on a compromise—he'd take her to spend time with the baby, at least.

When they'd arrived at the town house after the soirée, Augustus was asleep, but seeing Modesty lean over his cot with tears in her eyes eased Constantine's heart.

Watching her gaze lovingly at the little one as he snored lightly, wrapped in his muslin swaddle, Constantine couldn't bring himself to tell her they wouldn't be able to bring Augustus home in two days.

For the first time, he'd seen a glimpse of what could be...a vision of a happy life with Modesty and Augustus.

Now, in her bedchamber, he finally turned to her, and his breath stuck in his throat at the sight of her. Still in her indigo silk gown, she dragged one long, white glove down her arm. Mesmerized, he followed the brush of silk down her forearm.

She slowly removed one glove, then the other, the intimate gesture making her intentions clear. His mouth went dry.

Octavius's unwelcome words flooded his mind. *A redhead... looked so timid but must be fire in bed.*

The way her body had responded to his touch, the way she was looking at him now, he agreed.

He needed to speak now, before her seduction stripped away his resolve entirely.

He walked to her and offered a glass.

She took it and smiled. "Thank you."

She had the most beautiful smile.

He nodded and clinked his glass against hers.

He wanted to tell her everything—about his true parentage, about Augustus's claim, about the blackmailer and why it was important to keep Augustus hidden longer. But every time he opened his mouth, her trusting gaze stopped him. How could he destroy that trust when it was so new and so fragile?

"How did you enjoy tonight?" he asked.

"I enjoyed some of it." She chuckled. "Dancing with you...I didn't mind that."

Their eyes locked as she sipped her wine, staring at him over the rim of the glass.

He swallowed and chuckled. He was hard just being in this room, where her scent always lingered. "I didn't mind dancing with you, either."

It was more and more difficult to think with her so close. But he needed to tell her. He wanted to.

My mother had an affair. I am not my father's son. Augustus is the real heir because Ophelia was the duke's daughter. My father left a will issuing his intentions that the title must only pass to a blood heir.

I am not the blood heir.

Augustus is.

After all, all titles were permitted to descend to the next generation at the good will of the monarch. Constantine was sure the Regent would love nothing more than to remove the title and bestow it on the child.

He opened his mouth.

"Perhaps we could have a real marriage," she said.

Her eyes were bright and sparkling as she took one step closer. She laid her hands on his chest. All thoughts of telling her the truth evaporated like steam. He inhaled her sweet scent, and his blood simmered.

His lips were suddenly so parched he had to empty the entire glass of port down his throat. "A real marriage?"

She cupped his face, her touch soft and gentle, and even that gentlest of touches sent a pull of desire straight down to his groin. "Sometimes, people marry for love. Sometimes, they fall in love with each other after they marry. Why can't that be us?"

"Love was never part of this marriage," he managed.

She stroked his cheek. "But it can be."

A realization struck him.

Damn it all, it already was—for him.

His heart drummed against his ribs, full and light. That ache to make her happy, the need to see her smile, the compulsion to go against his own better judgment and risk losing everything.

All of it was because he loved her.

"I—" he started but couldn't say another word.

God, he wanted to agree with her. To turn this marriage of convenience into a marriage of love.

But if she ever learned the truth—the secrets he was hiding, the battle he was fighting against the baby she protected...

She'd never speak of love again.

"At first, I thought you were selfish and cruel, but I see now what a good man you really are."

Every word was a blow straight to his gut. He was still selfish and cruel. Still the most prideful man in England. He was going to destroy her trust—it was only a matter of time.

"I refused you when you came to me on our wedding night," she murmured, running her other hand up his chest, leaving a trace of fire on his skin even through the layers of clothing. "I won't refuse you anymore."

And then the little minx stood on her toes, leaned forward, and kissed him.

Her lips were soft and warm. Her taste, her scent, her touch ignited something deep within. Perhaps it was because he'd wanted her for what felt like forever. Perhaps it was because she offered herself so freely.

Something snapped inside him.

An honorable man would stop her. Explain the whole truth. Tell her he couldn't let her love some false version of him.

He was not a good man.

He was a bastard in every sense of the word.

But he'd dreamed of having her for far too long.

He wrapped his arms around her waist and took their kiss deeper, claiming her mouth as he would soon claim her body.

18

He kissed her with urgency, his lips like fire, his arms around her waist like iron rods. She moaned as she melted against his granite-hard chest. He groaned into her mouth, and his tongue tangled with hers, setting all of her senses on edge.

Her hands were in his hair, around his neck, and she had the urge to grind her sex against him like she had before, to rub her breasts against his body and purr like a cat.

Did she just say she wanted a real marriage? To the Duke of Pryde—the man she'd once thought as cold as stone?

But she knew there was more to him. She'd seen him with Augustus and with Mr. Hawthorne. He'd paid a fortune so she could have the Pictish mirror, and he'd been protective of her with the Regent...

Despite her reservations, deep in her heart, she wanted nothing but to bring him happiness.

And she was weary of resisting her body's desire for him.

She was ready.

He was breathing hard now—they both were. He leaned back and looked her up and down. "Modesty... I..." He shook his head, as though trying to shake off some kind of a fog and gather his thoughts.

"What?" she murmured.

His eyes were so dark they swallowed her whole. "I can't think straight... God... What are you doing to me?"

She? She was doing this to him? She'd never seen him with a single hair out of order. Even when he was hurrying out of the house on some secret mission, he was still meticulously collected.

Beads of sweat formed on his forehead. "Are you certain about this?" he asked.

She licked her lips and looked up at him from under her eyelashes. As she worked one button of his waistcoat free, he exhaled a ragged breath.

"I am very certain, Constantine," she said as she began working on the next button. "I want you to fulfill your promise to put something big inside me."

He closed his eyes and inhaled sharply, a visible tremor passing through him. "Good Lord, woman, you don't know what you're asking. I am not a gentle lover. There's a certain way I like things so that I don't lose control... I don't know that you can bear it."

A deep ache in the pit of her stomach made her squirm and clench her thighs together. She didn't know what he meant. But she knew she wanted everything. "I can handle it."

He fell on her lips again, and, with barely restrained force, walked her backwards. Behind her, something heavy thumped against the rug, followed by the distinct sound of crystal rolling across wooden floorboards. The port decanter, her mind registered distantly, unwilling to focus on anything except his touch.

Her back met with a wall, and she felt the fabric of the curtain on the skin of her upper back. As he kissed her, ground against her, his hands in her hair, his hard body flattening her against the wall, she heard a slight ripping of the curtain high up by the ceiling.

He growled into her mouth like a wolf. His hands roamed her body with desperate hunger, kneading her breasts until she arched into his touch, wanting more, needing more. Each caress sent tingles through her body, making her gasp against his mouth.

"I'm going to hoist you up," he murmured against her lips. "And I want you to wrap your legs around me."

"What?" she asked.

"Wrap your legs around my hips."

He ran his hands down to her waist, then he yanked her dress up. Lifting her by the hips, he pinned her to the wall with his pelvis, and she wrapped her thighs around his hips as he thrust his hard and impressive bulge straight against her sex.

"Good girl," he rasped, and his praise made her inner muscles tense sweetly.

She moaned as friction brought the delight she craved. She was surrounded by him—nowhere to go—and she wanted nothing more than this. She began moving her hips with the rhythm of his soft thrusts, meeting his pelvis, and he groaned like an animal.

Suddenly the wall was gone from behind her back, and he was carrying her. She loved that, despite her height, he could carry her effortlessly. He threw her onto the bed and loomed over her, his arms supporting him, his face above hers.

He did not wear the cold mask of a statue anymore.

There was raw emotion on his face.

Adoration. Hunger.

Longing.

He scanned her body, breathing deeply, quickly, unevenly. And embarrassment hit her, mixed with a burning excitement when she realized her skirt and her petticoat were still pulled up to her hips. Her legs were covered only by her stockings and her shoes.

His gaze on her sex was so intense, she felt like he was already touching her. "Open your legs for me, darling."

She squirmed, and her folds wettened. She squeezed her thighs together, her face heating.

"I don't know if it's appropriate... To look there..."

He fumbled with his coat, but his hands were shaking. "We're past propriety, darling." His voice was even, but deep and raspy. "You're about to become mine forever. I want to see you. All of you."

Another sweet spasm had her inner walls tightening in anticipation, her blood heating. What was his commanding voice doing to her?

She did as he asked, feeling herself become vulnerable and bare, heat creeping down her face to her neck. As his gaze dropped to her very core, he let out a sharp exhale and something animalistic crossed his features.

He growled deeper than before.

His Adam's apple bobbed as his chest rose and fell faster, the tendons in his neck bulging.

"What a pretty seashell..." he murmured. "All mine."

He shrugged off his waistcoat and tossed it aside, yanked his white shirt out of his breeches, and pulled it over his head so harshly, she heard the fabric tear. He kicked off his boots and shoved down his breeches and stood completely bare before her.

Besides a glorious show of broad, muscular shoulders, a hard chest with defined muscles, a finely carved abdomen going into narrow hips, and muscular thighs, there was...

Her breath hitched. A very long, thick organ stood upright amid a circle of dark hair.

She supported herself with her elbows as she craned her neck to see it better. She opened her mouth in shock. "Is this the hard thing you spoke of? The one that would bring me pleasure?" she asked, recalling his words from before when his fingers had introduced her to such bliss.

He swallowed hard. "It is."

She couldn't find her words for a moment. "How is it ever going to fit?" she managed finally.

"It will...and I'll make sure you'll love it. But first I'm going to make a feast of you."

And then he fell straight onto the bed between her thighs, his face so close to her sex she shifted away in embarrassment.

"Constantine!" she demanded in alarm. "What are you doing?"

He grasped her hips with his hands and looked up at her. "I'm going to kiss your pretty shell, darling. Keep your thighs open for me."

"No! Surely, you don't have to do that..."

He took a deep breath and closed his eyes for a moment, and when his gaze met hers again, it was strangely tender. "I understand you feel shy. I wouldn't want to do anything you don't want me to. And I don't have to do anything, Modesty. But I'm dying to kiss you there, dying to put my mouth on your pretty wet lips. I want to taste you, feel you tighten and shudder and fall apart from my touch. I don't remember wanting anything more."

Oh, dear heaven... Just his words had a wave of heat rushing through her, sweat hitting her skin.

His eyes were warm on hers. "Tell me to stop and I will. What will it be? Do you want me to kiss you there?"

A tremor rushed through her as she opened her mouth to say the most decadent words of her life. "Yes, I want you to kiss me there."

"Good girl."

And then his lips were on her... And he kissed her sex like he kissed her mouth...desperately, hungrily, his tongue swirling and exploring her folds.

She moaned as intense bliss spilled through her.

First his hands...and now this... Was there any end to the exquisite torture he could put her through? And how would it feel to have his hard member deep inside her, where his fingers had been...

She felt her walls squeeze deeply, heat taking over her body.

He teased her and gently sucked her flesh and all she could do was take it and try not to die from bliss. He was making noises of his own: desperate growls, masculine moans, and words of encouragement and adoration slipped through his lips like he was in a fever.

She was about to fall apart when he withdrew from her, and looked up, his fingers gently rubbing her heated, achy, needy flesh.

"Sweet girl, I can feel your walls tightening for me, can feel how drenched you are."

He rose to his knees, his hands shaking as he held his large member. It looked so thick and swollen, long veins running along its sides. He stroked himself up and down, looking at her. Then he had her sit up, unlaced her dress and pulled it down, then unlaced her corset and pulled it over her head. And finally, with his hands that refused to cooperate, he removed her chemise.

Finally, she was left in only her stockings and slippers, which she kicked off.

He stood over her, his hair tousled, so unlike the Duke of Pryde. He looked so young and vulnerable. So different... And she loved him like this. This was the man beneath the mask.

Passionate.

Honest.

True.

He cupped her breasts and bent his head to lick and suck on them until she was breathing raggedly. Then he positioned himself between her thighs, and instinctively, she moved her hips, rubbing herself against him, wanting him to come closer. His member felt silky and hot and hard against her.

He groaned and was visibly shaking. "I am going to take you now. God help me to keep control..."

"No, Constantine. Don't hold yourself back. Lose control. I want you to."

"I don't want it to hurt for you."

"Will it?"

"It might. That's why I wish to be gentle with you," he whispered, his fingers trembling as they traced her cheek. "I'd rather suffer a thousand wounds myself than cause you a moment's pain."

He pressed his member into her entrance, and she moaned, welcoming the strange but pleasant invasion. With one hand, he rubbed her folds in that beautifully sensitive place while he slowly entered her with small, controlled thrusts.

She was stretching, stretching, and then she felt it, the pain, the snap of something inside her, and then he was in.

He cried out and shook in her arms. She gasped, overwhelmed by the wonderful sensation of him inside her. She felt so full, and the slight sting was dissolving as she tightened around him.

"Does it hurt?" he asked.

He was supporting himself with his elbows, and his hands cupped her face, gently stroking sweaty strands of hair from her forehead.

"It did a little," she said as she moved her pelvis to meet him, to bring him deeper. "But not anymore."

He kissed her, dozens of small, soft kisses on her lips, her eyes, her cheeks. "I'm sorry, darling girl. I'm so sorry for hurting you. I promise, this will only get better. A world of delight. Anything you want is yours. I'll do anything..."

His care made her heart tighten, and she reassured him with a deep kiss.

"Then don't stop," she murmured against his lips. "Show me this world of delight. I want you to take me. Do whatever you please with me."

He gave out another wolfish growl and began moving his hips. Slowly at first, in and out, in an exquisite torture. The pain left completely as deep satisfaction took over, and she wanted him to go faster.

They were as close, as connected as two people could be. He was looking into her eyes, and she into his, and she more sure than ever she was seeing the man behind the walls he'd erected around himself.

And then he came undone, thrusting into her with ferocious abandon, and the tension was building, building, and he was groaning and murmuring: "How did I ever resist you?" and "I want you. All of you," and "I need you," and "I've never wanted anything as much as I want you."

He was taking her to heights she never thought possible. Something tightened inside into unimaginable bliss, and as she cried out and arched her back, he bucked and growled and held her hips, pounding into her quickly. And as she fell apart, so did he. For a few moments, they both shook, and then he fell into her arms, burying his face in her neck, his arms wrapping around her.

They were locked together, he was still inside her, and she was melting in his arms as they breathed one breath.

Their hearts beating as one, she marveled at the transformation before her. Gone was the icy mask he always wore, replaced by something raw and real and beautiful. His eyes held such tenderness as they met hers, such vulnerability, that her heart swelled with love. This was the true Constantine—not the Duke of Pryde who the world knew, but her Constantine, who trembled at her touch and whispered endearments against her skin.

And she loved him, every part of him, even the parts he had only now dared to show.

19

"I'M GOING to wash you now," he murmured into her ear. "You'll tell me if it hurts, will you?"

Steam rose from the bathtub in the middle of Modesty's room as Constantine took the washcloth and dipped it into the warm water.

She reached for the cloth. "You do not have to do that. I am perfectly capable."

His wife was so pleasantly situated between his thighs, her back leaning against his chest. Earlier tonight, he'd rung the servant bell and asked them to bring the bathtub and hot water. The footmen and the maids had thrown curious glances at him as he'd paced his wife's bedchamber in nothing but a dressing gown while she'd hidden under the sheets.

Let them talk.

"Of course you are. I'd like to do this for you. I know I hurt you before... I'd like to take care of you."

She inhaled deeply and exhaled, easing back against him.

He loved her, even more now that she had given herself to

him. And he'd been much rougher with her than he'd intended.

But his control shattered at her touch. He didn't recognize himself with her.

He lowered the cloth down to her thighs.

Lit candles surrounded them in candelabras, their flames reflected in her large mirror.

It was so peaceful here. So quiet, with just the water dripping, the coals crackling in the grate, and Modesty's even breathing as she nestled against him. He could feel the smooth skin of her back, the slight weight of her. And her wet hair pooled in the water around them, clinging to him.

"All right," she said, and he saw a slight rise in her upper cheek as she must have smiled. "If you wish."

He lowered the cloth and placed it on her inner thigh. The sheets were bloody as well as her inner thighs. A sign she was truly and irrevocably his.

Someone he treasured. Cherished. Adored.

He never wanted anyone else as long as he lived. She was his now, and he was hers, and that was it.

Softly, he ran the cloth closer to her sex. He kissed her cheek, her ear, her neck. "Is this all right?" he asked.

She chuckled and wriggled her behind against his groin, sending an onrush of heat straight into his cock, which quickly began to let him know *it* appreciated the attention.

"Very much so, indeed," she said.

When the cloth reached her sex, she tensed slightly. "Too much?"

"It stings a little. But do continue."

He chuckled and patted her very gently between her thighs, acutely aware of her body. She didn't flinch or pull away, and that told him she was all right.

"You must know your way around virgins," she said.

He ran the cloth over her other thigh. He couldn't see what he was doing, but he wanted her to feel cared for.

"Yours is the only virginity I have taken," he said.

"Oh?"

"You are the second woman I have known in such a way. And whatever happens, you will be the last one I'll ever know."

That made her go rigid, and he stopped patting. She craned her neck to meet his gaze.

"Does that surprise you?" he asked.

"Yes. Second woman, really?"

"Yes. Before you, I had a regular lover at Elysium. She was my first."

She didn't move, barely breathing. "Aren't you forgetting Ophelia?"

Stunned, his mind raced as he searched for something to say.

Damnation. This lie was still haunting him. He wanted to tell Modesty the truth, but she trusted him, thought him a good man. She'd never look at him the same way if she knew he'd lied to her about something so monumental as Augustus's parentage, that he'd never corrected her misunderstanding. And that wasn't even the biggest lie he was living...

"And Ophelia," he said, hating himself. "But that was just once. The woman in Elysium was my lover for ten years. And now I have you."

He waited for her reaction. It was quite a confession, he knew. And it must not be easy for her to hear about any other women in his life. He certainly hated to see or hear about Mr. George Lockhart, who Constantine was sure harbored much more than *friendly* feelings towards her.

She made a circle in the water with her finger. "And...you stopped it?"

"Yes. After I proposed and you accepted, I knew the only woman I could ever have in my life was you. My wife."

"Was she...was she more than just a lover? A body?"

He swallowed. "She was a friend, in a way. Just someone I talked to. As well as someone who allowed me to satisfy... certain needs. I never wanted to sire a bastard..."

"But you did."

Wrong. But, of course, he couldn't admit it.

He lightly ran the cloth over her sex. "Could be worse. Testament to how right I was to restrict myself to only one... two women."

She looked at him over her shoulder. "And you will not miss your lover at Elysium?"

He shook his head. "No. I don't need a lover when I have my wife."

How could he ever miss another woman when he had her —the most beautiful, kind-hearted, challenging, and intelligent woman he'd ever met?

She was everything he could ever wish for. And he wanted to make her happy.

Only, one day he'd shatter this fragile happiness like glass.

He let go of the cloth and wrapped his arms around her, pulling her closer. She turned to him in the water, sleek, her movements tickling his thighs and stomach. He met her eyes, like molten malachite in the candlelight.

She cupped his face, taking a lock of his hair between her fingers. "Let me wash you now."

He chuckled. Her washing him felt like a seductive, forbidden delight. "Very well, my duchess."

Dripping water onto the floor, they switched sides, and he nestled comfortably between her thighs as she cleaned him with the warm cloth.

"Tell me about that woman from Elysium," she said.

He frowned. "Are you certain? It might not be pleasant to hear."

She dipped the cloth into water. "I am stronger than you think."

He inhaled deeply. "There's not much to tell, in truth. My experience was...mechanical. Clinical, even. It was necessary to satisfy my body to maintain control over my emotions. My father taught me I must do whatever it takes to ensure the honor of the bloodline. I never wanted my relationship with a woman to be different...until you."

The words "because I love you" almost slipped from his tongue.

She ran the cloth down his shoulder. "You must have had quite a strict childhood."

"Yes," he said bitterly. "My father made it very clear that I was supposed to be a certain way. I've always liked horses. That was encouraged, but only if they were purebreds. Once, when I was seven, I cried when my favorite horse died. Father found me in the stables. 'Dukes of Pryde don't weep,' he told me. 'Tears are for common folk who have nothing to offer the world but their emotions.' Then one day—I was twelve, I think—I found myself in the stables at night, and one of the mares had a difficult foaling. The stud groom asked me to help, and of course I did. When that foal finally emerged, alive and healthy, I felt like I had touched a miracle."

She dropped the cloth and massaged his shoulders with both hands. "That sounds wonderful."

Her touch soothed the stiff, achy muscles of his shoulders, his back, his biceps, and his neck. If heaven existed, he was in it. As his body relaxed, it became easier to talk, to share the worst things that had happened to him. He wanted her to know, to be part of him.

"After that, I became absorbed with learning everything I

could about horses—their anatomy, their care, their illnesses. I'd follow the grooms whenever I had a free minute. I'd sneak books into my room, draw horses from memory."

She lightly pressed his head back onto her chest. Picking up a pitcher standing on the table by the bathtub, she filled it, then poured water over his hair. "You were a passionate boy."

Constantine chuckled softly. "Obsessive, more like. When I found something that interested me, I had to master it completely. Know everything. Do everything correctly."

She poured more water over his hair. "That is where your drive for perfection lies, does it not?"

"Hm. I've never thought of it that way. But of course, when my father noticed my involvement, he told me dukes did not doctor horses. Dukes rode them."

A small, indignant huff escape her lips. Her reaction, so protective and understanding, made his heart swell with affection.

"So I had to hide my obsession from him," he continued as she picked up a cake of soap and foamed her fingers. "I secretly helped in three more foalings. When I was sixteen, I heard about the Royal Veterinary College opening in London. I wanted to study there. But when I told Papa, he said it was unworthy of a duke."

She dug her fingers into his hair and began massaging the soap into the wet strands, her fingertips sending delicious sensations across his scalp. "I am sorry to hear he thought that way."

"I suppose I shouldn't have been surprised. Whoever heard of a duke who was a horse surgeon? Certainly that would have been beneath any Duke of Pryde. But I had a different idea that I thought Papa might approve of—to establish a small horse hospital right here on our estate. Can you imagine what a difference it would have made? We'd have employed graduates from the college, cared for our horses and those of our tenants. And I...well...I secretly hoped to learn alongside them."

She tipped the pitcher again to wash the soap out of his hair, and he closed his eyes as one or two rivulets ran down his face. "I was overjoyed when I told my father. I thought he'd be proud, you see, to establish something so new and so honorable."

"That is a most excellent idea," she said, melting his heart. "It *is* new and honorable."

He smiled softly at her sweet acceptance and support as she rinsed away the rest of the soap. He felt free. Warm. Happy.

Then he chuckled bitterly. "But he laughed at me."

He felt her go still.

"I am sorry he crushed your dream like that," she said as she picked up a soft linen cloth and massaged his hair with it to absorb the water.

He didn't reply, just enjoyed the movements of her fingers over his head. He'd never felt this connected, this intimate with anyone in his life. God help him, it felt wonderful to set his pride aside and just be who he was. To stop trying to always be right and win at all costs. To stop pretending that he never made a mistake.

To stop pushing people away.

She picked up a comb from the table beside the bath and began running it through his damp hair.

"I've never told anyone about this before," he said, "but because of that dream, my father thought I stole his diamond tie pin."

"Was that the pin you wore at our wedding?"

"Indeed it was. My mother had given it to my father, and one day he wanted to wear it as a gesture of reconciliation, but he couldn't find it."

She kept combing his hair. It never felt so good when his valet did it. "Do you know who stole it?" she asked.

Constantine nodded. "Mr. Hawthorne."

She froze, the comb positioned against the side of his head. "Mr. Hawthorne?" she asked, shocked. "He seems so kind, why would he ever do such a thing?"

"He had a younger brother who was in deep trouble due to gambling debts."

Modesty's hand tightened around his.

"When Father discovered the pin was missing and ordered every room and drawer to be searched, I took it from Mr. Hawthorne and hid it among my own belongings. I just couldn't have Father sack the only friend I ever had."

"Did you really not have any friends your age?" she asked softly.

There was an edge of pity in her voice that made him bristle up with wounded pride internally. But he could also understand her pity.

"Pathetic, isn't it? I was not allowed to play with the tenants' or servants' children, and my father preferred to make political connections in the city rather than entertaining guests in our house. So, yes, Mr. Hawthorne was the only friend I had."

Modesty smiled. "I wish I could have been your friend."

His throat tightened with a raw emotion, tears prickling his eyes. He thought of Chastity and Lucien, who had known each other all their lives and had been friends for years. How would it have been to have someone like that in his own life? Someone who understood and accepted him, who'd be his partner in mischief and by his side in the most difficult moments?

Instead, he'd always been an adult in child's clothes.

"I wish that, too. I would have secretly climbed out of my window at night to spend time with you."

She smoothed his hair, humming softly. "So what happened with Mr. Hawthorne?"

"To protect him, I confessed to taking the pin, claiming I wanted to have something that reminded me of my mother close to me. My father was furious. He saw it as further proof of my unworthiness. I was too sentimental about horses *and* people. He punished me, but it was nothing. Mr. Hawthorne stayed."

Constantine fell silent. He was acutely aware of her skin against his, her breath against his back, her fingers on his shoulders now, a silent sign of support. In this moment, she felt more precious than any title or estate.

She moved like a sleek water creature and was soon straddling him, her gaze locked with his.

It was terrifying to look into her eyes after everything he'd shared. But there was nothing but love and acceptance in her gaze.

His heart shriveled with fear. Perhaps she thought well of him now, but when the truth came out, she'd know what he'd done—lied, robbed a babe of his true inheritance, and lived the life of someone he was not.

And yet, like a coward, he allowed himself to selfishly enjoy more of her affection, her touch, her support.

She cupped his face with both hands, and he was lost in her eyes. Her skin was luminous, water droplets glistening on the tiny freckles on her shoulders that he adored. "You're a wonderful man, Constantine. Under that hard chest of yours is the kindest heart."

All lies. The man she described was who he wanted to be. But not who he was.

But he didn't contradict her. He let her kiss him, melting his bones like honey.

He only wished he deserved her high esteem and regard. In that moment, he knew he couldn't go back on his word to her, even if it harmed him. Even if gossip would spread like wildfire, he'd return Augustus to her as he'd promised. He'd told her he couldn't bear to hurt her, and he meant it.

As he kissed her back, his blood waking up with desire, he knew perhaps he didn't have the kindest heart.

But his heart most definitely beat for her.

It had for longer than he cared to admit.

And it would always belong to her.

20

"Forgive me, but this is out of the question," said Thorne Blackmore, leaning back in his chair the next day, his eyes as dark and bottomless as wells.

Constantine's jaw tightened. He checked his pocket watch again. He needed to return home for Modesty, then continue on to Eccess's Mayfair house—Dulcis Court—where all six of his fellow dukes would be waiting. The annual autumn dinner party was not an event to be late to, especially when the other dukes had been so supportive of his marriage. He had anticipated his business with Blackmore would be accepted quickly, but there was clearly something going on that he didn't understand.

There were three more men in the study besides Mr. Blackmore. Blackmore's associate and good friend, Mr. Brace Sterling, who leaned back against the desk, his fingers curling tightly around the edge, his piercing eyes on Constantine. He was muscular and ruggedly handsome, with blond hair tied back in a short tail. This was the unofficial doctor of

Whitechapel who had secretly permitted Chastity to conduct medical research in his clinic.

Two more men were present—twins, both with wavy chestnut-brown hair and hazel eyes. Tristan Nightshade always dressed in pale clothing and had a mischievous smile that softened his chiseled features. He sat on a red velvet sofa, his feet propped on the coffee table. Morgan Nightshade wore a dispassionate expression as he paced the room slowly. His arms were crossed over his black waistcoat, his hands tucked under his armpits, except when he'd stop to correct the position of an object: the marble bust on the mantel, books on the shelves.

The sounds from Elysium's main salon were almost impossible to hear from here, separated by a labyrinth of hallways. It was early yet at six o'clock in the evening, but there were quite a few clients gathered there already—drinking, laughing, gambling, watching women dance—and a small orchestra playing music. The crackling fireplace in Thorne's study burned real wood instead of coal, its warmth a stark contrast to the cold dread settling in Constantine's stomach.

"Mr. Blackmore, I hope you understand how much trust I've already put in you by asking for your help. No one knows."

Thorne's dark eyebrows rose while the rest of his angular face remained impassive. It was rare that someone of a lower social standing defied Constantine so openly and so coldly. The natural child of a baron, Mr. Blackmore mattered little in the ton.

But here in Whitechapel—in the world of forbidden pleasures, secret whispers, and criminal deals done in plain sight—he was the king. And he looked like one, leaning back in a large leather armchair, as calm and deadly as a python.

Tristan Nightshade rolled a coin across his knuckles, then flipped it high into the air with a flick of his thumb and caught it without looking, his amused hazel gaze on Constantine. "We already know more than you think."

Blackmore exchanged a look with his three companions. Constantine thought they might share the kind of intense friendship or brotherhood he and his six dukes had, and he wondered how it had started.

"His Royal Highness asked me to start an investigation into your true heritage." Blackmore picked up an ivory pen and tapped it against his desk.

The Regent's growing animosity was no secret, but to actually commission an investigation...

It was Constantine's own fault. If only he'd not indulged his pride at the antiquarian auction...

"Did he now?" he said, marveling at how calm his voice sounded while inside, his world was turning upside down.

"It seems your papa's will stipulates that should his true male blood heir appear, the title would fall to him. I suppose it's a curious clause. Highly unusual. It raises many questions, does it not?"

Constantine stared into the dark, glistening eyes, feeling like prey about to be consumed. "I suppose it does," he replied. He needed to collect himself and to get what he'd come for. "Mr. Blackmore, I've been a loyal and generous client for years. All my friends have been, as well."

Thorne gave a polite nod, knotting his fingers together on his flat stomach. "The Seven Dukes have been my very best clients."

"Can you help me, then?"

"It's a simple conflict of interest," said Morgan, standing as straight as a column. "You must see that."

Tristan rubbed the edge of his coin thoughtfully. "We wouldn't want to be caught in the middle of a manhood-measuring contest between His Royal Highness and yourself.

We lost you as a client when you married. We still have His Royal Highness."

Constantine's jaw worked. "Did you agree to help him? To investigate me?"

Thorne nodded slowly. "We did."

"I will give you whatever you wish if you work for me instead and feed him some false information."

Thorne's eyes narrowed. "Perhaps that could be arranged. I do not need money, as you know."

"What, then?" asked Constantine. "Anything. Name your price."

"There's a bill being proposed by Lord Saville in the House of Lords. The Licensing and Entertainment Venues Act. It imposes stricter licensing requirements, particularly on those operating late at night. If it passes next year, it would greatly affect my operations. I want it stopped."

Constantine swallowed. The bill had as good as passed already. Stopping it would require significant political capital from him—which he had, thanks to his reputation as a man of honor from a highly respected family. Something that would be completely wiped out if the scandal of his true heritage emerged.

"Consider it done," said Constantine.

The four men exchanged careful glances.

"How can I be certain you do work for me and not for His Royal Highness?" Constantine asked. "That you won't share the secrets you uncover with him? The Regent is a more powerful ally than a duke."

Thorne leaned forward, his elbows resting on the desk. "Secrets and trust are more valuable than gold, Your Grace. You of all people must know that."

Constantine had the feeling he was making a deal with the devil.

"One day, I might need another favor," Blackmore continued. "As people who trust each other, I am sure you would grant it to me. Would you not?"

Constantine nodded slowly. "Of course."

Throwing one last glance at his friends, Thorne nodded in satisfaction, stood, and walked around his desk to approach the sideboard with the whisky and the glasses. He poured five and handed one to Constantine and one to Tristan while Brace and Morgan took their own glasses.

Thorne raised his glass, looking straight into Constantine's eyes. "Nothing like a good Lagavulin whisky to seal the deal. To secrets—uncovering them and keeping them."

The liquid burned Constantine's throat.

Tristan stood up, empty glass in his hand. "Another drink? My sobriety was beginning to impair my judgment."

Brace poured some for him. "Of course. We need you sharp for the best sneaking ideas and evil machinations."

Tristan took the glass and plunked back down onto the sofa. He swallowed a generous sip with a satisfied exhale.

"Now that I'm sharp"—he lifted his glass to Brace in a mock salute—"allow me to fountain some genius ideas upon you."

His brother's eyebrows rose. "More like spew random nonsense, as usual."

Tristan's gaze lightened with humor. "Brother, tell me, does that stick up your arse ever get uncomfortable?"

Morgan's eyes narrowed. "At least I can stand upright."

Enough, Constantine wanted to roar, but he couldn't. He had to be polite and perfect. His hand curled into a fist at his side. "Please, Mr. Nightshade, do elaborate."

Tristan's gaze turned slowly to him, and he flashed a bright smile, then took another drink, hissing through his teeth. "Here's a novel idea that might just save your oh-so-noble arse. Why don't you toddle off to old Prinny, fall on your knees, and offer him your firstborn child? Oh, wait, that Andalusian you snatched from under his royal nose might do the trick instead. Nothing says 'please don't strip me of my ill-gotten title' quite like a prancing pony everyone wants, eh?"

A surge of anger clawed through Constantine. Him, begging forgiveness when he'd done nothing wrong? And giving the Regent such a treasure as the stallion when he'd envisioned starting a whole new line of pure Andalusians?

"Out of the question. That horse is mine."

Tristan shrugged. "Suit yourself."

Morgan meticulously adjusted the angle of a brass clock on the mantelpiece, ensuring it sat precisely parallel to the edge. "Your father's will practically shouts your secret... Why mention a blood heir otherwise?"

Constantine's hand tightened around the edge of the desk. "But it doesn't prove I'm not the blood heir."

Brace Sterling smiled at him sadly. "We might not know all of the circumstances of your situation, but bastards know bastards, Your Grace. It's evident you were attempting to gain control over the situation with your hasty marriage. And your decision to hide the babe that came with your new wife. Yes, we know about that. Miss Grace Lockhart asked me to look at Mrs. Ophelia Lester when she came to the almshouse. I always make my rounds there and pay special attention to the pregnant women. I also know that later, Mr. Fairchild and Miss Fairchild took her in. She died in childbirth. Miss Fairchild married you, and the baby—which obviously couldn't be hers because of the timeline—came with."

Mr. Blackmore observed everyone with a quiet calm while Constantine's world was crashing to bits. If these people could reach conclusions so fast, how fragile was his situation? And what had they told the Regent?

Constantine pinched the bridge of his nose. Whitechapel was a network of whispers, rumors, and dark corners where anyone could fish out secrets. It was a different world.

"The babe," said Morgan, "we assume, is Mrs. Ophelia Lester's. What we do not know for certain, but can deduce from your actions, is that the boy is your father's heir."

Constantine felt as if the floor had become very thin and very flexible and was now rising in waves under his feet. He weighed his options. These men already knew too much, and without understanding the full complexity of his situation, they might miss crucial leads. Better to have dangerous allies than powerful enemies.

He let out a long breath. "He is. Ophelia was my father's illegitimate daughter, though she was born to a marriage of her mother to Mr. Copeland."

Tristan chuckled. "The plot thickens."

"A legal father for the child," Morgan said, tapping his fingers against his crossed arms. "The Regent's investigation of the will won't overturn that. Roman law is clear. *Pater est quem nuptiae demonstrant*—the husband is presumed the father. So what evidence does this blackmailer have that could possibly threaten you?"

"They have my mother's letter. She wrote explicitly about her...indiscretion with a clergyman. About my birth."

Tristan clapped his hands together, grinning widely. "A duke, a parson, and an illicit affair walk into an inn... Oh, wait, that's not a jest, that's your life."

Constantine's fists tightened, his lips flattening into a straight line. "I need your help finding the blackmailer and retrieving the letter that they threaten me with. Here, I have the two letters the blackmailer sent."

As Morgan took the letters and read them, Blackmore's eyes were sharp on him. "I understand the seriousness of the situation now. Given His Royal Highness's dislike of you, he would be inclined to rule in favor of your father's will, declaring you the result of adulterine bastardy and appointing the boy the title out of spite, even if royals usually want to maintain stability in society. Am I correct?"

Constantine's teeth clenched. "You are."

Tristan swirled his whisky, then gestured at Constantine with the glass. "Looks like we've got ourselves a fellow member of the Bastard Brigade. Only this one's managed to snag himself a shiny little title. I say we help our noble impostor here keep his ill-gotten gains. After all, what's the point of being born on the wrong side of the sheets if we can't occasionally give society's precious rules a good, hard kick in the breeches?"

"I do not care for titles," said Mr. Blackmore. "Those who know me would say my sister is my one weakness. You are a friend of the family, and she and Lord Seaton were at your wedding. She'd want me to help you. Especially since you will help me to stop the bill."

Constantine remembered how Lord Seaton and Jane had attended his wedding, a gesture of support from Blackmore's family that felt particularly weighted now. He knew them through the Duke of Grandhampton and the rest of the Seaton family. When he'd heard of Jane's efforts in starting a school for the children of Whitechapel last year, he'd donated enough money to renovate the new school building. Knowing how fortunate he'd been to receive a good education, he wanted every child to have the same opportunity no matter their station.

"Thank you."

As Morgan passed the letters to Thorne, he asked, "What has been done to find the blackmailer so far?"

Constantine told them everything they had discovered and

the trail had led to a dead end. He finished by saying that even though he'd paid the second sum, the blackmailer had started a damaging rumor about his mother's infidelity, which had been published in the scandal sheets.

"So far, just the rumor," Constantine added grimly. "Publishing her actual letter would be something else entirely."

Tristan tapped his chin with his finger. "Those letters were delivered by street urchins, weren't they?"

"They were," said Constantine. "The dukes and I considered following that thread, but it's impossible to find the right child."

Blackmore's dark eyes glinted. "Impossible for you. Street urchins flock in every corner of Whitechapel. From the highest rooftops to the lowest cellars, they see everything. One word from me, and they'll find which child delivered those messages."

Constantine's chest lightened with hope. He was right. It was impossible for the dukes to find the child, but not for Mr. Blackmore, the king of London's underworld.

"Assuming it was just one," Morgan noted, producing his notebook. "A clever blackmailer would use different children each time. Make the trail harder to follow."

"And street children know every alley and hideaway in Whitechapel," Thorne added, his lips curving slightly. "They're impossible to catch—unless you know where they nest. And my starlings always come home to roost."

Morgan made another entry in his notebook. "I'm willing to bet you will soon receive a new blackmail letter. The published gossip was a sign the blackmailer was serious. They're preparing you for yet another demand."

Tristan lifted his glass to his brother again. "For once, I agree with my mechanical twin. And may I suggest that we deliver the money this time—false, of course—and do what you should have done when you first had to pay. Catch the bastard—no offense to present company intended."

Blackmore's eyes shone with mirth as he looked at Constantine. "As you see, Duke, you're in good hands."

Half an hour later, Constantine walked out of Elysium with turmoil roaring in his chest. He might just have bought his own freedom.

But he'd sold his most precious secret to the devil.

And added his honor like a cherry on top.

21

Modesty's gaze drifted to Constantine, who sat next to her at the Duke of Eccess's dining table.

Her body still hummed with memories of last night... The way she'd given herself to him, and he'd given her pleasure she never knew existed... The way he'd tenderly bathed her, sharing the deepest secrets of his past.

She felt closer to Constantine than she'd ever felt to another soul. Even his body revealed its secrets to her. As she combed and massaged his hair yesterday in the bath, she noticed a birthmark behind his ear. Hidden under his thick, dark hair, it was the color of red wine. Moving the wet strands aside, she discovered it matched Augustus's mark precisely—in the same location and in the same wolf's-head shape. Of course it was there—they were father and son.

Her chest grew warm as she studied it. There was something so incredibly intimate about it, it made her fingers tingle. Was it possible she was the only person on earth who knew of its existence? Even his valet might not know. The thought sent a thrill far more exhilarating than holding any Roman artifact or Pictish stone. Uncovering Constantine's mysteries was her own personal archeological exploration.

Yet now, watching him lost in troubled thoughts, she felt that intimacy slipping away like water through her fingers. Last night had changed everything between them—and nothing at all. He was still keeping secrets, still building walls even as he drew her closer.

Taking a deep breath, she determined to set that unsettling feeling aside and try to enjoy the evening. The vast dining room that would have intimidated her mere weeks ago now felt almost welcoming. The air was rich with the aromas of roasted game, exotic spices, and the subtle perfume of hothouse flowers arranged in gilded epergnes down the table's center. Everything was calculated to deliver the utmost pleasure and comfort. The walls, painted in deep russet and gold, reminded her of autumn leaves. The crystalline light from the chandeliers softened the edges of her lingering awkwardness rather than exposing it. Perhaps it wasn't just the comfortable dining room that put her at greater ease but her own sense of belonging. Not through her title, but through the moments of closeness with Constantine.

The Duke and Duchess of Luhst sat opposite them, Chastity's warm smile putting Modesty at ease as it had since their first meeting. The Duke and Duchess of Rath were placed near their host, Patience's quiet confidence an inspiration for the kind of duchess Modesty hoped to become. Even Lady Jane Seaton's presence felt more reassuring than intimidating now. All of these women had welcomed her as one of their own, despite her humble beginnings. The Dukes of Enveigh, Irevrence and Fortyne were here, too, as well as Lady Jane's husband, Lord Richard Seaton, and his brother, the Duke of Grandhampton, along with his duchess, Penelope. Unlike at

Lady Virtoux's event, where Modesty had felt as if she was walking on needles, here she felt that she was among friends.

There were no whispered conversations behind fans about the recent gossip columns, no sidelong glances when she or Constantine entered a room. These were the people who would always stand by Constantine despite the rumors about his mother's virtue that had been whispered at Lady Virtoux's party. They had closed ranks around him.

Still, Modesty noticed the shadows under Constantine's eyes, the slight tension in his jaw that hadn't fully eased since he read the article yesterday morning. That was likely why he seemed so distracted tonight, his spoon frozen over the bowl of turtle soup as his thoughts clearly drifted elsewhere.

"...wouldn't you agree, Constantine?" Eccess's voice cut through the air.

Constantine blinked, his brow furrowing for a split second before smoothing out. "I... Yes, of course."

Puzzled gazes and tense chuckles ran around the dinner table.

Clearly making a jest, Eccess had asked if women's education was a frivolous endeavor. But Constantine, so lost in thought, had completely missed it. Everyone at the table had been discussing the Duchess of Grandhampton's success in art and her school for women, as well as Lady Jane Seaton's free school for Whitechapel children—both girls and boys—which she had run for years.

Modesty knew he supported both.

After the intimacy and tenderness they had shared, she was no longer angry with him for keeping his secrets, but worried, aching for his well-being, and wishing to relieve his burden.

She was a duchess now, she told herself, and had every right to act like one.

Pushing aside her shyness, Modesty raised her glass with a smile. "I believe my husband is reminding us all of the importance of context in any jest. After all, agreeing to such a notion in this company"—she gestured gracefully to the women at the table—"is as unlikely as the Duke of Eccess serving anything less than exceptional wine." She turned to their host, who sat at the head of the table in his russet coat, his eyes sparkling with appreciative humor. "Speaking of which, this vintage is truly exquisite, Duke. Might we inquire about its origins? I'm sure Constantine would love to add it to our cellar."

Eccess gave a loud laugh, leaned back in his seat, and raised his glass to Modesty.

"I thank you for your compliment, Duchess. The taste you're fond of is the allure of the forbidden. This wine was smuggled from France and acquired through certain contacts in Whitechapel."

He raised his eyebrows suggestively at Lady Jane Seaton, whose eyes glinted behind her diamond-encrusted spectacles. No doubt Octavius meant the contact was her brother, the notorious Thorne Blackmore. The guests began jesting and talking, put at ease again. And under the cover of this distraction, Modesty finally turned to Constantine. In an instant, the tension in his shoulders eased. The corners of his eyes crinkled as a genuine smile spread across his face. To her absolute delight, he winked at her. A jolt of pleasure darted through her, and she beamed back.

She didn't know he could *wink*!

Constantine leaned towards her. His breath tickled her ear as he whispered, "Thank you for coming to my rescue, Duchess."

Discreetly, he rested his warm hand on her knee under the table. Modesty stifled a giggle, acutely aware of his inappropriate touch that spread fire in her blood. As he pulled away, his fingers trailed up her thigh, leaving goosebumps in their wake. Their eyes met again, and his held the same heat they had when he was buried deep inside her. Suddenly, she felt a little distracted herself.

As the night progressed, she found her gaze drawn to him over and over again. Each time their eyes met, his entire demeanor would brighten, as if her mere presence was a balm to some hidden wound. In those moments, the world around them faded, leaving only the two of them in a bubble of warmth.

After the usual separation of the sexes following dinner, the gentlemen and ladies rejoined one another. Footmen threw open double doors of polished mahogany to let the guests into one of the several drawing rooms in Dulcis Court. The house was the embodiment of its name—*dulcis* was a Latin word meaning "sweet" or "pleasant." Modesty's breath caught not at the grandeur but at the warmth that enveloped her like an embrace. A massive hearth dominated one wall, logs crackling and popping cheerfully, their flames casting dancing shadows across a brown bear skin spread before it. The sweet scent of woodsmoke was so much more pleasant than the scent of coal, which heated most homes these days.

Unlike any other sitting room she'd seen, the wine-red sofas had plenty of cushions that looked inviting and comfortable. Even the carpet beneath their feet was thicker, softer than the finely woven Aubusson rugs in Pryde House. Constantine guided her to one of the sofas, and Modesty sank into it. When Constantine's shoulder brushed hers, she felt warmed through to her very soul.

The rich, dark colors calmed her senses, a vast difference when compared to the austere white walls of her father's house, where comfort had always been secondary to propriety.

Octavius stood before the fireplace. His coat stretched across his shoulders as he raised a crystal glass of his finest brandy. His eyes shone with pleasure as the guests positioned themselves around the room.

"Is everyone comfortable?" Octavius called out. "The trick is to heat the brandy glasses before serving. It brings out the aroma and softens the flavor." He gestured to a footman who carried a tray of heated glasses, the crystal clouding slightly from their warmth.

A muffled giggle from behind the partially open door made him pause. Three heads quickly ducked back into the shadows —one dark, one fair, and one with unruly red curls.

"Sophie, James, Margaret," Octavius called out, his voice stern but his lips twitching. "I believe it's well past your bedtimes."

"We wanted to see the party," came a small voice. An eight-year-old girl ventured a peek around the door frame.

Seeing the sweet child reminded Modesty painfully of how much she missed Augustus. But tomorrow...tomorrow the two weeks Constantine and she had agreed on would conclude, and she could finally take Augustus home.

"And try the brandy," added a twelve-year old boy with a cheeky grin, earning him an elbow from a fourteen-year-old girl who must be his eldest sister.

She stepped into view. "We heard there would be riddles. Couldn't we stay just for one?"

Her spine was rigidly straight, and her hands were clasped precisely before her like a miniature lady of the ton. Watching her trying so hard to seem grown-up made Modesty's chest ache. Was that how Constantine had been at fourteen?

Octavius's expression softened. "Right. And how would you do that after your fifth governess this year left her post yesterday because she found a frog in her bed and her spectacles stained with ink? Off to bed, you rascals."

The children shuffled their feet, caught between pride and chagrin. Modesty noticed how their eyes kept darting to Octavius, seeking his approval even though they clearly knew they were naughty.

Constantine leaned to her. "They're the orphans of Octavius's deceased cousin. Since Octavius has no children as of now, James is the heir to the Eccess title."

Modesty's heart squeezed. "Poor children. I don't know what's worse, to have known your parents and lost them, or not to have known them at all."

Constantine sighed, his gaze drifting to Octavius. "He needs help. A good governess who'd rule them, rather than be ruled by them."

"And they need lots of love," she added thoughtfully. "All four of them, I think."

"To bed," Octavius grumbled to the children. They scampered away, their footsteps echoing down the hall. Octavius shook his head, returning to his place by the fire. "My apologies. They're quite impossible to manage. Now then, shall we begin our riddles?"

Around the room kind assurances came that there was nothing to apologize for.

Eccess cleared his throat and looked at a paper in his hand. "First riddle, ladies and gentlemen. 'I was a treaty of peace, a symbol of power. My hammer fell at a famous hour. Once split in two, my fate was sealed. My destiny, to the victor, revealed. What am I?'"

A hush fell over the room. Lady Jane Seaton ventured, "Is it the Magna Carta?"

"I'm afraid not, Lady Seaton," replied Eccess.

Modesty leaned close to Constantine. "It mentions a

hammer...and being split in two. That reminds me of the wax seals used in important treaties."

Constantine nodded, appearing intrigued. "What treaty would be significant enough to be called a 'symbol of power'?"

"Well," Modesty mused, "there was a major peace treaty in the seventeenth century... It ended a long war, didn't it?"

"The Thirty Years' War?" Constantine prompted.

Excitement stirred in Modesty's chest. That was the war between the Holy Roman Empire, the Habsburg Monarchy, France, Sweden, Spain, and various Germanic states. But it wasn't quite the right answer...

"The Treaty of Westphalia!" she exclaimed, feeling as if she would lift right off her seat. "It was signed in two cities—that's why it was 'split in two.' The hammer falling would be the wax seal."

"Correct!" said Eccess.

The room erupted in applause. She basked in Constantine's proud grin.

"This is why I love archaeology," she whispered. "Finding fragments, connecting patterns..." She studied Constantine's profile, noting the tension that still lingered in his jaw, though he seemed more relaxed than he had when they arrived. Like piecing together ancient pottery, she was slowly assembling the puzzle of her husband. What secrets did he keep buried beneath his careful façade?

Constantine squeezed her hand. "You're brilliant at it."

The Duke of Grandhampton stood up to take Eccess's place in front of the fireplace. He was tall and handsome, a stern man with hair almost as black as coal and dark eyes that lightened with incredible softness when he looked at his wife. He straightened the paper and read the next riddle. "'My name means glory, though battle I lost. A lover, a mother, but at great cost. Who am I?'"

"Joan of Arc?" called out the Duke of Fortyne.

His tall frame was elegant despite his imposing height. Candlelight caught the auburn hints in his dark brown hair, which was tied back with a black ribbon at his nape in the current fashion. His shrewd hazel eyes swept over the gathering as though assessing odds and advantages even in this friendly game.

"No, that is not it," said Grandhampton.

Modesty shook her head slightly. "It's not Joan... She was never a mother. The name means glory..."

Constantine furrowed his brow. "A female historical figure known for love affairs?"

"And motherhood," Modesty added. "Oh! Cleopatra!" she exclaimed.

Grandhampton nodded. "You're quite right again, Your Grace!"

The rest clapped their hands, and Chastity, who sat with the Duke of Luhst on the other sofa, leaned over the end table towards her. "Modesty, you're brilliant. You simply must join Misses with Microscopes!"

Modesty chuckled, her heart swelling with happiness. "I hope I can very soon."

Lady Jane Seaton stood to read the next riddle. "'My petals fall like winter snow, yet spring is when I choose to grow. My poison heart brings sleep profound, though beauty draws all eyes around. What am I?'"

While Modesty and Constantine looked helplessly at each other, she heard the Duke and Duchess of Rath whispering excitedly.

"Hellebore," cried out the Duchess of Rath not a moment later. "It blooms in early spring, has white petals that drop like snow, and contains poisonous compounds that can cause deep sleep...or worse."

"The answer is the hellebore," Lady Seaton announced, her eyes smiling from behind her glittering spectacles as applause filled the room.

The Duchess of Grandhampton read next. She was a beautiful woman with dark blond hair. "'I stand tall upon a land of stone,'" she read, "'from far I'm seen, though none may call me home. My secrets hidden in air and rock, though I'm watched by gods who never talk. What am I?'"

Modesty frowned, her mind racing. She leaned towards Constantine. "It's on a 'land of stone,' and it's watched by 'gods who never talk,'" she mused.

Constantine responded softly, "Could that be referring to statues?"

"Oh! Of course! And a land of stone...it must be Greece!"

"Acropolis," they said in unison, grinning at each other.

Modesty stood, addressing the room with confidence. "The answer is the Acropolis of Athens."

"That is correct!" announced the Duchess of Grandhampton, beaming at her.

As applause filled the room, Constantine squeezed Modesty's hand, his eyes shining with pride as he pulled her back onto the couch beside him. She chuckled as her body swayed closer to him as though drawn by an invisible force, their shoulders brushing as they leaned in close, already beginning to discuss the possible answers for the next riddle.

Out of the corner of her eye, Modesty noticed Chastity nudge her husband with a joyful smile. "Would you look at those two?" she whispered. "They're quite the team, aren't they?"

The Duke of Luhst gave his wife a boyish smile. "Indeed. I've seen statues look more animated than Pryde at most social gatherings. Yet here he is, practically grinning like a boy who's stolen all the sugared plums from the kitchen."

Modesty chuckled to herself. Surely she was not the reason for such a transformation of her husband...and yet...

For the final riddle, the Duke of Eccess returned to his place in front of the fireplace. "'A fire lit my streets, swallowed by flame, I fell and rose again to fame. My bridge fell first, then walls the same, yet still I stand and bear my name. What am I?'"

As the others began discussing between themselves, Modesty and Constantine leaned together.

"Paris!" cried Patience.

"No, I'm afraid not," replied Eccess.

Constantine smirked. "Wait...London burned to the ground several times, and now it's bigger than ever, isn't it?"

Modesty grinned, standing to announce their answer. "It's London!"

Eccess laughed. "Of course you'd know this. Ladies and gentlemen, allow me to announce the winning couple of tonight's evening. The Duchess and Duke of Pryde!"

As the applause exploded around the room, Modesty found herself caught up in the excitement of the moment. She turned to Constantine, her stomach flipping with enthusiasm. She'd never had such a partner, someone who brought out the best in her.

"Archaeology is fascinating," she said to him in a low voice. "It's like solving the most intricate puzzle imaginable. But instead of just words on paper, you're piecing together the very fabric of human history."

Constantine's chestnut eyes shone. "What a fascinating way to look at it. How did you come to this?"

"Growing up, I was surrounded by religious texts and sermons. You can probably guess how strict my father's upbringing was. I could read stories of ancient times, then started reading more books on history, and so on. Papa didn't mind it since religion and history come together. Then I met George."

Constantine's face darkened at George's name, that now-familiar flash of jealousy tightening his features.

"The Lockharts had a summer house in our parish," she continued. "George introduced me to antiquities, showed me little trinkets he found. Fossils. A medieval coin. That's how I came to love archeology even more than history. It allows me to touch the past, to see it with my own eyes, not just through the words of others."

"And your papa let you and George talk?"

"Grace was always with us. We didn't simply talk, he took me to my first excavation near Shepherdsbrook, even if it was only digging in the dirt. But I did find my own pieces of clay vases and dishes. There were also the ruins of the old Roman church where I found the mirror and Pictish stone. Can you imagine the implications?"

"With George?" he asked, his eyebrows still furrowed.

"Yes," she said, a little annoyed now. She was revealing such a profound thing about herself, and he was still asking about George? "But it wasn't about George or Papa or anyone. I made my own discovery. For the first time, I felt free," Modesty admitted, her voice barely above a whisper. "I made my own conclusions, could explore the world, challenge my mind, and feel connected to history. On my terms. I was not just accepting what I was told. I was discovering truths for myself."

She looked down, her cheeks heating. "I suppose that might sound terribly rebellious of me."

His face softened as he covered her hand with his. Around them, the guests spread around the room, talking, laughing.

And there she was with her husband, huddled on the sofa like two people in love...

"Rebellious?" he chuckled. "No, I'd say revolutionary.

You've quite transformed my understanding of the field. And perhaps...other matters as well."

His fingers tightened around hers, but even as warmth bloomed in her chest, doubt crept in. Her heart was swelling for Constantine, more and more every day.

But the higher she soared on hope's wings, the harder she feared she'd fall.

22

"Your Grace," came a voice from the doors.

The laughter that filled Eccess's red drawing room was still loud, and Constantine's own stomach quivered with laughter. The biggest, most beautiful grin spread on Modesty's face after a mildly inappropriate jest Irevrence had made about the hunger of some debutantes for a good match.

The faces of his closest friends and his wife were alight with genuine joy. For the first time in weeks, he allowed himself to forget everything else. The anxiety over the blackmail, the threat of losing his title and wealth, the danger to his reputation.

He just was. And he was with the woman he loved, with his friends who were like family.

Constantine turned his head to see Octavius walk to his butler. The man held a silver platter in his hand with a letter. While the room was still full of chatter and laughter, Octavius's face lost all humor when he read the letter. Octavius's gaze met his, and Constantine's stomach dropped, all previous lightness sucked out of him as reality crashed over him like a storm.

He stood, noting the five other dukes follow him with their eyes.

Octavius held out the paper for him. "This came from Pryde House for you."

Constantine took it, forcing his hand to remain still as he registered the blackmailer's handwriting.

The butler looked at Constantine. "Your footman brought it urgently, Your Grace. Apparently, a street urchin delivered it, and your butler thought you'd want to see it right away. He apologizes for the disturbance."

Constantine's windpipe was so tight he couldn't take another breath. "Quite all right. Simons was right to send it here. Can we go to your study, Octavius?"

"Of course."

Constantine looked back at his wife and saw concern replace the happiness in Modesty's eyes. He sent her a gaze full of regret.

Just one flick of his head towards the door was enough, and Rath, Luhst, Enveigh, Irevrence and Fortyne left their places as they apologized to the rest of the company.

In Octavius's study, when all seven of them had gathered, he unfolded the letter and read aloud.

London, 15 October, 1814,

To His Almost Former Grace,

. . .

I trust you enjoyed the society papers for the past two days? Consider that merely a taste of what's to come if you do not stop your surveillance. How entertaining to watch London speculate about your mother's "close friendship" with a certain clergyman.

This time, I require £5,000 in banknotes, delivered to the fishmonger's barrel at Whitechapel Market. I understand it may take some time to procure this larger sum, but I am certain it must be possible by noon in twelve days.

Should you fail to comply, your mother's letter will find its way to His Royal Highness's breakfast table.

As always, your most humble and obedient servant,

Anonymous

P.S. Do not dare to have your men watch the appointed place again or you will face further consequences than a little gossip.

Constantine's jaw clenched so tight he felt he might crack his teeth. "Damnation. One of Blackmore's men said I'd get another letter."

"Five thousand..." said Fortyne, who stared into space. "You'd have to borrow that kind of money."

"We have to catch them," grumbled Octavius, thrusting his fist into the palm of his other hand.

Dorian slowly shook his head then laid his hand on Constantine's shoulder. His sky blue eyes looked deep into Constantine's. "Friend, this is serious. Once, you helped me conceal a murder, so you know I'll do anything for you. Five thousand is a fortune, no doubt. But there are more important things. What if Modesty is pregnant—or will be in a few weeks —and you lose everything? Can you not set your pride aside, go to His Royal Highness, and appease him? If he is on your side, he'd turn a blind eye to even a published letter. In that case, all you'd have to do is withstand the storm of rumors. But your title and your fortune would be yours. And eventually your heir's."

Pride. That was the hardest thing to give up.

"Beg him," added Lucien, who stood next to Dorian. "Get on your knees and beg him. Give him your horse. Give him anything he wants. Just get him on your side."

Constantine would never kneel for anyone. Not even his prince.

But they were right. A grand gesture was necessary. And Icarus was a small price to pay.

"Goddamn you two," he said. "Tristan Nightshade advised me the same earlier today. I couldn't agree to it then. But hearing both of you now... But I'll give him Icarus and I'll ask for his forgiveness. I'll request an audience right away."

23

"A GODFATHER?" Octavius gave a laugh, startling a flock of sparrows from a nearby oak. "You can't be serious. My own wards defy me. How would I ever take care of Augustus if the three children I am currently charged with are growing up to be little devils?"

They rode side by side through St. James's Park, their horses' hooves crunching on the gravel path of the Mall. Ahead, Carlton House's imposing façade loomed against the autumn sky, its Corinthian columns casting long shadows across the courtyard. Royal guards in their scarlet uniforms stood at attention, their muskets gleaming, watching the approaching dukes.

Despite the growing danger to his reputation and title, Constantine had kept his word to Modesty and brought Augustus home two days ago. The joy that had filled Pryde House ever since made him feel like he was walking on a cloud. Modesty was happily planning the christening. Since, as a boy, Augustus needed two godfathers, and Constantine was to be one of them, she'd asked him to suggest a suitable second godfather.

He adjusted his grip on Icarus's reins as the stallion danced sideways, sensing his tension. "But I know when it really comes to it, you will want the best for him."

Octavius threw him a dark gaze, his usually jovial face hardened. "Like you do?"

The jab made Constantine's gut churn. He was right. If he truly wanted what was best for the child, wouldn't he honor his father's will and allow Augustus to inherit the title and fortune as he should?

"If nothing else, please just stand in that goddamn church and say the words," Constantine burst out, his voice rough with desperation. "Augustus needs a powerful man who'd protect him. Who's on good terms with the Crown."

Octavius was silent for a long while, his gaze fixed on the palace ahead, a deep scowl on his face. Without taking his eyes from the path, he released one hand from his bay's reins and reached for his ever-present flask, taking a long pull.

"Fine," he spat out, wiping his mouth with the back of his hand. "I'll be his goddamn godfather."

The weight lifted from Constantine's chest. "Thank you."

Icarus's reins felt like lead in Constantine's hands as they reached Carlton House five minutes later. The autumn morning was crisp and clear, perfect for riding, though Constantine's stomach churned with every clop of hooves against the cobblestones. How had it come to this? Bartering away his pride, desperate to keep the secret he'd guarded his entire life.

They rode through the ceremonial archway into the grand courtyard. Beyond the palace's imposing Corinthian colonnade, a smaller courtyard led to the Royal Mews—a complex of stables and coach houses that rivaled many noble estates in grandeur. Two grooms in long tailored coats of royal scarlet with stand-up collars emerged to take their mounts.

As the head groom took Icarus's reins, Constantine's fingers lingered on the stallion's neck. He was perfect—the perfect sacrifice. The second groom led Octavius's gelding away, and their horses' hooves echoed as they disappeared into the magnificent stable block with its Georgian architecture. But would even Icarus be enough to appease the Regent?

As Constantine and Octavius were shown to the anteroom, the master of ceremonies told him the Regent would see him shortly. However, they sat in the spacious room—with rich silk damask walls of pale gold and light blue, elaborate plasterwork on the ceiling, and many portraits of the royal family in ornate gold frames—for what felt like hours. This was surely a deliberate slight, designed to put Constantine in his place.

A better version of him would have offered Icarus some time ago. But if he was lucky, this would be enough to satisfy the Regent without losing everything...

But "everything" had taken on new meaning since Modesty had entered his life.

His foot tapped against the polished parquet floors that shone in the dim light falling through the large windows. The clock was ticking. He had only nine more days until the blackmailer's deadline when he would either have to part with a quarter of his yearly income—a sum that could purchase a grand town house in Mayfair or a prosperous estate with tenant farms and hunting grounds.

He'd need to borrow that money. He'd already paid the blackmailer all he had and spent an exuberant amount on the mirror for Modesty. Fortyne would oblige, as well as his ducal friends, but it was humiliating to have to ask them in the first place.

But it was better than watching as his mother's letter

stripped him of his title, his lands, his very identity. Even worse, Augustus would be taken from them, placed under some court-appointed guardian until he came of age. The Regent would ensure Constantine was humiliated, ruined, exposed to all of London as an imposter who'd lived among them. And Modesty... God, Modesty would learn the full extent of his deception in the most public, devastating way possible.

The most blood-chilling thought of all was that he could lose her. Her affection, her trust, the intimacy she'd shared with him.

So he had to do this for her, for himself, and for a foolish belief that perhaps he could keep the happiness of the past few days for the rest of his life.

Only, was it even possible with this secret between them?

Finally, he and Octavius were bidden to enter the Regent's private audience chamber. At the door, he was announced in a less formal manner than his rank deserved. Yet another subtle slight that put his teeth on edge. Was it to show that the Regent had somehow uncovered proof that Constantine was not the rightful heir?

A shiver went down his spine as he went in.

The Regent was not seated formally as protocol dictated but reclining casually on a chaise longue, surrounded by five of his favorite courtiers. The Regent didn't even turn his head to them, instead finishing a conversation with one of the ladies.

"This is not like him," murmured Octavius. "He'd usually jump up and greet me with open arms."

Finally, the Regent dismissed his courtiers, stood up, and went to the tea table, which was laden with refreshments and drinks. He popped a sugared plum into his mouth.

"So," he said through the mouthful.

Constantine felt his lips press into a hard line. This intentional disrespect towards him left him with two questions.

Did Regent know for sure?

And had Thorne Blackmore and his team betrayed Constantine?

"My dear duke," said the Regent, eyeing Constantine coldly. Then his gaze darted to Octavius, and he gave a curt, guilty nod. "Eccess."

"Your Royal Highness." Constantine and Octavius bowed.

"I hope we find you well," added Octavius.

"Oh, I am very well. Forgive me, Eccess, I am very fond of you, but I'm afraid there are matters with Pryde I would like to discuss in private."

Constantine and Octavius exchanged a long look. Not good. Not good at all. Octavius was supposed to be a jovial intermediary to smooth things over. And now he was being sent away.

"Must I, Your Royal Highness?" asked Octavius with a friendly smile. "I was hoping to have you taste this latest French cognac I got my hands on..." He lifted the wooden box he carried.

The Regent's face lit up with a genuine smile. "I'd be delighted. Later. Please."

He gestured to the door. After another moment of hesitation, Octavius put the box on the table, bowed to the Regent, and retreated with a sorry glance at Constantine.

The Regent had just eliminated Constantine's strongest defender on the chessboard. Now his king was vulnerable.

When they were alone—save the footmen—Constantine's heart pounded. There were no signs at all this was going to go well.

"Is your dear wife in good health?" asked the Regent slowly. "You should have brought her. Or even better, sent her here alone."

Constantine felt a jab of fire cut through his body. "The duchess is perfectly fine. I thank you."

"Marvelous. I suppose the marital bliss is still strong between you two? Does she know of this?"

He lifted a sheaf of carefully written papers from the desk. Constantine recognized it at once. A copy of his father's will.

Blood drained from his face.

"She does," he lied. "Of course she does. We have no secrets."

The Regent's eyebrows arched in surprise. "And what does she think of it?"

"She does not think anything of it. There's nothing to think."

"Oh, I disagree. It would be a great disservice to your deceased papa to dishonor his last wishes."

"Indeed," said Constantine, his back growing damp with sweat, anger roiling in his gut. *Keep your composure*, he told himself. *You've done it all your life. Just a little longer.* "His will has been respected for all these years. There's nothing there that contradicts the current situation."

"Isn't there?"

Constantine's pulse drummed hard. The man took pleasure in torturing him. Constantine's own fault, really. All he had to do was to let the Regent win. Let him have a bigger budget, the horse, and the Pictish mirror. He had to put an end to this. It was not too late. But how could he have supported using the people's money to pay for more elaborate parties and racing debts while children starved in the streets?

The thought was a bit hypocritical, he knew. Constantine himself could have done much more for the poor—like Modesty had before she married him.

"Never mind the will, Your Royal Highness," said Constantine, gathering his restraint and self-control. "I brought a gift."

The Regent's eyebrows rose, and he laid the will back on the table. "Oh? I did not expect that."

"The Andalusian. Icarus. He is yours. He is awaiting you in your Royal Mews."

The Regent's expression shifted. He looked pleased. Victorious.

"Why, thank you very much, Your Grace. I appreciate the gift. It must have been quite hard for you to part with the stallion. You paid so much for it."

He inclined his head submissively, hating every moment. But hope took root in his chest. This was helping. Mr. Nightshade, Dorian, and Lucien were right. Icarus was an easy price to pay compared to the alternative.

"Yes, it was, but I wanted to extend this gesture to you as a show of my respect, loyalty, and appreciation for Your Royal Highness. It is time to set aside our disagreements and be at peace. I hope the gift pleases you, now and in the future. I am your loyal servant, just like my father was to the Crown, and all my ancestors before."

The Regent inclined his head and chuckled. "A grand gesture. One I accept gladly." He picked up the will again. "I think this can be forgotten." Constantine's chest warmed and expanded with relief. Was this all it took to make the threat go away? If the blackmailer publicized his mother's letter, the scandal would be damaging and unpleasant, yes. But it would be the Crown's decision what to do with this information. Whether to ignore it and rule that according to "pater est quem nuptiae demonstrant," he was the rightful heir or to honor the will and start the investigation into who the true blood heir was, causing Constantine to lose everything.

"Thank you, Your Royal Highness." He bowed. "That would be most welcome."

"Very well," said the Regent, slapping himself on the thigh.

"And naturally, you will support the Crown's request for additional funds?" The Regent's smile didn't reach his eyes. "After all, the royal household's expenses have only increased since your...passionate speech against the allocation."

The decision that had started this feud. It would be humiliating—not to mention wrong— to go against his earlier statement. His standing in the House of Lords would be devastated.

His pride was groaning as he bent and twisted his own principles. Who even was he anymore?

"Yes," he said, his teeth screeching. "You will have my support."

"And one more thing...another gift I'd like from you," the Regent said.

Constantine's windpipe constricted. This was not good. Nor was the mischievous glint in the Regent's eyes.

"Anything," Constantine said.

"The final gift...the price...is your wife, Your Grace."

No. Surely, Constantine hadn't heard correctly. Surely, the Regent wasn't so bold as to actually say this to his face.

"I'd like to become the best of friends with the Duchess of Pryde. Make it so, and the will is forever forgotten. Whatever happens, the Crown will always highly favor you and protect you at all costs."

Constantine couldn't move. Couldn't feel the floor under his feet. Somewhere deep within him, a tremor started.

The fire of rage consumed his very being.

Control yourself, commanded the voice of duty and discipline that had governed his every action since childhood. *A duke must remain beyond reproach at all times.*

A duke does not slight his monarch.

But the voice was too weak now, and the image of Modesty being intimate friends with this man painted his world red.

He supposed that was all it took.

Modesty.

Abandoning thirty years of control and composure, he marched towards the Regent, grabbed him by the lapels, and roared straight into his face: "Never!"

The Regent's eyes widened, his skin paled, and a pathetic squeal escaped his throat.

"Do not touch her, talk to her, even think of her or, so help me God, you will regret this."

"Unhand me!" cried the Regent.

Through the fog of rage, Constantine became aware of cries behind his back, and quick, heavy footsteps. Then hands clasped his arms and dragged him away from the Regent.

The guards. Octavius.

Good God, what did he just do?

"What have you done, you fool?" grumbled Octavius in his ear, echoing his own thoughts.

But he had not a shadow of regret. Modesty's honor couldn't be threatened—and that was the end of it.

"You," spat the Regent, his face reddening as he straightened his clothes. "You will be so very sorry about this." He clasped the will in his hand once again. "I will do everything in my power to find out why the will stipulates what it does. And if I get the slightest chance to leave you with nothing, I will. You have no notion what a grave mistake you have just made. Get him out of here!"

Every word was like a stab into his gut. Victory had been so close.

And now he had made it all even worse.

"Leave at once," barked the Regent.

"Let's go, Constantine," murmured Octavius, tugging him to the door.

Constantine turned around. "Icarus is coming with me."

Then he let Octavius drag him out.

"You should be happy I'm not calling this treason!" the Regent shouted after him. "Threatening your own Regent! I could throw you into prison and have you hanged for this slight!"

But Constantine didn't look back.

He knew the Regent could do it, and he'd have a good case against Constantine.

But as he and Eccess marched down the opulent hallways, all he thought about was how he wanted to see Modesty. How he longed to tell her everything.

And then an even more bizarre thought came: Was his title worth the cost of losing her?

Would surrendering to the truth actually be as bad as he'd feared all his life?

But as Icarus was brought to him outside in the courtyard and he looked into the stallion's eyes, stroked his white coat, his father's words—repeated countless times throughout his childhood—echoed in his mind. *Better no duke at all than one who brings shame to the title.*

Without his position he truly would be nothing, just as his father had warned.

The deserving heir. The perfect duke. That was what he had to be. That was the whole point of his existence.

As he and Octavius mounted their horses and walked towards the exit gate, he knew he had to work even harder to find the blackmailer. He'd send word to Mr. Blackmore.

And he had to protect Modesty. The Regent's sexual appetite was legendary. He didn't stop at anything; no lady was safe once she caught his eye, regardless of her rank or marriage. He'd destroyed countless reputations, broken up marriages, all for his own amusement. And now Constantine had just revealed Modesty as his greatest vulnerability.

He'd double his efforts to find both the blackmailer and his mother's damning letter—despite the threats about further consequences. The blackmailer clearly wouldn't stop until Constantine was destitute. If he didn't fight, he might as well just give up everything—his title, his holdings, and now, most terrifyingly, Modesty's safety.

24

CONSTANTINE HANDED Simons his top hat and then swiftly removed his greatcoat. "Where's the duchess?"

"In the drawing room, Your Grace."

Excellent. Constantine hurried there, crossing the hallway in long strides. He couldn't wait to see Modesty.

Waves of anger had coursed through his body after his visit to Carlton House. Octavius's steed couldn't match Icarus's pace, but he had followed Constantine, leaving only after they'd both reached Pryde House and discussed what had transpired.

At least the quick gallop through London's streets had helped to ease some of Constantine's tension. But nothing would relieve him quite like burying his face in the smooth skin between his wife's neck and shoulder.

"But Your Grace—" called Simons, but Constantine didn't want to hear anything more.

His body thrummed with urgency to be near her.

Through the open door, he saw her standing with her back to him looking out the large window. He crossed the space between them, wrapped his arms around her waist, and pressed his lips against her skin.

Just inhaling her scent made him feel so much better.

"Modesty..." he murmured. "I missed you."

She stiffened and turned around in his arms, facing him now. Something was wrong.

He didn't like the strange glint in her startled eyes, the flaming blush on her cheeks.

A careful cough behind him made him freeze. He turned to find Mr. George Lockhart standing awkwardly next to the sofa, fumbling with his hands. Two teacups sat on the table along with a teapot, biscuits, and pastries.

Jealousy blazed deep within Constantine's gut. He suddenly understood Dorian so, so well. A corroding rage clawed deep inside him. The thought of driving his fist into the other man's face was darkly seductive, licking at the skin of his hands.

Showing physical affection in front of others was considered vulgar. Something a well-bred duke would never do.

Something the old Constantine wouldn't have done in ten lifetimes.

And yet, there he stood, his arms still around Modesty's waist. She was positioned very securely right against his chest.

A statement.

He stared straight into George's eyes. "Mr. Lockhart."

George licked his lips, avoiding Constantine's stare and looking anywhere but at the two of them. This was *his* home, goddamn it, and *his* wife. He could do what pleased him.

"Your Grace," mumbled George.

"What are you doing?" Modesty pushed against him, trying to free herself.

Oh, no. Not yet. He glared at George.

"You can let me go now," murmured Modesty softly but

with a stern undertone. At least one of them was maintaining their social manners.

Statement sufficiently made, he released her.

"I didn't know you were here, Mr. Lockhart," said Constantine.

"Yes, I—" George sent a meaningful look to Modesty, eyes wide.

Constantine didn't like any meaningful glances passing between them at all. Modesty straightened her posture, a proper duchess in the making. She met Constantine's eyes.

"Mr. Lockhart applied to be part of an excavation in Egypt," she said. "He got the position, and he even secured a place for me."

The floor under Constantine's feet moved like a deck in a storm. Egypt...excavation...

George sent Modesty a sheepish look. "I only got the position because of the Roman ruin you let me take credit for."

She chuckled. "It's nothing."

That was most certainly not nothing! She'd let him take credit for the ruin she'd found, the one with the mirror and the Pictish stone? And now he was getting all the glory?

No wonder she looked agitated. That was everything she'd ever wanted.

And he was not the one to give it to her...

He nodded, that was all he could do. A hollow ache bloomed in his chest. He should have been the one to make it possible for her, to make her dreams come true—and yet he was the one to forbid her to dig. Because of the rigid rules of propriety.

Was he right to do so? Was he not overthinking this situation? Could a duchess truly not participate in an excavation, search for ancient relics, be on the brink of a scientific discovery?

She was right. Both Patience and Chastity were duchesses and neither Dorian nor Lucien forbade them a single thing. On the contrary, they supported their wives in any way they could, celebrated their achievements, were proud their wives defied social expectations laid on women.

He wanted to do the same.

But if he did, he'd draw yet more attention to the family name. More scrutiny meant more questions. More questions meant someone might find that one crack in his ship...

The crack that would split into a gaping hole and sink him.

Or was he already going down?

"Tell me about the expedition, Mr. Lockhart," he said.

"Certainly. The British Museum is funding my project to continue excavating the Valley of the Kings near Thebes. I will be the lead archaeologist, and I already have the artist to sketch our discoveries including hieroglyphics. I've hired the surveyor, the interpreter, and two guards. Two excavation assistants are ready to go. I only need the duchess as my main assistant. My aunt is ready to accompany us to ensure all propriety—and, perhaps, the duchess could ask a friend to come."

Constantine met Modesty's gaze. Her eyes were shining and her smile spread on her face. "It's not the Picts, of course... but it's a once-in-a-lifetime opportunity. And you could come with me."

Constantine nodded. He could practically see her bouncing with excitement. Seeing her that way made his own heart soar. Under different circumstances, he would have laid the world at her feet. He'd fund an excavation to Egypt from his own fortune; he'd go with her and dig by her side.

Only, he couldn't. His heart broke at the thought that the villain standing in the way of her achieving everything she ever wanted was he.

He who loved her.

"You know I can't. My duty is here. How long is the excavation going to be?" asked Constantine.

He didn't know how much longer he could hold his composure. The rigid rules he lived by were a stone sarcophagus, his pride sealing him inside, trapping him in a prison of his own making.

George frowned slightly. Perhaps he'd never expected Constantine to let Modesty go; perhaps he'd expected him to say no immediately. Constantine would have expected the same.

Except, the word just wouldn't come out of his mouth, not when Modesty looked so full of life, enthusiasm, and happiness. How could he be the one to take that away?

"I estimate it will be two...maybe three years," said George. "Of course, I understand your concern would be the duchess's safety. And I assure you, it is my first concern, too. The guards will be with her at all times."

"When will you leave?" asked Constantine.

He was completely numb. He felt like he was an observer now, watching himself from a distance as he prepared to ruin his own life and shatter his own heart. But he'd rather break his own heart than hers.

He loved her.

That was his way of loving her. He needed an heir, but her happiness was more important.

"In roughly two weeks," replied George.

Constantine nodded, and just couldn't say anything. Neither yes nor no. If she wanted to go, a few days more would be all he'd have with her.

"That's when Augustus's christening is," she replied, looking into Constantine's eyes. "I can't."

"We can have the christening earlier," he said softly.

She frowned. "Are you not opposed to—"

He gave her a gentle smile. "The christening isn't as important as spending three years in the Valley of Kings."

"Oh, heavens..." she said and pressed her palms to both her cheeks. "Three years... I can't. What was I even thinking? I can't leave Augustus alone... I promised his mother. I'm his guardian."

Constantine forced down the knot in his throat. "He'll be perfectly safe with me."

"I know... But..." She looked at George and straightened her shoulders. "I can't come with you, George. I am very honored and pleased you invited me, but there are other obligations keeping me here."

George's shoulders sagged slightly as he stared at the Persian carpet, fingers clenching and unclenching at his sides. When he finally looked up, his features had settled into careful blankness, though his eyes betrayed his hurt.

"Of course," he said. "I quite understand. You're one of the best people I've ever known, Duchess. Augustus is very fortunate to have you as his guardian." He bowed. "However, should you change your mind, the ship *Aurora* will leave from the London docks. I bid you both good day."

And then he left.

Modesty turned to Constantine with a calm smile on her lips, but it fell when she met his gaze. He must have been a hard sight to behold—with Mr. Lockhart's departure his resolve to keep his face in a polite arrangement disappeared.

She closed the two steps between them and cupped his face, searching his eyes. "What's wrong?"

Constantine wanted to tell her everything about his true parentage, the blackmail, the Regent's threats. But fear gripped him, choking the words before they could form.

Images flashed through his mind—Modesty's face twisted

in revulsion, society ladies whispering behind fans, his peers turning their backs, Augustus being torn from their care and raised by a stranger, Mr. Hawthorne losing the comfort and privacy of his home. The Regent's triumphant sneer as he stripped Constantine of his title.

The worst was the thought of losing Modesty's affection. The realization hit him like a physical blow. When had this woman become so essential to his existence? When had her happiness become more important than his pride? He'd spent his life building walls to protect his secret, yet she had somehow slipped past every defense and claimed his unworthy heart.

And now the very deception meant to protect everything he held dear threatened to destroy the one thing he couldn't bear to lose. Because he loved her more with each passing moment. The emotion resonated through his body and soul, terrifying in its intensity. He'd never expected to find this bone-deep need to worship her, cherish her, make her dreams come true. To be worthy of the trust she placed in him.

So instead of confessing, he pulled her into a fierce embrace, burying his face in her neck. He breathed her in, making the scent of her part of his very being.

Modesty wrapped her arms around his neck. "You're shaking. Because of Egypt?"

He shook his head.

"What's happened?"

He pulled back, cupping her face in his hands. "I can't tell you all of it, not yet. But I need you to know something." He took a deep breath. "I'm terrified. Not of you going to Egypt, but of you realizing one day that I'm not the man you think I am."

Modesty shook her head and smiled. "I know you have secrets, and you have your reasons... But whatever it is you keep private, I've seen glimpses of the real you—the man behind the duke. That's the man I'm falling for."

Falling for... God knew, he didn't deserve her love...her faith in him. He could only hope one day he would earn her high regard. He kissed her, claiming her mouth with all the fervor of the words he couldn't say.

As they pulled apart, Constantine said, "I want you to go to Egypt. It's part of who you are, and I don't want to stifle you. I want you to be happy."

She smiled. "I am happy. You make me happy. And I cannot wait for Augustus's christening."

"Me, either," he said softly. "Octavius will be the godfather...well, second godfather after me."

She beamed. "I only hope I'll do the christening justice even if it will be very small, with only our friends and family in attendance."

"You will, Modesty. You're a duchess now. You can do anything."

25

CONSTANTINE JOLTED AWAKE. A baby cried. He blinked, disoriented, before realizing Modesty was no longer beside him. The sheets on her side were cold.

He stood, grabbing his dressing gown.

Augustus. Something was wrong.

The chill night air nipped at his bare chest and shins as he hurried towards the nursery. He'd just made love to Modesty and usually slept naked after.

When he pushed open the door, the sight before him made his heart clench. Modesty paced the room, cradling Augustus against her chest. "Shh, my darling. It's all right."

The baby's cries were weak and pitiful.

Constantine moved to stand by her side, looking at Augustus's flushed face. "What's wrong?"

"He's burning up. I can't get him to settle."

He laid a hand on Augustus's forehead. The skin was far too hot for comfort. "He needs a doctor."

"I've already sent for one."

Constantine nodded, his mind racing. "We need to cool him down. I'll fetch some water and cloths."

"Mrs. Walcott is fetching them."

"Well, it's taking too long."

He hurried down to the servants' quarters and found the astonished Mrs. Higgs and Mrs. Walcott, who was preparing the linens, dark circles under her eyes. Feeling pity for the woman, he told her to stay and take a break. He asked for the supplies, and Mrs. Higgs helped him carry them back upstairs.

Returning to the nursery, he found Modesty rocking the feverish Augustus, shushing softly.

Mrs. Higgs set the basin of water on the chest of drawers. "Ah, poor child."

Constantine went to stand by Modesty's side. "Let me take him. You should rest a little."

Gently, he lifted Augustus from her arms. The baby whimpered, his little body still radiating heat. Constantine's chest tightened with worry.

"Shall I fetch Mrs. Walcott?" asked Mrs. Higgs.

With his free hand, Constantine dipped the cloth into the cool water. "No. In fact, please make sure she gets some sleep. We'll require her in the morning when we surely will need a rest. She must be exhausted. We'll take turns, wiping him with cool cloths, try to bring the fever down."

Singing old lullabies he barely remembered, Constantine cradled Augustus against his chest. He paced the nursery, his bare feet silent on the carpet, willing the fever to break.

This child, so small and vulnerable, was the biggest threat to his station. By all logic, he should resent this innocent babe, fear him even. Yet, as Augustus's tiny fist curled around Constantine's finger, the thought of any harm coming to the babe was unbearable. When had it happened? When had this little one wormed his way so deeply into Constantine's heart?

His gaze drifted to Modesty, her brow furrowed with concern as she prepared a cool compress. She was the piece he never knew was missing. For her, he wanted to be better, to be worthy of the love she offered so freely.

Soon, the physician came and suggested it was fever and the inflammation of the throat and sinuses. What they were doing helped, he said, so they should keep at it. Mrs. Walcott came and fed the child, then went back to sleep. A small bath of lukewarm water was brought.

The night wore on. When Augustus's cries grew particularly distressed, Constantine found himself telling stories, just as Mr. Hawthorne had done for him when he was a boy.

"And then," he said, voice low and soothing as he dabbed Augustus's forehead with a cool cloth, "the clever hare outran the wolf, leaping over hedgerows and ducking under fallen logs."

Modesty, curled up in the rocking chair, smiled weakly. "I didn't know you were such a storyteller."

Constantine chuckled softly. "Neither did I. Mr. Hawthorne's education runs deeper than I thought."

While he rocked the child, his mind returned to the practical arrangements he had been taking care of since the confrontation with the Regent five days earlier. The claws of dread dug deeper into his spine each day. The Regent was after him. Investigating. And more determined than ever to see him suffer.

Yesterday, Blackmore had given him both bad and good news. The Nightshade twins had found the lad who'd brought the second blackmail letter demanding £2,000. The urchin had been hired by a beggar, Three-Finger Bob, half-mad with ramblings. Clearly, he wasn't the blackmailer but an intermediary used to hire the urchin.

According to Blackmore, Three-Finger Bob described the

man who hired him as neither young nor old, neither tall nor short, neither slim nor fat, neither rich nor poor. After he'd said that, he'd sunk deeper into ramblings, and his gaze had grown cloudy. How he could have been trusted by the blackmailer to do anything was beyond Constantine.

Blackmore's search for other urchins, or "starlings," continued. And his men observed the market stalls in case they saw something suspicious leading up to the payment date.

But Constantine felt like he was losing.

Therefore, he had asked his solicitors to transfer the property that wasn't tied to the Pryde title to Modesty's name. He'd also made sure most of the assets he had accumulated as duke would be hers, so that she could be independent, fund a dozen excavations, and also take care of Augustus and Mr. Hawthorne.

And even though she'd want nothing to do with him, there would still be six dukes to watch over her. They'd protect Constantine's family as their own, according to their credo. His destruction wouldn't have to devastate the people he cared about most.

As the first hints of dawn began to lighten the sky, Augustus finally drifted into a fitful sleep. Constantine settled into the window seat, the baby nestled against his chest. The last of his defenses crumbled. In this child's feverish face, he saw how connected they were. Augustus was another soul marked by his father's ruthless pride. Ophelia had been cast aside, Constantine was forever striving to prove worthy of a title that wasn't rightfully his, and now this innocent babe was heir to a legacy of pain and unhappiness. He deserved better than to inherit their family's wounds.

No. The cycle would end here, with him. Augustus would know something Constantine never had—unconditional love and acceptance, without the crushing weight of expectation. Because of Modesty. Because somehow, in trying to protect his carefully constructed world, Constantine had found something far more precious: a real family.

26

MODESTY OPENED her eyes and rubbed her stiff shoulders. She was warm, though uncomfortable, sleeping in a chair. Someone had put a blanket over her. She didn't remember falling asleep, and now morning light was seeping through the window.

Augustus!

She sat up, madly looking around the nursery. The cot was empty.

And there was no Constantine in sight, either.

Oh, please God, please do not let Augustus have passed away from fever while I slept!

She jumped to her feet, her skin prickly with terror. She ran out of the room, through the hallway, and straight to Constantine's bedchamber.

She swung the door open and froze on the threshold.

In the vast, rich bedchamber, by one of the tall windows, Constantine was sprawled on the bed, asleep. Augustus was cradled safely in the crease between his chest and his arm.

Relief made her limbs go slack. Her heart swelled at seeing them this way.

Slowly, so that the floor didn't creak under her feet, she moved across the room.

Last night, Constantine had taken care of Augustus like the babe was his own.

Like a true father to his child.

He was a good man. Whatever secrets he held, and however much he protected them, she loved him.

She leaned down and pressed the back of her hand against Augustus's forehead. Clammy, but not scalding hot like last night.

Letting out a slow, steady sigh, she gently lifted the baby.

Constantine stirred, but didn't wake up, thank heavens. He needed sleep.

She left the room with Augustus and put him into his cot in his nursery. Mrs. Walcott was back, looking much better after a few hours of rest.

With the baby taken care of, Modesty went down into the kitchen, surprising all of the servants, and asked the assistant cook to prepare tea for the duke. Bearing a tray laden with a teapot and cups, biscuits, and buttered toast, she returned to her husband. Her mind drifted to the christening as she ascended the stairs. Only three days away. Invitations had been sent, All Saints Church secured, and Papa was preparing for the event. But if Augustus would still be unwell, she'd cancel it in an instant.

As she placed the tray on the night table, Constantine stirred and opened his beautiful chestnut eyes. They were flecked with gold, she now knew, and were steady like the ground under her feet.

He was so handsome and looked so vulnerable with his face free from the social mask of a duke. His hair was tousled from the night before, and his cheeks were a little flushed. His chin and jaw bore stubble. She didn't like the dark circles under his eyes, and she knew they weren't just from the night of poor sleep. For days now, he had been more worried than ever.

Fear of gossip must be draining him, and she ached to support him, to bring him relief.

"Would you like some tea?" she asked, brushing a lock of dark hair from his forehead.

Instead of answering, he caught her hand, pulled her to his chest, and kissed her.

She sank into his embrace, his body hard and hot and beautifully familiar.

His arms wrapped around her as his mouth claimed hers. His tongue played with hers, and her body was already hot and pliable for him. Her nipples hardened, her intimate muscles tightened, and her blood heated.

"I would like some of you," he murmured.

With that, he rolled, pinning her under the weight of his body, urging her thighs apart. She giggled as he looked her over, his hands gliding over her breasts, down her waist, and gripping her hip.

He kissed her, deeply and with intention. And she wrapped her legs around his hips, feeling his hard member long and hot against her sex. Instinctively, she moved her hips to rub herself against him, and he moaned into her mouth.

"Little minx." He chuckled. "You seem so correct and proper during the day...but you're fire in bed."

She kissed him. "Because you are the spark that ignites me."

He growled slightly and turned to kissing her neck. He pulled her nightgown over her head then cupped her breast and kissed her nipple, playing his tongue over it, circling it, biting it gently, so that fire shot through her blood. She arched her back, giving him more access.

He lavished the same attention on her other breast until her senses whirled, every inch of her alive to his touch.

She unfastened the breeches he'd pulled on at some point during the night, then pushed them down his hips with her feet. She hooked her legs around him, bringing him tighter against herself.

There were no more barriers between their sexes, and he looked deep into her eyes.

"Are you—?"

"I want you," she said and moved her hips to direct the head of his member into her opening.

He hissed in pleasure as she managed to position his tip against her, but he held back when she tried to take him in with a thrust.

"Slowly, darling," he murmured as he lowered his head to hers.

He gave her the most tantalizing kiss, which made her inner muscles clench as she ached for him to fill her, desperate for release.

"I want to savor you," he said.

Then very, very slowly, he pushed into her, and she let out a long breath. He looked into her eyes—worshipping her—and she couldn't look away.

Her muscles clenched around him, sucking him deeper.

They were connected now as deeply as two people only could be—bodies, hearts, souls.

She loved him... Good Lord, she loved him! And he seemed to tell her the same, with every movement of his body.

Still looking deep into her eyes, he began moving in and out, spilling pleasure through her veins like liquid honey.

She couldn't stop, couldn't look away, couldn't do anything

but be held captive in his gaze, and feel him slowly move in and out of her, teasing her nerves and stroking all the right places. Slowly, he increased his pace, and her body betrayed her by reaching the edge of her pleasure before she wanted things to finish. He let out a curse as she cried out and her muscles convulsed around him.

"Hold on," he murmured into her ear. "This is not the end."

While she moaned and trembled against him, he restrained himself, but as her release subsided, he began moving again, faster and faster, pumping into her harder and murmuring sweet things into her ear.

How beautiful she was, how dear to him, how he craved every day to have her in his arms, how her smell drove him mad, and he wanted to inhale her forever...

He whispered other things she couldn't remember or understand, as he masterfully brought her body to yet another peak, which she didn't think possible. And she quivered again in sweet agony, harder and longer than before. Another wave flooded over her directly after the first one, and she couldn't stop as she cried out his name.

Constantine...

That undid him, too, and he groaned, sounding pained and almost hurt, as he found his own release inside her.

They lay together like that, kissing softly, looking into each other's eyes. He was stroking her hair, kissing her lightly on her nose and her cheeks and her eyelids.

Who knew that a man as prideful and rigid as he would be the gentlest and most generous lover?

When he stretched out by her side, she laid her head on his chest, and he wrapped his arm around her, holding her to him tightly.

"I am sorry I've been distracted," he said. "I didn't want to... It's this matter... Very urgent...and it's not getting better."

"Why can't you tell me?"

He swallowed hard. "I want to... I suppose I can tell you part of it. But I can't tell you all of it, though you deserve to know."

She raised her head and supported it with her hand, looking at him.

He furrowed his eyebrows, his Adam's apple bobbing. His face looked so young and yet completely torn with worry and... regret...pain...

"Augustus is not my son. He's the grandson of my deceased father."

Modesty blinked. "Pardon?"

"Ophelia and I were never lovers. She was the illegitimate daughter of my father and a woman who had stayed with our family. My mother's friend."

Modesty sat up, her mind reeling. A feeling of devastation was opening in her chest like a chasm. "Why couldn't you tell me that from the beginning?"

He drew in a deep breath. "I am sorry. There are very few people who are aware of my father's illegitimate daughter. I couldn't just tell this secret to a person I didn't know. But now I know I can fully trust you."

"Is that what the blackmail is about? When you accused me of blackmail, is this the secret that concerned you?"

A pained expression crossed his face. "Yes."

"Oh..." Her thoughts were running, escaping, galloping. "Wait...but that means... When you refused Ophelia, pregnant and impoverished, you sent away your own sister..."

He sighed and closed his eyes, nodding. When he opened his eyes, he was searching her face.

"Why did you?" she asked.

He looked away. "Because I didn't want a scandal."

"So Augustus is your nephew... How is that a scandal?"

"My father's reputation has always been impeccable. The Buccleigh line has always been pure and honorable. I can't have anything otherwise."

"But how is a scandal more important than someone's well-being? Especially a mother carrying a child—two lives, Constantine!"

His face twisted with something that looked like shame. "It's not that simple—"

"Then explain it to me," she demanded. "Because the man who just spent all night caring for Augustus can't be the same man who abandoned his sister to the streets."

He reached for her, but she moved farther away. "Modesty, please—"

"No. There's more you're not telling me. I can see it in your eyes."

"I offered her help," he said, his voice strained. "But there were conditions—"

"Conditions?" The word tasted bitter. "What conditions could possibly justify abandoning your own blood?"

He flinched at the word "blood," something dark and painful flickering across his face. "You don't understand—"

"Then help me understand!" She was nearly shouting now, all her confusion and hurt pouring out. "Because I've seen how gentle you are with Augustus, how much you clearly care for him. Yet you let his mother die alone and desperate. The Constantine I know wouldn't do that without a reason."

His face went stark white at her words. For a moment, she thought he might finally tell her everything. But then he seemed to fold in on himself, that familiar mask of the duke sliding back into place.

He was silent, his gaze averted.

He wouldn't tell her anything else.

The walls were up.

And she was not inside them.

She rose from the bed to put on her chemise. Then she would go and check on Augustus. The darkness at the edges of Constantine's eyes felt like a weight on her soul. He may have told her some of his secrets...

But not all.

27

"CONSTANTINE, DO YOU HAVE THE SHAWL?" Modesty asked from the darkness of the carriage, little Augustus cradled against her chest and cooing sweetly.

Descending the front steps, Constantine walked to the carriage and handed Modesty the Norwich shawl of rich indigo with hand-embroidered patterns in golden thread. It had been his paternal grandmother's, and he was proud Augustus would be christened in the family heirloom.

"There you are," he said as the soft silk left his hand.

Thankfully, Augustus had improved greatly, but he was still congested. Every time the babe gave a chesty cough, Constantine wished he could take the sickness away. He would rather be ill himself than see the child suffer.

But instead, he was taking Augustus's future away from him.

Modesty barely met his eyes as she took it. The three days since that terrible night when Augustus was so feverish had been spent in tension. That was exactly what he'd feared. His lies, his secrets, would ruin their happiness, wouldn't they?

He ached to reassure her. All morning, Modesty had been fidgeting, fussing over Augustus, tugging at her gown, checking her appearance in the mirror. She'd been increasingly on edge leading up to the christening, except when he'd held her in his arms at night. Though their hearts grew ever more estranged, their bodies met in the darkness with the desperate urgency of laudanum-seekers, each knowing their medicine was also their undoing.

"You don't need to fret, Modesty," he said softly, and she met his gaze this time. "You couldn't be more perfect."

For the first time since that night, the softness he craved warmed her eyes. Her copper hair was done in fashionable curly tendrils under her bonnet, framing her pretty face. And she wore a silk indigo gown and pelisse, silently announcing to the world that she was his. Just the thought had him growing stiff in his breeches.

"Thank you, Constantine," she replied, and the increasing blush on her cheeks hardened his member further.

That was how she was in his arms, in their bed, when he took her to her next peak. Flushed. Those pretty lips swollen. Eyes dark and glistening.

"I am so glad you'll be his godfather," she said. "You know how important it is for me to have him properly christened publicly without shame. I just wish you—"

He swallowed. "What?"

She looked over at Mrs. Walcott, then leaned closer to him. "I wish you could tell me everything. We're husband and wife. I'm yours, aren't I?"

His mind reeled. "You are." He reached out and brushed her cheek with his knuckles, and she leaned into his touch like a kitten. "I wish I could, darling. You just need to wait a little longer."

He needed only one more day to remove the biggest

danger. Tomorrow the payment of £5,000 was due, and with Blackmore's help, he'd finally get the blackmailer.

Thorne had informed him that a washer woman had sent the last messenger. She'd said the man who'd hired her was wearing a top hat so low she couldn't see his face, and since he'd paid her handsomely, she didn't ask any questions. Blackmore assured him the trap would be set tomorrow at noon, when the false money was supposed to be dropped into the fishmonger's barrel.

"Tomorrow," he promised. "I'll tell you everything tomorrow."

She searched his face and nodded. "Very well. Now come, we should go to Shepherdsbrook. We must be on time for the meeting with my father."

Right. The meeting with the vicar to go over the responsibilities of the godparents and raising the child with the church's values.

He put one leg on the carriage step, his heart lighter with the resumed connection between them. "Of course. I can't wait."

"Are you His Grace, the Duke of Pryde?" asked a boyish voice.

With a prickly sensation at the back of his neck, Constantine turned. A boy of about ten, with a dirty face and threadbare clothes, stood in front of him with a folded paper.

A dark premonition sank like a stone in Constantine's gut.

He stepped down onto the pavement. "That is me."

The boy shoved the paper into his hand and darted down the street.

"Get him!" he yelled to the footman who stood by the carriage.

Constantine started after the boy, his legs pumping. The footman, Davidson, ran by his side down the paved road.

They followed him down to the next crossing, then the one after.

But the urchin was too fast. At the second crossing, he turned sharply to the right and then again right into an alley. But when Constantine and Davidson turned there, it was empty. Constantine called for the boy, saying he only had a few questions about who gave him the note, but there was no one.

He cursed, breathing hard, dreading to open the note.

But he had to.

He unfolded the paper.

Sir,

I regret to inform you that your time is at an end. Circumstances compel me to alter our arrangement; the date is now advanced to this very day. You have but one hour to deliver the money to the specified location or prepare to lose all. Your mother's letter lies ready to be dispatched.

Anonymous

It was written in a rush, without the usual formalities. Constantine's fingers trembled, his heart pounding so loudly he was sure the whole street could hear it. The world around him faded, leaving only the stark reality of the words on the paper. In one hour—the same time as the meeting with Modesty's father.

There was his choice.

Go with Modesty and risk everything: his position, his title, his fortune, and perhaps even her good regard and custody of Augustus.

Or finally get the blackmailer and save his title, his fortune... And his pride.

He needed to choose Modesty, he thought as he walked back to the carriage. There were other ways to deal with this, weren't there? He could send the note to Blackmore, urging him to set the trap immediately.

But they may not be able to arrange things in time.

"Constantine?" Modesty's voice cut through his haze. "What is it? Who was that boy?"

He looked up, meeting her eyes. He had reached the carriage without realizing. The sight of her, so beautiful, rocking little Augustus in her arms, made his heart constrict painfully. How could he choose between them and everything he'd striven so hard to preserve?

"It's..." he began, his voice catching. "It's nothing. Just a message about some business matters."

The lie tasted bitter on his tongue. His mind raced, weighing his options. If he went to the christening, he'd be there for Modesty and Augustus, supporting them as he'd promised. He'd see the fruits of Modesty's hard work, watch her shine as the duchess she was becoming. But the letter...if it was published, everything would come crashing down. His very identity would be stripped away.

On the other hand, if he caught the blackmailer, he might finally end this nightmare. He could secure his future, protect his family from scandal and ruin. But at what cost? Missing this crucial moment, breaking Modesty's trust, letting down the little boy he'd come to love?

"We must go," she said. "Please. We don't want to be late."

"Of course."

Climbing into the carriage felt like moving through molasses. He settled beside Modesty, forcing a smile that felt like a grimace.

"Is anything amiss?" she asked.

Constantine looked down at Augustus. The baby cooed

happily, oblivious to the turmoil raging within his guardian. Those innocent eyes, that sweet face—how could he risk losing this?

But then the weight of generations of Buccleigh pride pressed down on him, judging, demanding that he protect the family name at all costs.

His mother's voice echoed in his mind: *Beyond reproach. You must be beyond reproach.*

The carriage lurched forward, and with it, Constantine felt his resolve crumble. He couldn't do it.

He was too proud to give it all up while he could still fight.

"Stop the carriage!" he called out, his voice cracking.

Modesty startled beside him. "What's wrong?"

Constantine turned to her, his heart breaking at the confusion and worry in her eyes. "I'm so sorry, Modesty. There's an urgent matter I must attend to. It can't wait."

Modesty's eyes widened. "But the christening!"

"I know, I know," Constantine said, the words tumbling out in a rush. The meeting with her father would take some time, then the christening itself... He might make it. "I'll be there, I promise. I just need to take care of this first. I'll meet you at the church."

Before Modesty could protest further, Constantine was out of the carriage, ordering the driver to take his wife and Augustus to All Saints. As he watched the carriage pull away, Modesty's hurt and bewildered face burned into his memory, and Constantine felt a piece of his heart shatter.

He ran around the house and into the mews, crying for the grooms to prepare Icarus right away. Then he barked instructions for two grooms to gallop to the houses of Dorian and Lucien and ask them to meet him in Elysium. They were all probably getting dressed, soon to leave for Shepherdsbrook for the christening.

Eccess would be needed as the second godfather. And it would be good to have the other three present in the church to help with anything Modesty required.

He ran back through the servants' door and to his study to collect the bag that held stacks of paper cut to the size of pound notes. It was already prepared for tomorrow, thank God. As he picked up the leather bag, he was still trying to convince himself he was doing the right thing. He was protecting Modesty and Augustus, wasn't he? Securing their future?

But as Icarus flew through London's streets, all Constantine could see was Modesty's face, all he could hear was Augustus's soft coos. And as he felt the distance between them growing with every hoofbeat, he wondered if he'd just made the biggest mistake of his life.

And if his pride was going to be his downfall once again.

This time, forever.

28

"Where is he, Modesty?"

Sunlight filtered through the church's tall windows, illuminating her father's starched white surplice as it hung over his black cassock. She'd never seen such a thunderous expression on his face. His bushy reddish eyebrows were snapped together over his small eyes, reminding her of an indignant owl.

Augustus was cradled in her arms, feeling heavier than usual in the thick shawl. The empty space beside her felt like a void, growing larger with every second that ticked past. Constantine's absence was a physical ache, a hollow pit in her stomach that threatened to consume her. How ironic that this was the very place she'd first met him. He had rejected Augustus that day—and today he would formally accept him into his family. Wouldn't he?

She'd smoothed her gown a hundred times, adjusted Augustus's lace cap, anything to keep her hands busy and her mind from spiraling into despair.

Instead of her husband, the Duke of Eccess—the second

godfather—stood by her side, his boulder-like shoulders seeming to fill the space beneath the chancel arch.

"He said he'd be here," she whispered, and even her whisper echoed from the walls. "Please, Papa, let's just wait a moment longer."

Papa cleared his throat, displeased. "He wasn't there for the pre-christening consultation. He isn't even prepared."

She felt compelled to defend her husband, though she was as angry and concerned as her father. "The christening was set for one o'clock. It's five to one. He must be on his way. He promised he would make it."

Father sighed. "Fine."

Only the first two pews were occupied with their small circle of guests. The rest of the wooden pews stretched back empty and dark, worn flagstones between the rows. She was grateful there were no more members of the ton present to witness her humiliation.

The Duchess of Rath and the Duchess of Luhst had positioned themselves strategically near the front to offer support. Patience even caught her eye and mouthed, *You're doing splendidly*, which gave her comfort. Neither Patience nor Chastity seemed disturbed their husbands were also missing.

Grace sat in the front pew, as well, along with the Dukes of Enveigh, Irevrence, and Fortyne. But no George. Where in the world could he be? She felt a little hurt; she hadn't thought he'd miss Augustus's christening.

The Duke and Duchess of Grandhampton were present as well as Lord Richard Seaton and Lady Jane. Lord Spencer Seaton, Richard's oldest brother, and his wife, Lady Joanna Seaton, had accepted the invitation along with Lord Richard's sister, the Duchess of Kelford, and her husband, the Duke of Kelford. The Dowager Duchess of Grandhampton, who was the grandmother of the four Seatons, had arrived with Lady

Buchanan—Modesty's two unofficial godmothers. The presence of such dear friends only highlighted her husband's absence. She felt small and exposed before the altar.

What if he doesn't come like he promised?

She'd ask everyone to postpone, then. She wouldn't have Constantine miss such important event in Augustus's life.

Finally, the arched doors at the end of the aisle creaked open, and her heart lurched. She was still upset with him, but at least he'd finally come!

When Lady Virtoux appeared between the doors, shock sent a chill through her entire body. Numbly, she watched the lady walk down the aisle, accompanied by her husband and son, a poorly concealed smirk on her face. The rustle of clothes made all her guests turn around and watch the new arrivals with as much astonishment as she felt.

Eccess leaned closer to her. "Duchess, I was not aware you invited more people?"

"I'm as surprised as you are. I didn't invite them—Constantine must have."

Anger roiled in her stomach now. They'd agreed to keep the christening small and intimate. How could he invite one of the biggest gossips in London without mentioning it? And why would he do so when he wanted to avoid a scandal?

Worse, he wasn't even here!

Unease settled in her stomach as she felt Lady Virtoux's estimating gaze on her.

The doors opened again. *This must be Constantine! Finally...*

But no.

She recognized the faces of the lady and a gentleman coming through—she'd seen them at Lady Virtoux's soirée though she couldn't remember their names. Her gut squeezed to point of pain when more ladies and gentlemen of the ton followed the others into the church.

She could probably count on her fingers the number of times this church had seen aristocrats in the past century and within the ten minutes that followed, they filled it completely. So much so that many had to stand in the back. Silks of all colors, fine wools, bonnets with beautiful flowers, pristine white cravats were everywhere. A few had wet umbrellas—it must have started to rain.

Sharp eyes seemed to judge her. People leaned to each other, and whispers filled the church.

"Where could the duke possibly be?" someone said.

"Surely nothing could be more important than his ward's christening," came another voice.

"Perhaps he's reconsidered taking in the child."

"Perhaps it's not his *ward* at all..."

"'His distant cousin's orphaned baby...' Is that not the same explanation every other nobleman gives for the scandalous appearance of his natural child in his household..."

"He did wed the vicar's daughter in great haste..."

Modesty's cheeks burned with embarrassment and frustration. She and Constantine were supposed to be a united front.

A footman came down the aisle with a paper in his hand. A note from Constantine explaining his absence?

But he handed the paper to the Duke of Fortyne. He read it and whispered to Enveigh and Irevrence. Her heart sank. Surely this couldn't be Constantine's message. He'd send a note to his wife rather than his friends, would he not?

Octavius moved closer, standing slightly in front of her, as though to shield her from the crowd. Like a protective mountain.

"Do not fash, Duchess," Octavius kept telling her, though there was no conviction in his voice. "It'll be all right."

She felt like an imposter in her elegant gown, her new title ill-fitting without Constantine by her side.

The door opened again, and yet again her heart leapt with hope. *Please, let it finally be Constantine...*

But as the crowd parted and whispers of shock and awe rippled through the congregation, Modesty's heart sank.

The Regent himself walked down the aisle, head high, cold eyes on her. He wore a pristine black coat and breeches with a white cravat. His cheeks were ruddy, and his graying hair was in the windswept style.

Fortyne, Enveigh, and Irevrence stood up and hurried towards her, surrounding her protectively as the Regent approached.

"What is going on?" she demanded.

"Constantine is going to be further delayed," said Fortyne, smiling at the Regent.

Disappointment and anger fought within her.

She felt tears prickle her eyes. "He's not coming?"

"I'm afraid it's unlikely," said Irevrence, looking serious for once in his life.

Modesty felt her throat clench. "Why?"

Fortyne cleared his throat. "He's detained. Trust me, he'd be here if he could."

"What is the Regent doing here?" asked Enveigh quietly.

"Uh...that might be my fault," murmured Eccess.

He shot her a guilty look. Did he have any signs of the drunkenness so typical for him? She could smell the faint odor of alcohol, but he maintained a perfectly composed appearance.

"How so?" she barked out.

"I..." He let out a deep sigh. "There was an exclusive soirée at Elysium last night. The Regent often invites me to those. Says I'm a good sport. Claims he doesn't know anyone who shares his taste for fine wines and gastronomic delights so much as I do."

"And?"

"And...I don't remember most of the night. Goddamn it. I must have told him of the christening..." He paled. "I must have also told a few other lords who were in attendance..."

"Damnation, Octavius," growled Enveigh under his breath. "You must get this drinking under control!"

With her pulse drumming in her palms, Modesty wished for the hundredth time she could just run away. She couldn't have felt more abandoned and betrayed.

But, she supposed, she was made of stronger stuff than she had given herself credit for. Her father's shoulders slumped at the sight of the Regent. But she, contrary to her old instinct, straightened her back even more, setting her neck higher.

She curtsied deeply—not so easy with a baby in her arms. "Your Royal Highness," she managed, surprising herself with how steady her voice sounded. "We're honored by your presence."

Eccess and the three other dukes bowed. "Your Royal Highness."

"There's no need to guard the Duchess of Pryde like loyal dogs." The Regent chuckled, looking the four of them over. "I'm not going to bite."

Somehow, Modesty very much doubted he was as harmless as he claimed.

"Take your seats, gentlemen," the Regent commanded.

"I'm afraid the duchess requires our assistance—" Fortyne started.

"No, she does not. Return to your seats."

Modesty watched as some conflict was fought behind Fortyne's, Enveigh's, and Irevrence's eyes for a few moments. But they did as requested, no doubt reluctant to make a scene and worsen the situation. Octavius, however, took one step closer to her.

"You look quite well for what last night brought," the Regent said, looking Eccess over, but his smile didn't quite reach his eyes when his gaze returned to Modesty. "I wouldn't dream of missing such an...interesting occasion," he said, looking down at Augustus. "Though I can't help but notice we're missing the proud father. Or is it uncle twice removed? Thrice removed? I confess, I'm a bit unclear on the relationship."

Modesty felt the blood drain from her face. "Augustus is the son of Constantine's distant cousin, orphaned in a carriage accident just days after his birth."

The Regent leaned in close, his voice low. "Of course he is. That is what I heard. And church records will, no doubt, reveal the truth." Her skin prickled as he leaned even closer. "Might we have a private word, Duchess, if you please?"

"I should come, too," said Eccess, for which she was entirely thankful.

"No, I do insist that you stay here," said the Regent. "Take the child and wait."

"But Your Royal Highness—" started the duke.

"Is the duchess not to be trusted with her prince?" asked the Regent sharply.

Modesty stared at Eccess, who was blinking rapidly. He shot her an apologetic, helpless look and took Augustus in his arms. "I merely hoped to be of assistance."

The Regent nodded. "Then do so by holding the child." He offered Modesty his elbow. "Duchess, if you please?"

She laid her hand on his elbow, and he steered her towards a small chapel, leaving the confused guests gaping in curiosity. Once inside, he turned to her, his expression a mixture of false sympathy and barely concealed triumph.

"How are you feeling, Duchess, given everything?" he began.

"Everything, Your Royal Highness?"

"Well, the rumors, of course. The duke has always had a spotless reputation. But then his hasty marriage to you, the latest publication implying his mama had a lover. Scandalous. And now this child, and a christening for which he is absent... This whole situation does leave me puzzled. And given the suspicious will the late Duke of Pryde left..."

She felt as if she had been abandoned to steer a sinking ship in the middle of a storm. Should she keep up the pretense that she knew everything? That Constantine had shared this information with her? She drew strength from the thought of the Dowager Duchess of Grandhampton and Lady Buchanan. They'd advise her to handle the situation diplomatically.

"I'm certain it's only gossip," she said.

"Certain, are you? Given that the will stipulates the title must pass to the former duke's true blood heir?"

Modesty's fingernails bit into her palms. She could not pretend any longer. She had to know the truth. "I don't understand. Constantine is his heir."

The Regent arched an eyebrow. "Is he? Then why such a stipulation in the will? Why such secrecy around this child? Why the rush to marry you, a woman so far below his station? No offense intended, of course."

The pieces were starting to fall into place, but the picture they formed was still blurry. Constantine had told her Augustus was his father's grandson. But why would that matter unless...

"Your husband has gone to great lengths to keep this child's true identity a secret. One might wonder why, if there's nothing to hide."

Modesty's head spun. The secrets, the blackmail, Constantine's desperate need to protect his position—it all stemmed from this. The gossip about his mother and a clergyman, Augustus being his father's grandson, and now this strange clause in the will. She could almost grasp the solution to this puzzle. The most obvious conclusion—if all that was true— was that Constantine wasn't his father's true son. He was the result of his mother's rumored affair. But that couldn't be so...

Her knees were weak. Her ears rang louder than her own thoughts. There must be another answer to all this, but she just couldn't grasp it.

"I fear your husband may not be quite the man you believe him to be, my dear. Nor, indeed, the man any of us imagine. But do not distress yourself—all shall be revealed in due course. Rest assured, I am attending to the matter."

He reached into his finely tailored coat and retrieved a letter, which he offered to her. She looked at it, but couldn't take it, feeling as though it was a snake about to bite.

"I was hoping to give this to the duke personally. But I'm sure you will be so kind as to deliver it for me. He's summoned for a hearing in front of the House of Lords, in three days."

She took the letter in shaking hands. Was it possible to be angry with someone and yet want to protect them?

The Regent nodded with satisfaction. "For now, shall we return to the christening? Everyone is waiting."

As the Regent guided her back to altar, Modesty felt as though she were moving through a fog. She put the letter in her reticule. The faces of the congregation blurred before her, their whispers a dull roar in her ears as she took her place at the font.

She barely noticed Eccess asking if she was all right, if she needed to sit down. She looked into his eyes, searching for answers. Did he know the extent of Constantine's secrets? Did all of the dukes know?

She clutched Augustus closer as the weight of countless eyes pressed down on her. The whispers grew louder with each passing moment.

"What would you like to do, Modesty?" Papa asked. "Postpone?"

The suggestion sent a jolt of panic through her chest.

The ship was still sinking, but she was the one at the helm. She wouldn't sacrifice anything more. She'd take charge and guide it safely to shore.

"No," she said. "We have the godmother, and we still have one godfather. That is enough, is it not?"

Papa frowned as he eyed Eccess. "Are you certain, Your Grace? Will you accept the responsibility of being the child's only godfather?"

Octavius hesitated, then gulped. His large palm almost swallowed Augustus's little head as he patted it. "I will not let the duchess down."

The ceremony began. As she held the baby over the font, watching the holy water trickle over his forehead, Modesty was determined to be strong for Augustus, no matter what came next. But underneath her calm, capable exterior was an aching sadness for the family they could have been. And fury at Constantine for letting her down.

Her father had taught her well—a proper, obedient woman always put others first, excused their poor behavior, shouldered their burdens without complaint. For years she'd done exactly that, making herself smaller to lift others higher. But standing here alone, abandoned on what should have been their family's proudest day, she felt that old instinct dying inside her.

She didn't deserve this betrayal.

Augustus didn't, either.

The whispers and stares that would have crushed her

months ago now barely touched her. She'd faced down the Regent and conducted Augustus's christening with grace under extremely difficult circumstances. She was no longer that timid vicar's daughter who shrank from confrontation. She was the Duchess of Pryde, and she would not let anyone— not the ton, not the Regent, not even her husband—make her feel small again.

She held herself together through the final congratulations, through Eccess's concerned glances, through the slow dispersal of guests. But once she stood alone in the antechamber, her composure cracked. Her body shook as she held Augustus close, hot tears spilling onto his christening gown. Constantine's desertion cut bone-deep, but she loved him still, God help her. Regretfully, love wasn't enough to rebuild what his lies had broken.

29

THE STENCH of Whitechapel Market assaulted Constantine's senses. Rotting cabbage trampled underfoot, fish guts gleaming wetly on wooden boards, the metallic tang of blood from the butcher's stall. A cold drizzle fell, turning the packed earth between stalls to mud. Through the haze, peddlers' cries echoed off the close-set buildings: "Eels, live eels!" "Fresh mackerel!" "Apples, ha'penny each!"

Constantine's borrowed laborer's coat, threadbare wool scratching against his fine linen shirt, did little to ward off the damp. Around him, merchants haggled, people bought salt fish, ribbons, apples. His boots, though deliberately muddied, still marked him as different—they were too fine, too new for this world of desperate commerce.

In All Saints Church, Modesty would be standing alone, no doubt hating him. The image of her face when he'd fled the carriage haunted him. But he pushed the guilt down and forced himself to focus. If this worked, the torment might finally come to an end. He could keep his title.

Keep her.

"Your wife will never forgive you for this," Dorian muttered beside him, adjusting his worn laborer's coat.

Lucien gave a soft snort from his other side. "I don't know that I agree, Dorian. Both of our wives have forgiven far worse offenses. Especially in your case."

It was a wonder that Blackmore and his men had managed to arrange the setup on such short notice. Constantine had only to step inside Elysium, bark what happened, and Blackmore had sprung into action. Dorian and Lucien had arrived at Elysium shortly after Constantine, both out of breath, having galloped their horses. Then the three of them were given clothing to help them blend in. Blackmore had sent word to the rest of the dukes at All Saints Church.

They would make sure Modesty and Augustus were all right while he hunted the blackmailer.

Constantine's chest constricted. "She might forgive me. Once she understands I had no choice."

Three stalls down, he saw five of Blackmore's men—sharp and strong but blending in surprisingly well. All of them were dressed like regular inhabitants of Whitechapel, wearing worn-out and stained wool jackets, long frock coats, old breeches or trousers of wool or canvas. Dr. Sterling watched from farther down Petticoat Street, where it narrowed into an alleyway, leaning against the corner.

"Thank you both for helping me, by the way," Constantine said.

Dorian chuckled. "Considering what you've done for me, friend, helping you get your blackmailer is nothing."

"I am grateful to have my daughter, but I can't wait to look into the eyes of the person who used a blameless child to blackmail me," Lucien added. "And ask questions—for all of us."

Constantine nodded. They understood. They knew what it

was like to live with sin...and that a day would come when one had to pay for it.

"Is the bag in the barrel?" asked Lucien, casting a sideways glance at the stall across the aisle where people wound through the crowd carrying bundles and pushing carts. Children darted between the adults.

"Yes."

His palms were sweaty, his heart racing. At any moment, someone would come for that barrel. So far he saw only customers coming and going: a couple of women who looked like kitchen maids, a pie seller looking for cheap fish for his pies, a group of three washerwomen haggling over sprats for dinner, and sailors and mill workers.

"Be ready," Morgan Nightshade muttered as he passed, balancing an empty porter's yoke across his shoulders.

Across the way, his twin, Tristan, lounged against his knife-sharpening wheel.

The hair on Constantine's neck prickled as he darted a glance at the barrel. Casually, Morgan stood at the stall, and then he was blocked from Constantine's sight by a passerby.

But he could still see the barrel.

The person who came to the barrel was so smooth, Constantine might have missed them entirely. The movement was practiced and subtle, just someone looking at the fish.

But from the corner of his eye, he saw an arm sinking into the barrel.

His throat went dry and sweat broke through his skin.

He tensed to charge. It was a tall man, probably as tall as him. A poor coat with holes and patches covered his large body. A hat was pulled low over his forehead, and a tightly wrapped dirty cravat covered his mouth, concealing most of the man's face. Only a reddish nose protruded, indicating that he was perhaps a drunk.

"Is that—" began Dorian.

"The blackmailer," finished Lucien, already shouldering his way towards the big man.

The staged fight erupted right on schedule. "You bloody cheat!" one of Thorne's men bellowed. "I saw you palm that ace!"

The crowd surged towards the fight, creating the perfect distraction. Through the chaos, Constantine caught glimpses of their target moving down Petticoat Street. He was limping.

He was large, with a belly and broad shoulders. But there was something familiar about those shoulders, the way the neck was set, the angle at which the head was craned. Something nagged at his memory.

But the man was gone in the next moment, brownish coat melting into the crowd.

"He's heading for the alley," Lucien cried over his shoulder as he hurried after the blackmailer. "Sterling's ready."

Constantine charged after him, boots slipping in fish offal. The twins practically flew through the street, Morgan cutting left while Tristan circled right to flank the blackmailer. But the man snatched up a handful of oyster shells from a nearby stall and flung them underfoot. Morgan went down hard.

"Split up!" Dorian shouted. "Cut him off before the alley!"

Constantine's heart hammered against his ribs as they separated, weaving through the press of bodies. Rain dripped from the brim of his borrowed cap, running cold down his neck.

The man glanced over his shoulder and sped up. His limp was fading, steps becoming confident and broader in stride. He turned over a barrel of apples, and Dorian cursed as he crashed into it. But Constantine kept his eyes locked on the man, even as his trousers snagged on a nail, even as market women screamed and scattered.

The blackmailer glanced back once more. In that moment, the cravat slipped.

Constantine's blood turned to ice.

George Lockhart.

Modesty's childhood friend. The man who'd offered her everything Constantine denied her—adventure, discovery, freedom. Of course it would be him.

He wanted her for himself.

George broke into a full run, and it was clear that the big shoulders and stomach were nothing but rags that now flapped from under his clothes.

"Stop him!" Constantine shouted. He shoved through the crowd, no longer caring about maintaining his disguise. George disappeared down the alley where Sterling waited, then there was a sharp cry and a thud.

Constantine's chest burned as he ran. Modesty's face when he'd fled the carriage flashed in his mind—hurt, betrayal, confusion warring in those green eyes he loved. She was waiting for him...

But he couldn't stop. If he failed now, everything would crumble—his title, his marriage, the fragile happiness he'd found. And yet with every step guilt gnawed deeper. Was he choosing pride over love?

Constantine rounded the corner to see Brace Sterling sprawled in a puddle, blood trickling from his temple. George must have struck him. Beyond, the twins gave chase, but George was already scaling a stack of crates against a warehouse wall.

Dorian, the strongest of them all, followed George while Lucien stopped abruptly by Constantine's side, breathing hard. Dorian climbed one crate after another, but George was faster. Tristan was close on Dorian's heels, but as George reached the top of the wall, he kicked the topmost crate, and the whole construction tumbled down with a tremendous crash.

Constantine, Lucien, Morgan, and two more of Thorne's men darted towards the pile of crates, throwing them aside to get to their friends. Spitting curses, Dorian emerged from under the crates and threw a furious glare up towards the man silhouetted against the gray sky. A few scratches and bruises. Otherwise, Dorian looked fine. Constantine saw Tristan's coat, and he and Lucien hurried to help him up. He looked a little worse as he spat blood and favored his right leg. Morgan put his arm around him to keep him on his feet.

George watched them in silence, the bag in his hand. Rain plastered his hair to his forehead, now free of the cap he must have lost in the chase.

"You were her friend!" Constantine bellowed. "How could you do this to her?"

His face twisted with something like regret—or was it triumph?

"Do this *to* her? I'm doing this *for* her!" he called back. "To save her from your pride and your lies. Your secrets will destroy you. I won't let them destroy her, too. She must have realized what a rotten man she married by now. She should have agreed to come to Egypt with me. I would have given her the life she's always dreamed of."

Then George disappeared.

"The other side!" yelled Tristan. "Run! You might still catch him!"

Constantine, Lucien, Dorian, and two of Thorne's men burst into a sprint. Dorian limped slightly; he must have hit his knee. Seconds later, Constantine reached the other side of the wall.

The maze of Whitechapel's back alleys was completely empty.

Dorian and Lucien caught up, breathing hard.

Dorian gripped Constantine's shoulder. "We'll find him. No one can hide in Whitechapel for long with Thorne's eyes and ears on the lookout."

But Constantine barely heard him. His mind was already racing ahead.

"Modesty..." he murmured.

"You need to get to her," said Lucien, tugging his arm. "She might still be in the church."

He nodded, moving his feet as if trudging through a swamp. "God, he'll find a way to get to Modesty," he murmured. "Tell her everything I was supposed to and never did."

How much more would George reveal out of some misguided attempt to "save" her?

"His ship is leaving in a few days to Egypt," he told the others. "We'll need to keep watch in the port. Contact the captain of the ship."

The rain fell harder, soaking through his borrowed clothes, but Constantine didn't feel it. His mind raced. He'd need to stop to make sure Brace Sterling was all right, and then he'd fly like the wind to All Saints Church.

He ran, but he felt the weight of his choices crushing him. He'd abandoned his wife and ward to catch the blackmailer. Instead, he'd discovered the threat was closer than he'd ever imagined.

He had to warn Modesty, tell her George had been plotting against them all along.

But would she even speak to him after he'd left her at the christening alone? And would George now follow through with his threat to publish the letter?

30

"Where's the duchess?" Constantine barked, shoving his hole-ridden hat into Simons's hands. His workman's clothes were disheveled, clumps of wet mud still clinging to his boots.

He had practically flown to All Saints on Icarus only to discover the christening had finished without him.

Of course it had. He'd arrived two hours late.

Simons gave him a quick once-over, never having seen the Duke of Pryde in such a sorry state. Normally, that would have set Constantine's teeth on edge, the need to appear perfect, but today he couldn't care less.

"Your Grace, the duchess is upstairs. She's—"

But Constantine was already taking the stairs two at a time, his mind racing with all the things he needed to say. He pushed open the door to her bedchamber and froze, breath knocked out of his lungs.

Standing by the bed, Modesty was folding gowns and placing them into an open trunk. Her maid was busy on the other side of the bed, doing the same. Augustus lay in his cot nearby, cooing.

"Modesty, what are you doing?"

She turned to face him, and the look in her eyes made his blood run cold. There was hurt there, yes, but also a steely resolve he'd never seen before. She looked him over, frowning. "Why are you dressed like that? Do you know what, Constantine, it doesn't matter. I don't want to know. I'm leaving."

Leaving. Well, why wouldn't she leave him after all this?

The maid curtsied to him and threw a careful look at Modesty. "I'll go and prepare the boxes for your bonnets, Your Grace." She retreated.

Where would Modesty go? To Egypt? With George...? Goddamn it! Had he managed to reach her first? Had he told her everything?

George was going to give her the world when Constantine had locked her into a marriage she'd never wanted, into a position she despised. And even after he'd promised to be by her side, he'd abandoned her.

He had to alert her about George's true nature, but he would also need to tell her the whole truth... Could he finally do that?

Pride coursed through his veins, gripping his throat like a fist. His heart beat hard with love and fear, every slam against his ribs resonating in pain.

He crossed the few steps between them, took her by the elbow, and turned her to him gently. "Darling, please, don't go. Let me explain."

"Explain about your father's will? I already know."

Constantine felt his body grow cold. "How did you— Did he get to you?"

She took a folded letter from the side table and handed it to him. "If you mean His Royal Highness, then yes. He was kind enough to enlighten me and then asked me to give you this.

Even he came for the christening, while my husband couldn't be bothered to attend."

Not George but the Regent... His other adversary. He unfolded the letter with icy fingers and his heart sank.

Words sprang at him as he quickly scanned the elegant handwriting.

Your presence is required...
    hearing in the House of Lords...
    three days...
    grave concerns...
    right to the title of Duke of Pryde questioned...

Dread wound around his heart.

Shame and pride warred within him. "He had no right to tell you what was not his to tell."

"No right?" Modesty's voice rose. "I would argue he had every right to tell me the truth. The price of your secrets—of your pride—is finally catching up with you."

Constantine's jaw ached.

Drop to your knees, you fool. Tell her everything. Beg for her forgiveness.

His throat spasmed. Without reproach. He had to be without reproach.

"I was going to solve everything before I had to burden you with the truth. I wanted to protect you from this."

Modesty shook her head, her eyes teary. "You were protecting yourself, Constantine. Your title. Your precious reputation. That is all you have cared about all along."

She snatched her elbow out of his hand and turned back to her packing, picking up a gown then throwing it on the bed and folding it in sharp movements. "If you truly cared for me and Augustus, you'd have told me."

He loved her. But she was right, he should have told her long ago. Constantine's hands shook, itching to stop her. A dark abyss was spreading under his feet—the abyss he'd created with his own decisions and actions.

She threw the next gown into the trunk. "Do you know how foolish I felt, standing there alone? How embarrassed? I actually believed you cared for me, for Augustus. You promised me you'd be there."

Constantine couldn't stand it; this helplessness was killing him. She was slipping out of his grip, and he couldn't do anything.

She shook her head. "I even considered postponing so that you could be the godfather. Until the whole ton showed up!"

He frowned. "The whole ton?"

"Yes!"

"Not just the Regent?"

"No! Why did you invite them?"

"I didn't."

"Then who? Octavius said he might have spilled the news to the Regent, but others mentioned receiving invitations."

Constantine's mind spun. Written invitations... The black-mail payment deadline moved to the same day as christening without warning. *She must have realized what a rotten man she married by now.*

"George..." he murmured, realization hitting him like a fist. "It was all George Lockhart."

She stopped folding and stared at him as if waiting for him to sprout horns. "What about George?"

"It was him, Modesty. He blackmailed me. He made sure I had to miss the christening. He invited the ton!"

She exhaled sharply, blinking. "This is ridiculous. George

would never! Don't put the blame on him when nothing should have stopped you from being there for Augustus—from standing by my side like your friends did. I thought I had glimpsed a caring man under all those layers of stone. Clearly I was mistaken."

His friends had been there for her, while he'd abandoned her...

It was like the snap of a whip against his pride. He swallowed it. He shouldn't get defensive now. For once, he needed to tell her the truth. Lay himself bare.

Tell her what she and Augustus meant to him.

He opened his mouth to do so. But his pride had erected walls so high even he couldn't get past them. "I do care for you," he finally managed. "Both of you. More than anything."

Weak. Care for them? That didn't begin to describe what he felt.

They were his world.

He lifted a hand towards her, longing to pull her close, to stroke her hair, but she stepped out of his reach.

"If that were true, you would have trusted me with your secrets. But you didn't see me, did you? Not really. You saw a convenient solution to your problem. A simple vicar's daughter, willing to sacrifice everything for a child in need."

"That couldn't be further from the truth."

"Couldn't it?" Modesty's voice cracked. "I've spent most of my life trying to be whatever my father needed me to be. Then whatever you needed me to be. I married a man I barely knew because I thought it was the right thing to do for Augustus. I stopped going to the women's almshouse because you deemed it beneath a duchess. I was not allowed to do any more excavations. And for what?"

Constantine's face crumpled. "Pray, allow me the chance to make amends. We can resolve this. I'll do anything."

For a moment, Modesty hesitated. But then she looked over at Augustus, and something in her green eyes solidified.

"No." Her voice was quiet but firm. "I can't keep sacrificing pieces of myself, hoping that someday it will be enough. That someday I'll be worthy of your trust."

She met Constantine's eyes, and there was hardness in her gaze that he'd never seen before. "I'm more than just a convenient solution to your problems. I'm more than just a vessel for everyone else's needs and expectations. It's time I remembered that and put my own dreams first."

Egypt...she meant Egypt!

His stomach dropped to the floor.

"Don't go to Egypt with him, Modesty," he rasped. "George Lockhart was the man blackmailing me this entire time. I'm dressed like this because I've just chased him in Whitechapel."

She looked at him with a mixture of shock and disbelief. "Are you listening to yourself? You're trying to slander one of my closest friends? George would never blackmail anyone! He's one of the kindest people I know!"

Constantine's back was damp with sweat. "I know he may appear that way, but he has everyone fooled. And he said he was going to save you from me. You must be careful. Do not—"

Red eyebrows drew together; green eyes darkened with fury. "Enough!" She lifted Augustus from his bassinet.

"Don't go," he managed, his voice cracking.

Modesty paused, Augustus cradled against her chest. For a heartbeat, Constantine imagined she might change her mind, find it in her heart to give him a chance.

But she'd given him so many already.

She squared her shoulders, meeting his gaze. "I pray that you will one day come to choose love over pride."

He felt like she'd knocked all air from his lungs, and all he could do was gape.

"I'm going to stay with Papa for a while. Be well, Constantine."

He watched, frozen in place, as she swept past him, her scent of wildflowers lingering in the air. He heard her footsteps on the stairs, the murmur of voices below, the front door closing with a final, devastating thud.

And then, silence.

Constantine sank onto the bed without feeling his legs. He'd had a treasure he never knew he needed—a woman he loved, a child he'd grown to cherish—and in trying to protect the position he never should have had, he'd lost everything.

The grand bedchamber, with its opulent furnishings, felt hollow. Empty. Just like the space in his heart where Modesty and Augustus had been.

Constantine buried his face in his hands. The piercing pain in his chest sliced through his throat and shot up into his eyes. For the first time since that day in the stables as a boy, tears fell, and he didn't stop them. He didn't weep for his title or his reputation, but for the family he'd pushed away. For the love he'd been too afraid to fully embrace.

The price of pride was far higher than he'd ever imagined.

31

"WELL, AUGUSTUS," said Modesty as she put the baby on the patchwork quilt covering a narrow wooden bed, "this is where you were born."

Augustus cooed. He'd started moving his mouth in a way that made Modesty wonder if he was trying to smile for the first time, his dark blue eyes glistening as he looked up at her. He moved his chubby arms and legs inside the swaddle.

Modesty smiled softly at him. "Do you like it? I think you do."

She slowly walked around the small room, bare floorboards creaking under her feet. Sadness filled her, heavy and omnipresent. It was on this bed that she had sat, holding the hand of a dying woman.

The white plaster walls looked gray in the grim light falling through the small sash window, old cracks and imperfections looking like scars. A cross hung over the bed and an old gravure on the wall opposite.

"Is everything all right, Modesty?" Her father's voice startled her, and she turned to see him standing in the doorway.

The question seemed absurd. Nothing was right. Her world had shattered into pieces. She'd fled from the man she loved because his pride mattered more than their marriage. She'd taken Augustus from the only family he'd known.

"I scarcely know," she admitted. "I believed I was fulfilling my duty as duchess."

She'd accepted Constantine's half-truths and evasions. But the Regent's letter had changed everything. How could she go back to a marriage built on lies?

Three days ago, she arrived at her father's home, and she hadn't been able to sleep since.

Constantine came every day, asking if she was well, but she'd told Papa she didn't want to see him.

Papa walked towards her and sat by Augustus's side on the bed. He patted the baby on the cheek gently.

"I'd like to help you, child," he said to her.

She said nothing but turned to stare out of the window. The garden looked wilder, and the goat was nipping sadly at the last burdock protruding through the gap in the fence. With a sharp sting in her heart, she remembered how enthusiastically Bessie had chewed on Constantine's elegant coat. How the home she'd always loved could now seem so empty and desolate, she didn't know. Perhaps it was only reflecting how she felt.

"Of course, you're always welcome here," Papa continued, "but you've been very quiet since you arrived. What happened?"

She ran the pads of her thumbs over fingernails, now healthier and smoother than they ever had been. Since she'd moved to Mayfair, she hadn't been scrubbing the church and the house, tending the garden and the animals, helping in the kitchen and at the almshouse.

When she said nothing, he probed again. "Modesty, it's

hard to see you like this, dear. Matrimony is sacred. You ought to return to your place at your husband's side...or at least see him..."

Papa's words caused a familiar sense of guilt to weigh on her shoulders.

Her place at her husband's side...

Was it selfish to want more for herself? To demand honesty and respect? To want the man she loved to choose her and the baby he had taken in as a ward—and not his pride?

But how could she explain to Papa she was no longer the girl he'd raised? She didn't want to be obedient and modest—she wanted to be herself.

"The duke doesn't give me what I need," she said.

He sighed. "Although I would wish something different for you than marriage to one of the Dukes of Sin, what's done is done. What you must do now is be a good wife to your husband. That is your duty as a woman."

Duty as a woman... That was what she'd been taught all her life. Be small. Be supportive. Accommodate. Accept your role as a woman. Always put others first.

"What would people say, Modesty?" her father asked. "A duchess leaving her husband... Deception is a grave sin, but so, too, is the dissolution of a marriage. And what of the child? Have you considered the impact on his future?"

Of course she had considered it; she had gone through with this sham of a marriage for Augustus's sake. And she would ensure he had a good life, whatever it took. But she was increasingly convinced that growing up in a house of lies would only leave the child as wounded as her husband.

She had foolishly dreamed that things could be different. That she could be a true duchess—proud and respected, seen and listened to...

Loved by her husband.

She wanted to be part of Misses with Microscopes. She wanted to go to an excavation. She wanted to be like Patience and Chastity, who could go to balls and talk to diplomats and royals but also conduct experiments, study in libraries and laboratories, and debate hypotheses in reputable salons. But that would never be.

"I can't go back, Papa," she said.

But how could she move forward?

She was tied to Constantine forever. In the eyes of the law, she didn't exist without him. She was his property, an extension of him, dependent on his money and on his name.

"Why not?" Papa asked.

There were so many reasons, but she could share none of them with Papa—or anyone else.

She began pacing. "I don't know, Papa, but I do not want to restrict myself to the darkest corner of the room so that light will shine on everyone else."

He rose to his feet. "You don't know what you're talking about, child, but that's understandable given you're clearly going through a difficult time. I shall pray for guidance and wisdom for you. Perhaps, with God's grace, there may yet be a path to reconciliation. For now, you and Augustus are welcome here for as long as you need."

A loud knock sounded from the front door.

"Let me answer the door," Papa said.

Her breath caught at the thought of Constantine coming for her yet again. "If it's the duke, please tell him I won't see him."

Papa nodded and left the room. As she tried to coax Augustus into a true smile, her father called out from downstairs. "Modesty, Mr. George Lockhart is here for you!"

She wondered if she should heed Constantine's warning about George. But surely he was mistaken. Or it was yet another lie to manipulate her. George was one of her oldest friends, one of the people she trusted most. He would never hurt her, unlike her husband.

She picked up Augustus. "Let's go and see our friend."

As she entered the sitting room, George jumped to his feet. Something was different about him—there was a feverish brightness in his eyes, an almost manic energy in his movements. But she dismissed her unease. He must simply be eager to set out on his voyage.

George bowed, a wide smile on his face. "I hope you're well, Duchess. And Augustus." He came to her and wriggled his fingers over Augustus's nose, which made the baby frown as he tried to follow the movement.

"We are. As you see, I'm staying with Papa for now. We missed you at the christening."

"Right. I am so very sorry I couldn't be there. But...I hope all is well...with the duke?"

Papa cleared his throat. "The duke will always be well. It's those around him that might not."

Modesty straightened her back. No matter how displeased she was with Constantine, she was not going to spill intimate details of their conflict outside her marriage. "Papa is merely jesting. Augustus and I are just...in need of a break from the city, that's all. How's your sister?"

"She's very well. Sends her regards." George's eyes grew even brighter. "I—er—there's something rather exciting I came to share. One of antiquarians joining my Egyptian expedition told me traces of a Roman fort have been discovered just two miles south of here. They've uncovered parts of the foundations and have found some pottery fragments..." He leaned forward, voice dropping conspiratorially. "They even found what might be ceremonial objects—rings and amulets with markings similar to those Pictish symbols you're so fascinated by. I was rather hoping to show you before I sail. One last archaeological adventure together, like old times."

A familiar jolt of excitement ran through her. A new site!

"Papa, you wouldn't mind, would you?" she asked.

"No, of course not. You do need a change. Fresh air will do you good. The weather is very fine, as well."

"And is it safe for Augustus to come?" she asked. "He hasn't been outside yet today."

"Of course." George smiled. "I'm sure he'll develop a passion for antiquities, just like you. My gig is outside."

They went to the front door. She raised her brows at him as she handed him the baby and picked up her bonnet, tying it around her face. As she put on her pelisse, she asked, "Since when do you drive a gig?"

"My position on the Egyptian party is well paid," he said as he handed the baby back to her, put on his top hat, and opened the door for her. "They took me thanks to your finding, so I thought I'd spoil you one last time before leaving."

"I'm so glad for you," she said as he supported her by the hand to help her climb into the gig.

He nodded with a smile, then walked around to take his seat. He flicked the reins, and the horse walked forward.

They chatted pleasantly for a bit as Modesty enjoyed the passing landscape.

"Oh!" George exclaimed, reaching beneath the seat. "I nearly forgot. I brought something special." He produced a small silver flask. "One of my fellow antiquarians translated the most fascinating papyrus fragment—a recipe for a tea blend. Supposedly Cleopatra enjoyed it. I brewed it this morning and thought you'd like to try it?"

Modesty took the flask. "Tea that Cleopatra drank?" She opened it and sniffed. "What's in it?"

"Surprisingly, I could find most ingredients. Honey,

chamomile, mint, rosemary... Saffron, too. Wormwood, so it might be a little bitter. The only ingredient I couldn't source was blue lotus. It grows only along the Nile. But I hoped I might still capture something of the original essence without it."

Modesty hesitated. The scholarly part of her was intrigued by this connection to the ancient world, but something...a feeling in her gut...gave her pause.

"Come now," he urged. "Just a small taste. You're not coming to Egypt with me. This is my way to bring Egypt to you. We used to share treats as children, remember?"

The mention of their shared childhood made her concerns melt away. Surely, she was being foolish to doubt her oldest friend. She accepted the flask and took a small sip. The liquid was, indeed, oddly bitter beneath its honeyed sweetness.

"Interesting," she murmured, smacking her lips. Then she drank a few more gulps, trying to imagine if Cleopatra thought it strange, too, or if she enjoyed it. "That bitterness..."

"It's only wormwood, as I said." George flashed her a reassuring smile. "I wonder if blue lotus would change the taste."

She drank a little more. She thought the bitterness was slightly different from wormwood, but it must be because of the combination of herbs in the tea. "You have to try it in Egypt and write me with the results." She smiled as she handed him the flask. "Thank you for bringing it for me."

They continued chatting for the next half hour, but Modesty found herself growing strangely drowsy. Her thoughts became sluggish, her limbs heavy. She tried to focus on the passing scenery, but her vision kept blurring at the edges. Augustus's weight in her arms seemed to increase with each passing minute.

When she saw the outskirts of London, her stomach dropped.

She looked around. "Where is the site? If it's two miles away, shouldn't we have reached it by now?"

He looked at her with the warm, lovely smile of a friend who was about to give her the biggest gift of her life—something he knew she'd adore.

"I'm sorry, Modesty," he said, no longer bothering to use her proper title. "The site is a little more south than I mentioned. It's in Egypt. You are coming with me, after all. The ship is about to sail."

She gave out a laugh. "What? You're jesting, surely."

"No, dearest, I am not. I wanted you to be my wife. Had the duke not proposed first, I'm sure your papa would have given me his blessing. Then you and I would have been on this ship anyway. I would have never restricted you like he's restricting you—keeping you in a golden cage, making you into his image of the perfect wife and duchess."

Her mouth fell open. No. This was not the George she knew...

"You can't be serious! What about Augustus? Mrs. Walcott is back at home—what will he eat?"

"I've already hired a wet nurse for him. I recently came into some money... Your husband paid me to keep his secrets. Funny how things work out, isn't it?"

The memory of Constantine's warnings crashed over her. He'd tried to tell her, but she'd been too angry, too hurt to believe him. Now here she was, trapped in a gig with the very man who'd been plotting their destruction all along.

Fear dripped icy sweat down her spine as they entered Whitechapel. *He's the blackmailer. And now he's taking me away...*

The streets were getting increasingly crowded. Augustus squirmed against her chest, sensing her tension. She couldn't risk jumping—not with the baby. But the closer they got to the docks, the fewer options she'd have.

"Don't look so horrified," George said softly, his hand leaving the reins to cup her cheek. The gesture made her skin crawl, but she was too tired, her reactions too slow, to jerk back before his fingers reached her. What was going on?

Her eyelids were heavy. Augustus started slipping out of her hands, and she clutched him with all strength she had—which was diminishing with every sluggish breath she took.

"Your dreams are coming true, darling. Everything I've done—the blackmail, the gossip, destroying his pride..." He was talking but she was slipping down into some warm, dark place... "It was all for you. Our dream..."

No, she needed to remain awake. Run away from him. Keep Augustus safe.

But she was already sinking beneath the surface... Soft. Weak. Sleep.

"And now it's coming true," George added, and it was the last thing she remembered.

32

Constantine sat on the floor of the empty ballroom, his back against the wall. He held the decanter of cognac, Eccess's gift, in his hand, which rested on his knee. There were three more wine bottles discarded on the floor, glass shining in the dim light.

It was late...or early...

He was not certain.

His head spun as he replayed the vision of Modesty and him as they practiced the English country dance in this room. He remembered the feel of her warm waist through her clothes, her scent of wildflowers in his nostrils, her eyes glowing with the sort of fire that ignited his blood.

None of the chandeliers were lit, only a single candelabra burning low by his left boot.

Muddy footprints marred the pristine floor, perhaps for the first time in this house's existence. He wouldn't let the staff enter this room. His father's portrait—the length of the wall—glared at him from the dark background of an English landscape. Judging him. *Better no duke at all than bring shame to the title.*

Oh, he'd done that—and more.

The mirrors that had once reflected their first dance were now dark and empty. Sheet music was still on the harpsichord from their last lesson. The room's grandeur now felt hollow.

He was finally living in the nightmare he'd always feared.

A paper with George's exposé lay on the floor crumpled by his right boot. Confirming, exposing the truth.

He was never supposed to be the duke.

He still wore yesterday's clothes. He'd sent his valet away and refused to leave this room after the last time Mr. Fairchild had sent him away. The Pictish mirror he'd bought Modesty at that auction lay on the floor next to his coat. Was he cold? He didn't know. He felt numb.

He was also not sure if he'd slept at all. Perhaps he had dozed off at some point. He felt stubble on his face—he couldn't remember the last time he'd had so much stubble.

The exposé's aftermath was more devastating than he could have imagined. Although his mother's letter itself had not been published, the author claimed the report had come from "a trusted source close to the family." They'd revealed the details of the late duchess's affair with the parson. Dates and locations of their meetings that aligned perfectly with Constantine's birth—which Constantine couldn't verify or deny since there was no proof, but they seemed plausible enough for people to believe. Comments about how Constantine's appearance differed from that of his "father." Ophelia's true parentage and her connection to Augustus. The late duke's will specifically recommending a blood heir. And even Constantine's rejection of a pregnant woman when she'd come for help. There were church records, the details of his and Modesty's special marriage license and how quickly it was arranged, and even a testimony of a former servant who'd asked to remain anonymous.

His unblemished reputation had been left in tatters overnight. Yesterday, several letters had arrived withdrawing dinner invitations; another letter had suggested he should stay away from the House of Lords while "certain matters" were being investigated. His trading partners were suddenly requiring immediate payment. The bank demanded repayment of his investment debt. His solicitor had informed him that several contracts were now under legal scrutiny. His neighbor Lord Allen was raising an old dispute about the location of the boundary between their two properties. There would be more, he knew. More vultures circling.

Every fear he'd had since childhood was coming true. Every perfectly executed social interaction was now viewed as pretense.

His entire identity had crumbled.

But the biggest blow had come from the Regent, of course.

A letter had arrived stating that, in view of all the facts that had become clear in recent days, the Regent was concerned with the safety of the Pryde ducal title. And in the likely event that the Pryde title was stripped from Constantine, His Royal Highness was going to take Augustus as his own ward and raise him until he was of age.

The very thought made Constantine's gut wrench.

But what hurt him the most was losing Modesty. The biggest treasure of his life.

He should have spent every minute with her—talking to her, taking her to Pictish sites in Scotland, searching for ancient treasures. Time with her, that was what truly mattered.

True pride could not be gained in trying to be someone he was not.

His true pride was Modesty.

His wife.

The love of his life.

There were footsteps in the hallway, and he threw a glare at the doors. He should have blocked them with the chair.

"Go away, Simons!" he yelled and gulped the cognac.

He knew it was an exquisite one, but he could barely taste it through the pain in his heart.

"It's not Simons," boomed Dorian's voice.

"Go away, Rath!" he yelled, though with less conviction.

The doors opened; of course Dorian wouldn't leave.

Constantine leaned his head against the wall and closed his eyes. "Go away, please."

Even now, he hated for one of his closest friends to see him like this. How much lower could he fall?

But there were more heavy footsteps. And when he looked up, six tall figures were silhouetted against the candlelit hallway behind them.

"Not just Dorian," said Lucien.

"Then all of you, go to hell."

But of course, they did the opposite, spilling into the room until they surrounded him like walls. Something cracked in his chest. He'd been alone taking blow after blow when he really didn't have to be. He couldn't do anything. The gaping void where his heart used to be burst, and tears fell from his eyes as he sobbed.

Dorian dropped down and sat next to him, leaning against the wall. Lucien did the same on the other side. Both clenched his shoulders in silent support. The rest of them sat on the floor in a semicircle around them.

"Any word from Blackmore's men at the docks?" Lucien asked.

"Nothing," Dorian replied. "They've watched every ship for three days. Either George hasn't tried to leave yet…"

"Or he's already gone," Fortyne finished grimly. "Though my money's on him still being in London. He'd want to see the scandal unfold."

Octavius tried to better fit his large body into the gap between Dorian and Fortyne. He soon gave up and simply stretched out on his side, supporting himself with a bent elbow. Picking up one of the bottles, he nodded in appreciation and drank.

"Octavius, can you not?" asked Fortyne coldly.

"No sense of wasting a good smuggled bottle," he murmured as he offered it to Fortyne, who refused.

"Leave me," Constantine managed through his clenched throat, his chest convulsing uncontrollably. "I don't want anyone to see me like this."

"For God's sake, Constantine," murmured Dorian, still gripping his shoulder, "we've watched you maintain this perfect façade for years. You protected our secrets while drowning in your own. Did you think we wouldn't be there for you?"

The chasm in his chest ached. He knew in his head that he could rely on this mad circle of outcasts, but it was one thing to know and another to feel it as his truth.

"I haven't always been agreeable to you all." Constantine wiped his eyes. "I haven't always been your friend. I've judged you."

"You helped me when I needed you most," Dorian said.

"I was against your marriage to Patience."

"But you changed your mind. And now you'd protect her like we'd protect Modesty. Like we are going to."

Constantine exhaled, unable to see how anyone could do

anything to help him. That cognac quickly disappearing from the bottle in Octavius's hand seemed very appealing. "You don't want to be associated with me right now," he added, staring at the crumpled paper with the exposé. "I'm already ostracized. Everything is crumbling. You will crumble in association."

Lucien picked up the mangled paper. "First, we're not going to leave your side. If anything, we'll stand with you. Second, if you remember, only a few weeks ago, I lost everything when my scandal broke. Or so I thought. Instead, I found what truly mattered—love, family, redemption, and forgiveness. You're not losing your life, Constantine. You're finally starting to live it."

Constantine cleared his throat. "It certainly doesn't seem that way. I've lost my wife."

"It was my fault," Eccess admitted guiltily. "I must have told the Regent about the christening when I was in my cups. Maybe even told a few of the other lords who were in Elysium. God, Constantine, I'm so sorry."

"Secrets shared. Secrets sealed," said Enveigh with reproach. "You're our weakest link right now, Eccess. You must stop drinking."

"Go to the devil," Octavius muttered, casting him a dark scowl. "Yet another governess quit. There's truly nothing to do but drink. My three wards make my life a misery."

"Are you certain she quit because of your wards, and not because of yet another indiscretion of yours?" asked Luhst, winking.

"I'd never bed a good governess that can keep those three little devils under control," assured Octavius. "I'd treasure her and worship her and never touch her with a single finger."

"We'll see," murmured Lucien.

"Steady on, gentlemen," said Fortyne. "Eccess's indiscretion didn't help, but the Regent wouldn't have interfered if

Constantine hadn't been so proud. Besides, most of the ton came because someone sent them invitations."

"It was goddamn George. So you haven't caused my fall from grace, Octavius. But the truth is, your drinking might bring another of us to ruin."

Octavius's brows drew together. "Goddamn all of you."

The men were silent for a while, until Enveigh cleared his throat. "Look, Constantine, I've always envied your composure. That perfect mask you wore so well. But seeing you now, I realize what maintaining it must have cost you."

Irevrence chuckled. "Well, look at that—our flawless duke is human, after all. Rather refreshing, actually. Though your timing could use some work."

The jokes, the appreciation, the support, were like a balm to Constantine's raw, wounded soul.

Lucien sighed. "You're thinking like a duke trying to save his title. Start thinking like a man trying to save his family. Because no matter what you think now, you still can."

Constantine's shoulders hunched. "I don't know if I can. Modesty knows everything I am is a lie."

Dorian shook his head. "No. Everything you pretended to be was a lie. Who you are is the man who stayed up all night with a sick baby. Who bought his wife a Pictish mirror because her eyes lit up at the sight of it. Who took the blame for a stolen pin to protect his tutor."

"The man who would do anything to help a friend," added Lucien.

"Who saw worth in us when we couldn't see it in ourselves," said Enveigh.

"Who built this brotherhood on bonds stronger than blood," said Irevrence.

"Who should finally realize that being worthy isn't the same as being perfect," added Fortyne softly.

Constantine stared at the Regent's summons—the letter Modesty had given to him—and something shifted inside his chest. The lifelong fear that had driven his every action, every word...was not there.

What was he protecting anymore? He'd already lost what mattered most—his wife.

"Let them take the title," he said, and the words felt like freedom. "It was never truly mine. You're right, Lucien. I can still fight for my family. This time, I know the right choice. I choose Modesty."

He rose to his feet and marched to his study, the dukes following him.

His hands steadied as he reached for paper and a quill pen on his desk. No more masks. No more façades. For the first time in his life, he would do what was right, not what made him appear beyond reproach.

"Your Royal Highness," he wrote, the words flowing easily now. "I write to formally acknowledge Augustus as the rightful heir to the Duchy of Pryde..."

He outlined his requests: provisions for Augustus's care, protection for Modesty's position and reputation, guaranteed support for Mr. Hawthorne. The settlements he'd already arranged would ensure Modesty never wanted for anything, title or no title. He simply wished the Crown to know that and to make sure Augustus would be in her care.

Not the Regent's.

Strange how losing everything could feel like gaining something precious. Freedom. Truth. A chance to be worthy of love rather than a title.

He needed to tell her first. Before the court gossip, before the official pronouncements. Modesty deserved to hear everything from him. No more secrets, no more lies. He prayed she would forgive him and would see that he'd finally chosen love over pride.

He gave the letter to Fortyne and asked him to deliver it to the hearing for him.

Then at everyone's insistence, he bathed and allowed himself to be groomed and dressed properly.

But when he arrived at the parsonage in the afternoon, and saw Mr. Fairchild's ashen face, the hollow dread in his stomach returned.

"She's not at home," her father said, wringing his hands. "Mr. Lockhart came by earlier—said he'd learned of some ruins...or sites...just two miles south. She took Augustus with her... They should have returned by now..."

Constantine's blood turned to ice. "Two miles south? There are no ruins or sites south of here."

"Mr. Lockhart said they were newly discovered. Surely, something must have happened on the way—"

"The Egypt expedition," Constantine cut in, already turning. His heart pounded with a different kind of fear now.

He was running before the thought fully formed. He wouldn't let it be too late. Not when he'd finally learned what truly mattered. Even if Modesty never forgave him, even if she never looked at him with love again, he had to ensure his family's safety. Their happiness and well-being mattered more than his desires.

Perhaps that was what true nobility meant, after all.

33

THE GENTLE ROCKING pulled Modesty from unconsciousness. Her head throbbed, and there was a bitter, medicinal taste in her mouth. She tried to move, but her limbs felt heavy, uncoordinated.

Gradually, her vision cleared. She was in a small cabin, lying on a narrow berth. Through a round porthole, she could see the gray waters of the Thames, and beyond them the familiar silhouette of London growing smaller with each passing moment.

Terror shot through her. Augustus. Where was Augustus?

"He's here," George's voice came from behind her. "Safe and sound."

She turned her head too quickly, making everything spin. George sat in the corner, on the opposite bunk bed, Augustus cradled in his arms. The baby was sleeping peacefully, unaware that his world had been torn apart yet again.

She sat up, still groggy. "What have you done?"

George's face, so familiar and dear for years, now seemed

like a stranger's. "Saved you from him. From his lies. From that gilded cage he put you in."

"It was the tea, wasn't it?" she demanded. His betrayal tasted as bitter as whatever he'd given her. "Cleopatra's tea?"

His face showed real regret. "I am sorry about that lie. It's no more Cleopatra's than whisky. Laudanum is what you tasted."

Modesty shook her head in bewilderment. "You kidnapped me—and an infant!"

"I merely freed you. Everything is arranged for you, darling. The wet nurse, the napkins, clothes for the both of you. The captain was quite amenable once I offered him part of the money your husband so readily paid to protect his precious reputation. Though the notes in the final payment were false, there was still enough for our purposes."

"George, listen to yourself! What is this going to do to Grace?"

"Grace will be taken care of. I left her some money."

"Think of what will happen to her! People will come to question her. She'll be in trouble. Don't you care about your sister?"

"I left her money," he repeated. "She'll have funds to hire help if she needs to defend herself in court. Which she won't. She did nothing wrong."

"Give him to me." She held out her arms, trying to keep her voice steady despite her racing pulse. "Now."

"You're still unsteady. I wouldn't want you to drop him."

"Do I even know you, George?"

As she said his name, his face went pale and slack with a quick flash of joy. "I like that. Calling me George, like in good old times."

She stood up, her legs shaky as she walked to him to take Augustus, but he turned and walked out of the cabin.

"Do not fash about the babe, Modesty. He's perfectly safe with me."

Modesty stumbled after George, gripping the narrow companionway's wooden rails as she climbed. Her skirts brushed over the steps, smoothed by countless feet before hers. The passageway reeked of hemp rope, bilge water, and the sharp scent of salted fish that must be in the hold below.

Sailors in rough woolen jackets and worn linen shirts hurried past, their heavy boots thumping against the planks. A few merchant passengers huddled near their sea chests, watching her with a mixture of curiosity and discomfort. No one moved to help. Had George told them some tale to explain her disheveled state? That she was his mad wife, perhaps, or a fallen woman he'd charitably taken aboard?

They emerged onto the deck where canvas snapped overhead, the massive sails drawing taut in the wind. Coils of rope thick as her arm lay in precise patterns on the deck, while barefoot crew members scrambled up the ratlines into the rigging. At the helm, the captain stood conferring with his first mate, both pointedly ignoring the drama unfolding on their ship. The Thames stretched gray and endless around them, London now just a smudge on the horizon. Cold air whipped at her hair, her pelisse offering little protection against the chill.

"You must see reason, George," she said as she followed him across the deck, her heart pounding.

George stopped near the port side rail, his gaze fixed on the horizon as he adjusted Augustus in his arms. The railing, solid and weathered from years at sea, came up to his chest. Modesty's heart clenched as she saw him standing there, the baby's tiny hand peeking out from the swaddle.

Constantine... God, he'd been right this whole time. She'd thought he was the villain, but he was right to hunt the blackmailer, to protect them. Was right about George.

She was still mad at him. His actions still felt like a betrayal, but she knew he'd never do something like this. He was a proud man, but he had a good heart.

"Please, you can still put me and Augustus into a dinghy and send us back to London. It is dangerous for a newborn to be on board a ship! Even more dangerous in a country with a harsh, hot climate. An excavation in Egypt is not the place for an infant!"

"He'll be fine," George said as he pinched the baby's cheek slightly. "Won't you, little adventurer? He will have everything necessary."

"Necessary?" She caught up to him near the rail. "What is necessary? Was it necessary to blackmail my husband? To use my friend's death for your schemes?"

George's eyes hardened. "Ophelia told me everything that night, you know. When she was at her lowest, abandoned by her own brother—"

"Half-brother," Modesty corrected automatically. She knew this part—Constantine had told her himself. "The duke's illegitimate daughter." The Regent had implied that Constantine was not even the duke's son. But she knew that couldn't be true.

"Ah, but that's not quite the whole story, is it?" George's smile was cold. "Did your perfect duke tell you about the letter? About how he tried to buy Ophelia's silence?"

Modesty frowned. "What letter?"

"The one proving he's no more a Duke of Pryde than I am." George shifted Augustus in his arms as the baby stirred. "His mother wrote a very indiscreet letter to her lover. Which Ophelia's mother stole as insurance to keep herself and Ophelia safe. But all these years, there has been this proof of Constantine's adulterine bastardy out there. His biggest secret. That's why he demanded the letter as his price for helping her."

Modesty's mind raced. She didn't know about the letter proving his mother's affair... But it couldn't mean Constantine was illegitimate. When she had washed his hair, she had seen a birthmark identical to Augustus's. They had to be related.

"Ophelia was so alone, so afraid. All she wanted was Pryde's help—the only person left in the world that might take her in. Instead, he demanded she give him the letter before he'd lift a finger to save her."

"No..."

But even as she denied it, her mind was still trying to put together the pieces—Constantine's original belief that Modesty was blackmailing him, his insistence on taking Augustus after receiving that second letter, his reluctant proposal when she refused to let the child go with him.

"His Royal Highness knows now," George continued. "Everyone does. My exposé in the papers told the whole truth. Admittedly, I never had the letter. That was a farce. But I had all the facts from Ophelia. The great Duke of Pryde—nothing but a parson's bastard who let his own sister die to protect his lie."

Modesty's legs trembled. She gripped the ship's rail, the rough wood anchoring her. His mother must have believed Constantine wasn't her husband's son for some reason. And therefore, everyone who read the letter did, too.

But she must have been mistaken.

Poor Constantine.

"You used this information to blackmail him," she said.

"I did what was necessary," George said stubbornly, his gaze growing cold. "I also sent the invitations to the members of the ton for Augustus's christening. I'd make the same choice again—anything to free you from him. From the life of lies he trapped you in."

"This is not the way, George," she said, her voice rising. "Give Augustus to me. Now."

But when she reached for the baby, George stepped back. "Think, Modesty. What kind of life would you have with him now? His reputation in tatters, his title forfeit—because it will be, once the Regent enforces the old duke's will. Augustus is the true heir now."

"That's what this is really about, isn't it?" Understanding dawned, sharp and bitter. "You're not trying to save me. You want to control Augustus's inheritance yourself."

"I want to give you everything you deserve!" For the first time, George's composure fractured. "The freedom to pursue your dreams, to make your own discoveries. No more playing the perfect duchess, no more hiding your light to protect his pride."

"At what cost?" She advanced on him, anger lending her strength. "My ward's future? My marriage?"

"Marriage?" George laughed harshly. "To a man who's lived a lie his entire life? Who abandoned his own sister? Who cares more about his reputation than the people who love him?"

"You don't know him."

"I know he doesn't deserve you." George's voice softened. "I know I could give you so much more. You're angry now, but you'll see reason. We'll make incredible discoveries together. Raise Augustus away from all this corruption and pretense."

For one dizzying moment, she let herself imagine having the freedom to pursue her passion, to unlock history's mysteries without constraint. The life she'd dreamed of before duty and obligation had bound her to another path.

But then Augustus whimpered, his tiny face scrunching in distress, and reality crashed back over her. This wasn't about her dreams anymore. It was about a baby who'd already lost too much, about a man who'd spent his life believing himself unworthy of love.

"You're right about one thing," she said finally. "Constantine has lived a lie. But so have you. Pretending to be my friend while plotting all this? Using Ophelia's death, Augustus's future, my trust to satisfy your own ambitions?" She stepped closer. "At least Constantine's lies came from fear. Yours come from something far uglier."

George's face darkened. "You don't mean that. You're confused, still affected by the laudanum—"

"Give me my ward." She held out her arms. "Or I'll scream so loud every sailor on this ship will hear. Your excavation party must be gentlemen. No one will allow you to kidnap a woman against her will!"

"What do you think they're going to see?" His smile was frightening now. "A duchess trying to kidnap a duke's heir? A hysterical woman, unfit to care for him? Who do you think they'll believe—especially after I show them the letter from the Regent himself, granting me authority as Augustus's guardian?"

Horror washed through her.

"His Royal Highness would never give you guardianship," she cried. "Wait... Did you forge a letter from the Regent?"

She couldn't let George take Augustus to Egypt, couldn't let him use little Augustus as a pawn in his schemes. But how could she stop him? They were already miles from shore, surrounded by sailors who believed his lies...

And Constantine... God help her, she still loved him. Despite his lies, despite his pride, despite everything. She thought of his face when he held Augustus, so tender and uncertain. Thought of the vulnerability he had shown her when he'd talked about his childhood.

"The captain certainly believed it was authentic. Amazing

what people will accept when you wave enough money under their nose." He bounced Augustus gently as the baby began to fuss. "Now, I suggest you go back to your cabin and rest. The laudanum should wear off soon, and then we can discuss our future more rationally."

"I will do no such thing!" she roared, stepping closer.

"Sail!" screamed the sailor in the crow's nest. "Sail on port side!"

She leaned over the rail to see a sailboat drawing nearer with every heartbeat.

Even though it was still a hundred feet away, she saw a figure on board that she'd recognize even if he was only a speck on the horizon.

Constantine.

34

THE SLOOP CUT through the choppy waters of the Thames, spray stinging Constantine's face as they gained on the merchant ship ahead. His stomach churned, but not from the rough motion. From imagining Augustus and Modesty in George's hands.

The man who'd manipulated them all, who'd used Ophelia's death and Constantine's deepest secret to his own advantage, now held an innocent child and his wife hostage.

"We're catching up," Irevrence called from the helm, his lean frame braced against the tiller.

While Octavius stood in the center of the boat, his muscular legs wide apart, Dorian stood at Constantine's side, his icy blue eyes fixed on the merchant ship. "Thankfully, the *Aurora*'s too heavy to maneuver well this close to shore."

Constantine gripped the gunwale, his knuckles white. While Fortyne had gone to the hearing on Constantine's behalf, the rest of the dukes had commandeered this sloop from one of Enveigh's friends.

"There!" Lucien, who stood on his other side, pointed to

movement on the merchant ship's deck. "By the starboard rail."

Constantine's blood chilled. George stood at the ship's rail, Augustus in his arms. Standing by his side, Modesty was clutching her hands. Both of them were looking at the sailboat. Even from this distance, George's expression set Constantine's teeth on edge.

"Faster, Sylvester!" Constantine ordered Irevrence, shrugging off his coat. The weight of the garment would only drag him down if he had to swim. "Get us alongside."

"You're not thinking of boarding her?" Octavius asked. "In this chop?"

"Watch me."

Octavius started removing his own coat. The sloop was a smeller vessel, and Irevrence, who was an excellent coxswain, guided their boat into the merchant ship's wake, using the larger vessel's bulk to protect them from the worst waves. They were close enough now to hear George's shouts over the wind.

"Stay back!" George's voice cracked with desperation.

"Give him to me, George!" screamed Modesty, trying to snatch Augustus from George's arms.

George shoved her to the side; she staggered and fell on her behind. A snarl rose in Constantine's throat.

"Faster, Sylvester!" he roared again, never looking away from George.

"Hold on!" cried Irevrence. "Enveigh, ease the port sheet and haul in the starboard! The spinnaker's spilling wind— we're losing speed!"

"Understood!" Archibald loosened the port sheet just enough to reduce drag while pulling the starboard line tighter. The sail snapped taut as it caught the full force of the wind.

"Trim it tighter on the starboard," Sylvester called, his eyes fixed on the sail. "We need every inch of lift!"

Enveigh hauled the line with a steady pull, bracing himself against the deck as the sloop surged forward. The bow dipped and rose with the waves, spray flying as the renewed power drove them faster through the water.

Constantine steadied himself on the deck as the merchant ship loomed closer, its bulk growing larger with each moment.

"Another twenty yards, Constantine! Get ready."

Several long moments later, the sloop's bow was aligned with the stern of *Aurora*. Modesty was standing again, clutching at George's hands, trying to get at Augustus.

"Let go, Modesty! Pryde, turn the boat, or I swear I'll drop him!"

Constantine's heart stopped as George dangled Augustus over the rail. The baby's cries carried across the water, each wail slicing through Constantine's chest like a knife.

"No, you won't!" screamed Modesty, clawing at his arms.

"He's bluffing," Lucien murmured, his gaze sharp on the babe.

Constantine moved to the bow, calculating the distance to the ship's hull. "Closer, Sylvester!"

The gap was closing, but the waves made any jump treacherous.

"At least let me try first," Enveigh offered. "I'm the better swimmer."

Constantine shook his head. "He's my ward. My responsibility. And that is my wife up there."

His responsibility. Like Ophelia had been. This time, he wouldn't let pride or fear stop him from protecting his family.

The ships drew closer, their hulls nearly touching. Constantine could see George's face clearly now—the hatred twisting his once-friendly features.

Constantine eyed the cargo net hanging from the side. It swayed with the movements of the ship, but he saw no other option. He leaped, his fingers latching on to the rough and weathered ropes of the net. It was likely meant for hauling barrels or crates on board—now, it was his lifeline.

The big ship rolled with the waves, the net swaying and pulling taut as Constantine clung to it. His muscles screamed with effort as he began to climb, each movement jarring against the pitch of the ship. The coarse ropes bit into his palms, his hands slipping on the salt-crusted strands, but he gritted his teeth and hauled himself higher.

Behind him, he heard three grunts and felt the net sink. When he looked down, he saw Dorian, Lucien, and Octavius climbing after him. Irevrence and Enveigh must have stayed back to man the sloop.

Finally, he reached the rail and pushed himself over. He landed on his feet, breathing hard. Modesty's gaze was wide as she stared at him.

He beckoned to her to come to him, to safety, but she shook her head. She didn't want to leave George's side. He knew she'd leap into the waters to save the baby. He would, too. So would the other five dukes with him.

George backed away, still clutching Augustus. "Stay back! I'll do it!"

"No." Constantine advanced slowly, his hands raised. "You won't. Because deep down, you are not a man who kills babies. You know Augustus won't survive the fall—the water is cold and the tide is quick. You've helped in the almshouse alongside your sister. You do not have a bad heart."

Something flickered in George's eyes—grief or guilt or both. His grip on Augustus loosened slightly.

"I— I—" He looked at Modesty.

Using his distraction, Constantine lunged forward just as George's foot caught on a coiled rope. They both went down, Augustus slipping from George's grasp. Modesty caught the baby midfall, rolling to protect him as George scrambled to his feet.

But George had nowhere to go. Dorian and Lucien blocked one escape, Octavius the other. Only the rail remained behind him.

"It's over," Constantine said as Modesty ran to him, the baby held tight against her chest.

George looked at each of them, then at the choppy water below. His laugh was hollow. "You've taken everything from me. Everything. What's left but this?"

Before anyone could stop him, he vaulted over the rail. A moment later, there was a loud splash.

The *Aurora*'s captain bellowed orders: "Man overboard! Lower the boat! Thomson, Morris—to the longboat!"

As his crew scrambled to action, the captain turned to Constantine. "Your Grace, we must search for him. The current's swift but he may have surfaced downstream."

"Of course," Constantine replied grimly. They couldn't leave even George to drown, no matter his crimes. "We'll aid in the search from our vessel."

The *Aurora*'s crew lowered their longboat with practiced efficiency, four sailors taking up the oars.

"Modesty..." he managed.

Her name was mixed with his breath, in his blood-stream, embedded in the very flesh of his heart. The deck shifted under his feet, and it had nothing to do with the waves.

He looked at the baby, who was squirming but calming down now. "Is he all right?"

She kissed Augustus's forehead. "I think he's fine."

"And you?" He looked her over. "Are you hurt?"

She pursed her lips. "I'm fine."

Her red hair was ablaze in the sunlight, tendrils ruffled in the wind. And the most beautiful green eyes he'd ever seen were almost emerald now.

"Take us home, please," she murmured.

Home...

His throat constricted, he nodded. She was no doubt shaken, and all he wanted to do was take her and Augustus to warmth and safety. The rope ladder had been tossed over the rail by the sailors. Constantine helped secure the baby to his chest then started picking his way carefully down the swaying ladder, testing each rung. When he reached the sloop's deck, Enveigh and Irevrence steadied him while Dorian and Lucien stood ready above to help Modesty descend.

She gathered her skirts with remarkable composure and made her way down the swaying ladder as though she'd done it a hundred times before, though Constantine could see her knuckles were white on the ropes. Rath and Luhst followed.

"Set course downstream," Irevrence called, taking the helm. "We'll search the south bank while they take the north."

They looked for George for some time but found no sign of him. If George had survived the fall, he'd already made it to shore. If he hadn't... Constantine pushed the thought away. He had his family safe. That was what mattered.

"We're setting course to return," Irevrence called from the helm.

As they returned to the docks, Modesty sat quietly, protected from the cold by the wool blanket he'd wrapped around her and Augustus. She'd asked him to take them home...was it only to say a final goodbye?

He may have saved her...but that didn't mean she would ever forgive him.

35

MODESTY HELD AUGUSTUS, who was now asleep. There was a tremor in her hands that she couldn't stop.

The warmth of her bedchamber in Pryde House enveloped her like a protective cocoon, so welcome after the biting wind and the churning waters of the Thames. The familiar scent of the lavender sachets her maid liked to lay between her clothes and the beeswax candles situated around the room gradually steadied her racing heart.

Seeing the baby so close to death... It would have all been her fault. Trusting George had been a terrible mistake.

Constantine had been right all along.

If only she had believed him... But how could she when he had held so much back?

She caught her reflection in the window—spine straight, chin high, the perfect picture of a dutiful daughter turned proper duchess. The image blurred as tears threatened. No. It was time to stop playing the role everyone expected of her.

It was time to stop blaming herself for everything that

happened around her. Yes, she should have never entered George's gig, never have believed him about a new Roman ruin, never have taken that tea.

She was still in shock about George's betrayal.

But had Constantine told her his secrets from the beginning, she would have been more likely to trust his warnings.

She lowered Augustus into his cot, smoothed the creases of his swaddle, and brushed her knuckles down his rosy cheek.

Was she still angry with Constantine?

She was. Though she couldn't help but understand his actions. The fear he'd lived with since he was a child. Constantly trying to compensate for his perceived flaws by striving for perfection—something no human could ever achieve.

And what had he done all this for?

For a title. For fortune. For status.

No. That wasn't him.

She knew, at his very core, his actions weren't for title, money, or reputation. It was his father's approval he'd been seeking, long after the man's death. His father's—and generations of dukes before him. He'd thought his very existence made them ashamed.

What a miserable life.

The clock in the hallway struck the hour—it reminded her that Constantine should have been standing before the Regent, defending his title that morning. Instead, he'd chosen to come after her and Augustus. Her heart gave a peculiar flutter at the memory of his face when he'd reached for her on the ship. No mask of ducal perfection then—just raw fear and desperate love.

He hadn't gone to the meeting to save his pride. When it mattered most, he chose her. Her and Augustus.

He was ready to sacrifice everything for them.

The door creaked open. Constantine stood there, hair still windblown, cheeks ruddy. His perfect ducal façade had been cracked wide open. He was holding a tray with a tea set, pastries, and biscuits, like a servant. Their eyes met.

~❦~

Constantine hovered in the doorway. He had gone to the kitchen himself to give Modesty time to settle Augustus into his cot. To give her time to recover from the shock.

He thought she'd like some hot tea to warm up.

Though the floor wasn't careening as it had on the ship, he still felt unbalanced. He didn't think he'd feel steady ground under his feet again until he held his wife in his arms.

But soon, she'd want to separate from him in any way she could—once his resignation went through and he'd lost most of his possessions and his position.

He proceeded deeper into her room and put the tray on the round table as quietly as he could. She was standing by Augustus's cot, following Constantine with her eyes. Outside, dusk was settling on London, and the candles that were lit around the room brought a golden-auburn glow into her hair. Augustus slept, adorable baby snores filling the quiet bedchamber.

"Would you like some tea?" he asked gently. "You must want to warm up."

She nodded. "Yes, please."

He poured the tea and brought it to her. She took the cup from the saucer, wrapping her hands around it and sighing deeply in satisfaction. He watched her plump, rosy lips curl around the edge as she sipped, closing her eyes briefly.

"Thank you, Constantine," she said as her eyes met his. "Aren't you having any?"

He cleared his throat. "No."

Truth was, he couldn't imagine taking a single sip or a bite.

He allowed himself to run his gaze over her body. "How are you feeling? You must still be shaken."

"I'm fine. I should have believed you about George. If I had, none of this would have happened. But I was too vexed to listen."

He shook his head. "No. Don't say that. You were right. George was one of your oldest friends, and I've behaved like a complete ass. I hid things from you. I kept secrets. I...I betrayed you. It's all on me, Modesty. None of what happened is your fault. And I'm just glad that you and Augustus are safe and well."

Her shoulders sagged as if she was relieved. "It means a lot to hear you say this, Constantine. But still..."

There was a sharp pang in the center of his heart. "No, you have every right to be furious. I abandoned you and Augustus when I should have been there for you."

Her shoulders lifted again. She put the cup on the table. "You should have. But then you wouldn't have known the truth about George. I only wish you'd shared your secrets with me from the beginning."

He nodded. "You're right. I am so sorry I didn't. This will always be the thing I regret most in my life. I was afraid to lose you. I have fallen in love with you, Modesty—and I was terrified that if I told you the worst things about myself, you'd think poorly of me. All my life I've lived terrified of the world learning my secret. Of losing everything that I felt lucky to have but that was never truly mine."

She stepped closer to him, her gaze warming with empathy. "Oh, Constantine..."

He didn't deserve her empathy, no matter how good it felt. "But I've corrected my mistake. Fortyne went to the House of Lords in my place to give my letter of resignation to His Royal Highness. I've given everything up for Augustus, it never belonged to me anyway. I should have done it the moment I learned of his existence. No. I should have done it the moment Ophelia came seeking my help. I'm so sorry. I made sure you're always going to be his guardian."

Modesty's eyes clouded with confusion.

But before she could speak, he needed to say one of the most difficult things in his life. He loved her. And if it meant letting her go, he'd do it, no matter how much it would destroy him. The words poured out of him. "I am not asking for your forgiveness. I wouldn't blame you if you could never forgive me, if we can never return to the happiness we once knew. And now, with my title gone, you have every right to seek an annulment. I misled you—committed fraud by concealing the truth about my identity. The Bishop of London would surely understand and grant an annulment. If freedom from me is what you desire, I will not stand in your way."

He knew he'd never be able to forget her, though. She'd become a part of him. Even if she wished nothing to do with him, he'd watch over her and Augustus from a distance, protecting them if they needed him to.

Whatever she wished, he'd give her, expecting nothing in return.

"An annulment?" Her eyes widened, and she blinked, looking hurt. "I didn't realize that was something you wanted."

"No, I don't want it. But if you wish it, I will not oppose."

She sighed and shook her head. "Constantine..." Then she cupped his face in her hands. Her touch... He hadn't thought he'd ever feel it again. It was heaven, simple and sweet. "I don't want an annulment."

Something loosened in him, and he exhaled deeply. Relief.

"You don't?" he asked. "Why?"

"Because I love you."

"You...love me?" he repeated, struck dumb. "After everything I've done?"

She shook her head with a soft smile. "I've loved you for some time now. And I understand why you did what you did. You've been chasing something unattainable your entire life. Your father's approval. His love."

Everything he was tightened in a spasm and then released. It was like the armor he'd worn all his life had dissolved. Like he didn't need to fit into a mold anymore.

It felt strange. New. Completely foreign.

But wonderful.

He felt free.

"How did you know?" he began.

"Because I felt the same thing, darling." She smiled. "Only, I chased approval by trying to fit the role of an invisible, obedient woman. But neither of us needs to be shaped by those molds anymore."

"But..."

He was speechless. She understood him...when he couldn't even understand himself.

"I've seen the real you," she said. "Because you showed him to me. I saw the man behind the mask. And I've loved you since that day."

His entire life he was sure he'd never kneel in front of anyone. Not his father, not the Regent, not the ton.

It was love that did it. His knees loosened, and something he'd never felt overcame him.

Surrender.

Love for her filled him to the brim, and a complete gratitude spread through him. There were no more barriers, no more walls, nothing more to defend.

He barely felt the impact as his knees connected with the floor. Modesty gasped softly in surprise—he was surprised, too. But there he was, wrapping his arms around his wife's hips, burying his face in her soft stomach, inhaling her scent —lavender, wildflowers, and the heavenly sweetness of her skin. She knew him like no one else, and she fully accepted him.

"I love you, Modesty," he murmured against her. "I'm yours—fully and completely. And if you let me, I'll spend the rest of my life making you happy. Without a title, without a large fortune, but I'll make up for it, I promise."

Her hands caressed his hair, and he reveled at the touch of her fingers.

"No." She chuckled. "I mean, I don't care about the fortune, the title, or any of that. I will stay with you no matter what. What I meant was..."

She tugged him up to stand in front of her. He looked deep into her gorgeous green eyes, sinking in them.

"You didn't have to resign," she finished.

"I did. I want Augustus to take his rightful place."

She shook her head. "You think you're not your father's son. But that's not true, and I have proof. Your mama was mistaken—we will never know why she thought the parson was your true father, but we do know one thing."

Constantine's skin tingled in protest. Not true? No, he knew it like he knew his own body. That had been his reality for most of his life.

She wrapped her arm through his elbow and led him to the cot. Augustus was sleeping, his lips half-opened as he snored softly, still a little congested. She gently undid the laces of his baby cap and lifted it on the right side of his head so that Constantine could see the birthmark in the shape of a wolf.

"Do you see that?" she asked.

"I do. I noticed it long ago."

The baby's hair was starting to come in, fine blond strands beginning to cover the mark.

"You have the same one," she said.

He frowned, touching his head. "Where?"

She went to pick up the hand mirror from her dressing table. "In the same exact spot. Come here," she said as she beckoned him to stand by the big mirror. "This will take a little maneuvering..."

She positioned the mirror at an angle behind him, and when he could see the back of his head in the polished surface, she parted his hair with her free hand. It was a little hard to see at first through his thick, dark hair, but then he could distinguish a shape...a mark the same wine-stained color as Augustus's...

The wolf's head.

"What does this mean?" he asked.

"It means you two are connected by blood. Some birthmarks are passed down through families, like other traits such as hair color, eye color, facial features. A birthmark in same shape and location cannot be a coincidence. It means you must be your father's true son, after all."

"No," he murmured. His world was tilting on its axis. "That can't be. I don't look like Papa. He had blond hair, blue eyes, and a Roman nose—same as Ophelia, same as Augustus..."

She chuckled as she watched him with a calm smile. "Yes, you have your mama's coloring, and maybe that's why she assumed you were not your father's son. But the birthmark is clearly from your papa since Augustus has it, too. I noticed it when I combed your hair after...well..." She blushed.

Oh, Constantine remembered... In the bathtub, after she had fallen apart around him, and he'd felt for the first time that he could be himself with her.

She put the mirror away and looked at him, empathy shining through her eyes. "I didn't say anything because I didn't think it was significant that you and your son would have the same birthmark. Then when you shared that Augustus was your father's heir, I thought it was also obvious that you both are your father's descendants. So I didn't pay it any mind. But now that I know you doubt your blood relation to your father... There's nothing else that can prove your blood ties better than this."

His world was careening, transforming.

Relief...anger...regret...rushed through his heart and stayed in a strange mixture of swirling emotions.

All he was trying to be—desperately, obsessively—all he could never be...

He already was.

What a jest.

What a complete and utter jest.

His hands dropped to his sides.

"I am the Buccleigh heir..." he murmured. "My father's true son..."

"You are. And Ophelia was your half-sister. So Augustus is your true nephew."

"So George was powerless."

"He was. And he never had your mother's letter. He was bluffing all along."

He stared at his reflection in the large mirror, trying to make sense of all this. "I left everything to Augustus and you. I wrote a letter resigning my title for Augustus's sake. And I made sure a significant part of my fortune that wasn't tied to the title belonged to you."

She smiled as she cupped his face, and he met her eyes. "You're a more generous and thoughtful man than you let others believe. But I'm sure the Regent will not be bold enough to take away your title when he is shown evidence that you are the rightful heir. Especially since there is no actual proof to suggest otherwise. Only gossip."

Constantine exhaled. "Fortyne took the letter to the House of Lords this morning, but nothing will be signed or decided upon today."

"So you can ask for an audience with the Regent and show him the birthmarks. Tell him the scandal was started by a jealous suitor not in his right mind. I'm sure your six dukes will support you, as well as the Duke of Grandhampton, the Duke of Kelford, and the rest of the Seatons."

His throat relaxed and softened. The man he used to be would have protested, too proud to ask for help. But he no longer felt the need to justify himself, to prove anything to anyone. All he wanted, all he needed, was already his.

"I am sorry you had to go through all that," she said, laying her hand on his chest, "just to discover you were the heir all along."

He drew in a slow lungful of air. For the first time, his heart was full and peaceful, all its broken, jagged pieces glued together. "I am not sorry," he said, wrapping his arms around her and drawing her to him. "I don't care. Let them gossip. I would go through all this again if it led me to you."

A slow, happy smile spread her lips. "Oh."

"With the exception that I would have helped Ophelia and would have never sent her away. That decision will always be my reminder of pride's consequences. But thanks to you, I have realized who I really am and have come to peace with myself."

"You are a good man." She cupped his face. "The best person I know."

"I disagree. That position will always belong to you, my duchess. You healed me. I've been convinced my whole life I needed to be perfect to be happy. To be appreciated. To be respected. But you showed me I don't need to be perfect at all."

She was melting in his arms. Warm and soft and so wonderfully his.

"I love you, Constantine," she said. "Perfect...imperfect... you. For all that you are."

He breathed out and felt like he was about to burst with lightness and joy. Words poured from a warm place in the middle of his chest. "My darling, 'love' doesn't begin to describe what I feel for you. You're the reason for my existence. My heart began to beat for you the moment I saw you in that church, even if I kept denying it. I may have offered you a marriage, but it was never for convenience. I've wanted you— in my bed, in my house, in my life—since that day. My future doesn't exist without you in it. Somewhere, someone designed me and made it so that I could never be complete or happy without you. Please know this, darling, in me, you have a trusted friend, a husband, a lover, a protector, and a servant bound to your happiness. I don't need anything from you but you, existing, breathing, living somewhere in this life. I love you. I've always loved you. I always will."

Tears filled her eyes, but before she could respond, he pressed his lips to hers in a long, slow kiss that had his whole body tingling with love for her. There were no more secrets in his soul. He stood bare and open—for her, for the little boy he'd accepted as his family, and for the best friends he could ever have in the world.

They were the true treasures of his life, not his title or his fortune or his reputation. Not his father's approval—or society's.

This woman had seen straight into his heart and chosen

him and made him see that he didn't need anything external to feel worthy and loved. Didn't need masks and rigid defenses to belong.

He already did. Thanks to her, he'd found his home was where he'd been all his life, even though he hadn't felt it.

He knew it now. Her love had showed it to him.

From this day forward, he had a lifetime to make her just as blissful as she made him.

EPILOGUE

Pryde Manor, August, the following year...

The sun filtered through the foliage, warming Modesty's cheeks as she watched Augustus. He stood in the lush grass, his chubby hand pressed against the trunk of the ancient oak that soared above them, his eyes fixed on Modesty and Constantine. He desperately wanted to walk to them but wasn't yet allowing himself to let go of the trunk. Unsatisfied with his slow progress, he grunted, his pale eyebrows drawn together over his blue eyes, which were so like Ophelia's.

He'd been tottering along while grasping on to pieces of furniture and walls for weeks. The next step would be letting go of them and walking on his own.

Mrs. Walcott was dozing on a chair a few steps away, and Modesty didn't want to wake her. Lucien and Chastity as well as Dorian and Patience with their eight-month-old baby, Edward, were positioned on blankets next to theirs, arranged in a triangle around the larger blanket that held food and drink. The spread included glazed ham, cold game pies, various terrines, fresh bread, sweetmeats, and bowls of seasonal fruit and berries. Silver wine coolers held bottles of champagne and claret.

The palatial three-story Pryde Manor with tall columns and windows was fifty or so yards away, across a large lawn often used for activities like archery and cricket. A park with rolling hills and woods surrounded them.

Modesty was lying on her stomach on the picnic blanket, Constantine's head nestled in the valley of her lower back. She had received a letter from Sir Joseph Banks, trustee of the British Museum, and was reading it aloud to the gathered company.

"'Your interpretation of the mirror's symbols opens fascinating new avenues of research into ancient British societies. The museum would be particularly interested in your thoughts on similar symbols found on recently discovered stones in Morayshire...'" A small explosion of fireworks burst in her heart as she read the words.

The company erupted in joyous exclamations of approval. For months she had been comparing the mirror's symbols to other feminine imagery in ancient British art, developing a theory about women's roles in Pictish society.

She'd compared the carved spiral patterns among a few Pictish stones and objects—including her mirror—to the spiral carvings on Knocknagael Boar Stone, which had been found in Inverness. That stone's spirals were thought to signify cycles of life or eternity. Often, they appeared alongside the boar—a symbol of strength and protection. In combination with the knowledge that Pictish kings were crowned through the female line, she argued that women had played a much more important role in Pictish society than was currently believed.

In her essay, she theorized that Pictish tribes associated women with both resilience and spirituality.

And her work had garnered the attention of scholars in the field. More antiquarians had become interested in the history of their own country.

Perhaps she hadn't proven her theories yet, but she looked at the past with a fresh perspective. And—for the first time— her voice mattered. It was respected, acknowledged, and appreciated. She contributed to the understanding of humanity, just like she'd always wanted, and she was not going to stop there.

Augustus's grunts had become more determined, pulling her attention from the letter. The mere sight of him, as ever, caused her heart to overflow with love.

"I think he's about to walk," she muttered to Constantine, her stomach squeezing with excitement.

She felt his head shift as he looked at the child.

"Oh, indeed. Go on, lad!" He sat on his haunches by her side, setting down his copy of *The Gentleman's Stable Directory: Or, Modern System of Farriery* by William Taplin.

He was studying treatments for lameness caused by hoof abscesses, which was afflicting his tenant Mr. Greenbow's mare. Constantine has already cleaned and poulticed the abscess, showing a gentle touch that had the farmer's teenage son watching in awe. The new veterinary surgeon, one of the first graduates of the Royal Veterinary College, would arrive tomorrow. But Constantine planned to continue learning and helping where he could.

"Go on, Augustus!" four-year-old Stella, Lucien's daughter, cried out as she jumped up from her blanket and rushed to the boy, her golden locks bouncing. In her excitement, she threw a piece of cake, which landed in Lucien's hair. He was stretched on his side next to Chastity, wooden horses, blocks, and figures spread on the blanket in front of him.

Stella stopped two steps away from Augustus and held her hand out to him. "Just one little step! You can do it!"

Lucien grimaced as crumbs rained down on him, and Chastity burst out laughing. The rest followed, even Dorian's expression transforming into an amused grin. Modesty thought it was a rare but welcome sight that made him look boyish and carefree. Patience lit up with joy from within like a candle sconce.

Little Edward was sitting nearby, carefully picking individual blades of grass and studying each one with a look of concentration that was not unlike Patience's. He had Dorian's dark hair but Patience's angelic face. Everyone jested that he would be a botanist like his mother.

Lucien shook his head with a grin and removed the piece of cake from his golden locks. "The joys of fatherhood are clear to all present," he said with a kind chuckle, his gaze, full of love, on Chastity and on Stella.

"Papa!" Augustus called, his gaze on Constantine.

Of course, Constantine was his uncle, but when he'd started saying Papa—his first word—no one had had the heart to correct him.

With a determined frown, stretching his chubby hand straight towards Constantine, he took his first shaky step.

Modesty's gasp froze in her throat. Everyone cheered and called out encouragements as the child took three steps before plopping back onto his plump behind.

"Well done!" Constantine said as he made his way to Augustus.

"Marvelous!" echoed Stella, who came to stand by Constantine—only a few more baby steps from Augustus.

"Go on," said Constantine. "Come here."

"Come here, Augustus!" Stella bounced up and down.

Her Whitechapel accent had disappeared after almost one year living with Lucien. And she was an adorable little lady, with a striking combination of a strong character and indomitable charm—both from Lucien.

Augustus grinned, grunted as he stood up, and took five more steps before falling into Constantine's waiting arms.

Everyone erupted in cheers and clapping, waking up Mrs. Walcott, who joined in.

Modesty chuckled as she watched Constantine fall onto his back with a giggling Augustus safe his arms. Stella giggled, too, and launched herself onto Constantine, tickling him. Even Edward joined in, and Constantine was a wriggling mass of a male completely taken over by three children.

As Modesty smiled, tears of joy in her eyes, she looked at Patience and Chastity, both of whom exchanged understanding gazes with her. He'd changed so much since the first day she'd met him.

He was now soft, and relaxed, with inner peace radiating from him. Even his formerly impeccable windswept hairstyle now looked a bit unruly at times, with a few hairs often sticking up at the back of his head.

That look of contentment had been with him every day since the failed kidnapping. Not even the scandal that had raged through London for some time afterward had affected him.

He'd met everything with a calm, stoic acceptance.

Before, he had been as cold as a stone. Now, he was as unbreakable as one.

When His Royal Highness had summoned him to the palace, Modesty and the six dukes had refused to let him go alone. They'd stood by his side before the Regent, who had demanded to know if the rumor was true. He'd said he had every intention to honor the former duke's will; he only needed proof.

Constantine had apologized for his previous behavior and told him he regretted his actions and his futile rivalry with the Regent. The rumor was false. There was no proof because it was not true. But the Regent could, of course, rule otherwise as was his privilege. Or he could reject Constantine's letter of resignation. With Constantine so calm and respectful, it seemed the fight no longer interested the Regent. Modesty suspected his change of heart had more to do with Constantine's gift of Icarus and the duke's new humble demeanor than any real forgiveness.

Constantine told him Icarus was his and was waiting for him in the courtyard. He apologized that he had taken the gift back before, but he could now see how futile his pride was and that there were more important things in life.

That left the Regent completely speechless. He had made a few jabs at Pryde's character, but seeing that it had no effect, he said he would not accept Constantine's resignation and that he would need to continue to fulfill his duties as a duke and not try to pass them off to a baby.

The Regent had never again made any overtures towards Modesty. Whether it was Constantine's fierce defense of her that day in Carlton House or simply that His Royal Highness had found new amusements, she was grateful the matter had been laid to rest.

"Who would have thought, Constantine," said Chastity, who was dressed in the most gorgeous yellow color that made her look like the goddess of spring. There was a fluffy feather decorating her hair. "One year ago, on this very lawn, we were shooting arrows at your house party. You were so correct, so faultless as a host. I could never imagine you rolling in the grass with three children, with smudges of butter and jam on your clothes and laughing from joy."

Constantine winked as he set Augustus on his feet. Then he rolled over onto his stomach and said, "I know, Chastity. Allow me to shock you even further. Children," he exclaimed and neighed, "I am a unicorn—who would like to ride me?"

As the grown-ups roared with laughter and the children squealed in excitement and began to crawl onto his back, Modesty shook her head. Could her heart be any lighter? Could love fill her very being any more than it did now?

She was among friends, people who'd become her extended family. The Misses with Microscopes club had become a weekly gathering where Patience, Chastity, and she chatted about their latest theories and discoveries...and sometimes about their husbands. She felt like she'd found a home with two new best friends. She also went to help Grace in the almshouse regularly, and Constantine joined her from time to time.

"Say, Constantine," said Lucien as he gave his wife a meaningful gaze, "does your groundskeeper still enjoy his new cottage?"

"Yes, he does," Constantine replied between neighs as he slowly walked on hands and knees in the grass with Stella and Augustus on his back. Little Edward crawled after them, giggling and making a funny sound that could be a neigh, as well.

"So the old one is still unused?" asked Lucien, holding Chastity in his heated gaze. Modesty noticed Chastity's cheeks were flushed, and she was sending him the same gaze straight back!

"It is," said Constantine. "Why do you ask?"

Lucien finally averted his eyes when Dorian began glaring at him. "No reason. Keep on with your horsey nursery."

"I must say," said Patience, who leaned against her husband, and earned an arm wrapped around her shoulders, "I much prefer this house party to last year's! We have Modesty now!"

Everyone cheered her and nodded their agreement. Modesty beamed. "All of you are welcome here anytime. And please stay as long as you wish."

Lucien picked up a grape and crushed it between his teeth. "Thank you, Duchess." He winked at Chastity, who grinned back at him. "We certainly have much to look forward to on Pryde territory."

⁓⋅⋆⋅⁓

The night air was heavy with the scent of blooming jasmine as Constantine followed Modesty's laughter through the twisting paths of the maze. The children were in bed—sound asleep, he hoped. And they'd enjoyed a wonderful dinner with their best friends, who had now retired to their rooms.

Moonlight silvered the perfectly trimmed hedges, creating an ethereal glow.

"This way," her voice called, drawing him deeper into the labyrinth. "Unless the mighty Duke of Pryde is afraid of getting lost?"

He chuckled, quickening his pace. "I grew up here, darling. I know every turn."

"Then why haven't you caught me yet?"

A year ago, he would have bristled at such teasing. His pride would have demanded he prove his mastery over his own grounds. Now, he delighted in letting her lead this dance.

He rounded another corner and stopped short. The center of the maze opened before him, transformed. She'd laid out a thick blanket scattered with pillows. Candles in glass lamps cast a warm glow, and a bottle of wine sat cooling. But it was Modesty herself who took his breath away.

She stood beside a telescope she must have borrowed from their library, her copper hair loose around her shoulders. She'd discarded her spencer, leaving her in just her thin muslin gown.

"I thought we could study the stars," she said with a hint of shyness in her smile that made his heart ache. "The ancient Romans believed the summer constellations told stories of pride and redemption."

He moved closer, drawn by the sparkle in her green eyes. "Is that so?"

"Yes." She gestured upward. "See there? That's Cassiopeia, the queen who challenged the gods..."

Constantine wrapped his arms around her waist from behind, breathing in her familiar scent of wildflowers. "And was humbled for her pride?"

"Yes." She leaned back against his chest. "Though some say she found greater glory in accepting her true self."

"Like someone else I know," he murmured, pressing a kiss to her neck.

She turned in his arms. "We both had to learn that lesson, I think. I was nothing but the humble daughter of a vicar."

"You were always much more than that, darling. And now here you are, leading your husband on a moonlit chase through the maze." His fingers traced the curve of her cheek. "What happened to that vicar's shy daughter?"

"She fell in love with a duke who showed her it was safe to be herself." Modesty's hands slid up his chest. "Who proved that true nobility has nothing to do with birthright or title..."

"And everything to do with decisions we make and the actions we take," he finished, lowering his mouth to hers.

The kiss was sweet, unhurried. They had all night, all their lives, to explore this precious thing between them. When they finally parted, Modesty's eyes were luminous.

"Make love to me under the stars?" she whispered.

Constantine's breath caught at her boldness—not because it shocked him anymore, but because he treasured how far they'd both come. "Here? In the open air?"

"Everyone's asleep." When he hesitated still, she added, "Live a little, Duke."

"Mmmm," he murmured as he planted a kiss on her collarbone. He could feel her pulse beating faster under his lips. Good. His own heart drummed for her. "I like seeing you happy like this. Are you happy?"

She chuckled. "Very. Are you?"

"I couldn't be happier."

She leaned back slightly. "Let me see if I can show you how I feel."

He couldn't stop a grin. "I was told redheads are fire in bed. You certainly are."

He loved when she took control like this. She saw him— and he felt seen. Not just as a duke, a title, and a number of pounds earned per year.

But as himself.

She walked him towards the blanket, her hands on his chest, and then they both dropped to the soft pillows.

He thought she'd lie down next to him, but she knelt by his bent knees instead. He propped himself against up with his elbow, watching her settle between his thighs with a sparkle in her green eyes. He wanted to lick every inch of her. Her skin tasted divine on his tongue.

"What do you have in mind, darling?" he asked. "I know that glint in your eyes. You are planning something."

He remembered her the night he made her his...sensual

and yet afraid of her own body, of her reactions, of the pleasure she could experience.

Modesty then would have never imagined taking initiative the way she did now.

He had never imagined letting her do so.

Now they were both complete.

She licked her lower lip. "You know me so well."

She began fumbling with the buttons of his breeches. He swallowed. Seeing her this way, leaning over his crotch, her breasts practically falling out of her dress, had his semi-erection hardening to stand at full attention.

"Modesty—" he said, his lips parched.

"Hmmm?"

"What are you doing?"

He knew exactly what she had in mind, and the mere thought of her touch sent desire coursing through him.

"I am freeing you of your clothes." She pushed his breeches down his thighs, and his cock appeared before her.

She stared at it, the wicked minx, and licked her lips again. He couldn't stop a growl.

"I can see that..." he said, his voice low and throaty.

"Let's see if I can make you even happier."

Her hand circled his erection, and his head fell back. Even her lightest touch brought him intense pleasure.

"Where do you get such ideas?" he managed as he watched her hand move up and down.

"Well," she said, "the Misses with Microscopes don't just discuss science."

The shock of hearing that almost made him sit up—except at that moment, she took his cock in her mouth, and the questions died in his throat. All he could do was moan, watching those lush pink lips wrapped around him.

"Wha—?" he choked out as her tongue glided up and

down, swirling around. "Who—? Are you ladies talking about this—?"

"Mmmm," she murmured against his cock, sending vibrations through his flesh. "No talking now."

"Damnation," he managed as she encircled him again and pushed against his chest so that he lay flat on his back.

He wasn't sure he liked her discussing things that went on in the privacy of their bedchamber, unless...

Well...

They resulted in new experiences like this one.

A year ago, he never would have allowed something like this. He'd have needed to be the one in control.

But look at him now...wonderfully helpless...trusting...free.

He hadn't just surrendered his body to her but his whole self. Fears, flaws, the darkest, most shameful things he hadn't even dared acknowledge to himself.

And she still loved him.

Still wanted to please him.

She amplified the sensations now by pumping him with her hand while her tongue was working around him.

He didn't think he could get any harder, any bigger. Good God, he'd face a thousand scandals to protect this woman, to keep her and their family safe.

"Modesty," he groaned as he sat up. "I must be inside you."

Her face was flushed, her lips red and glistening, and he kissed her as she straddled him—just like that night when he'd lost control for the first time with her. She guided him into the tight, hot heaven of her body, and he looked into her eyes as he entered her, feeling as if he were swimming in the sea of stars above them.

Thousands of people had come before them, and thousands would come after them. These eternal stars had witnessed countless stories of pride and redemption. But none, he was certain, quite like theirs.

Soon, he could feel her trembling, her knees giving in, and he himself was pure fire.

He couldn't hold back any longer. She was too good. He was always completely undone when it came to her.

"Darling," he said as he leaned back a little, "I am going to — Ohhh..."

The grip of her body around him tightened as he knew she was reaching the same blissful point he was, and her arms gripped his shoulders harder. He couldn't stop himself from plummeting over the edge. But as he was writhing with pulsing need, he stroked her slick sex with his fingers until she cried out. And he felt her clench around his pulsating cock, her thighs shaking.

Heavens above, he loved this woman.

Never could he have enough of her...never.

They both collapsed onto the blanket, and she nestled her face on his chest. They were breathing hard, and he kissed her sweaty forehead.

"You little scientists." He chuckled.

"What?" she asked innocently. "The study of pleasure is science as well."

"Please don't tell me you are sharing intimate details with them."

She shrugged. "Nothing concrete. We don't gossip about you dukes. But we do share what pleases us...what surprises us...and what we wonder about."

"You can always ask me."

She kissed him on the cheek. "I can, and I do. But sometimes I like to surprise you. Didn't you enjoy this?"

"I did. All right. Permission for surprises granted."

She laughed softly and put her chin on his chest, looking

into his eyes. "Oh, Duke of Pryde. Could you ever imagine saying that when we had just married?"

He shook his head thoughtfully. "No, that Constantine could have never allowed himself to be surprised. Least of all by you."

"Why is that?"

"Because...because you intrigued me. I didn't know what to do with your incredible selflessness. Your kindness completely disarmed me."

"I thought you despised me because I was lowborn and so easily controlled."

"I never despised you, darling." He kissed her. "Never. Truth is, I think I was in love with you long before I allowed myself to admit it—even to myself."

She sighed. "You're not the only one who was afraid to be in love. I was, too, darling. I was sure a duke like you could never love someone like me. That I'd always be just a means to an end for you."

He wrapped the blanket around them and held her closer. "I suppose we both had our own demons to overcome. I will always love you, Modesty. You're the love of my life."

"And we both became better people," she said. "I love you, Constantine. My humble Duke of Pryde."

He traced the curve of her cheek, marveling at how the moonlight caught the copper in her hair. "Do you know what makes me proudest now?"

"What's that?"

"Not my title or lands or bloodline, but that I'm worthy of your love. That I can be both the duke society needs and the man you deserve."

She lifted her head, her eyes shining. "And I'm no longer just a vicar's daughter. I'm a duchess and I know my worth— in the library, in society, and in her husband's arms."

"You're everything, Modesty." He kissed her softly. "My heart, my home, my redemption."

Above them, the summer stars wheeled in their eternal dance, witnesses to how the challenges they'd faced together had transformed both pride and modesty into something far more precious.

Love.

•✦•

Thanks for reading **DUKE OF PRYDE**. If you enjoyed Constantine and Modesty's story, make sure to get your exclusive bonus epilogue - available only here:

https://mariahstone.com/sds3-bonus/

Don't stop now. Find out how what happens next, when Octavius drowning in excess hires a mysterious governess who is hiding her own dark secrets in **DUKE OF ECCESS**

His wards have driven away five governesses in one year. She's the "Mad Heiress" with a bounty on her head.

When he discovers his miracle governess is London's most hunted woman, will he turn her in—or risk everything for love?

Continue reading DUKE OF ECCESS now >

Available in Kindle Unlimited, ebook, print, and audio!

ALSO BY MARIAH STONE

MARIAH'S TIME TRAVEL ROMANCE SERIES

- Called by a Highlander
- Called by a Viking
- Called by a Pirate
- Fated

﹏

MARIAH'S REGENCY ROMANCE SERIES

- Dukes and Secrets
- Seven Dukes of Sin

﹏

VIEW ALL OF MARIAH'S BOOKS IN READING ORDER

Scan the QR code for all ebooks, paperbacks, and audiobooks.

ENJOY THE BOOK? YOU CAN MAKE A DIFFERENCE!

Please, leave your honest review for the book.
As much as I'd love to, I don't have financial capacity like New York publishers to run ads in the newspaper or put posters in subway.

But I have something much, much more powerful!

Committed and loyal readers

If you enjoyed the book, I'd be so grateful if you could spend five minutes leaving a review on the book's sales page.

Thank you very much!

ABOUT MARIAH STONE

With over one million books sold worldwide, bestselling author Mariah Stone captivates readers with emotionally intense historical romances that balance passion with deep character growth.

Readers describe her books as "unputdownable," "heart-wrenching," and "the perfect blend of adventure, mystery, and passion."

Mariah's books are available worldwide in 7 languages as ebooks, audiobooks, and print.

Fall in love with Mariah's world - Get your FREE book today at mariahstone.com/signup

facebook.com/mariahstoneauthor
instagram.com/mariahstoneauthor
bookbub.com/authors/mariah-stone
pinterest.com/mariahstoneauthor
amazon.com/Mariah-Stone/e/B07JVW28PJ

Made in the USA
Coppell, TX
28 February 2026

72956038R10208

VOM KOMMEN UND GEHEN

Burgenland

Betrachtungen von Zu- und Weggereisten

Herausgegeben von Peter Menasse, Wolfgang Wagner

Böhlau Verlag Wien Köln Weimar

Gefördert durch das Land Burgenland

Bibliografische Information der Deutschen Nationalbibliothek:
Die Deutsche Nationalbibliothek verzeichnet diese Publikation in der
Deutschen Nationalbibliografie; detaillierte bibliografische Daten sind im
Internet über https://dnb.de abrufbar.

1. Auflage 2021

Korrektorat: Anja Borkam, Jena
Umschlagabbildung: Das Cover zeigt ein Bild des Malers Robert Lettner
aus der Serie „Das Spiel vom Kommen und Gehen"
(www.robertlettner.info)
Umschlagsgestaltung: Bernhard Kollmann, Wien
Layout: Bettina Waringer, Wien
Druck: Finidr, Český Těšín

Vandenhoeck & Ruprecht Verlage |
www.vandenhoeck-ruprecht-verlage.com
ISBN 978-3-205-21275-1